INSURRECTION

A Novel of Moreauvia

BYRON STARR

Insurrection
By Byron Starr

ISBN 9781894953863

Trade paperback edition
Published by Creative Guy Publishing
Vancouver, Canada

INSURRECTION

A Novel of Moreauvia

BYRON STARR

creative guy publishing
vancouver | canada

Foreword

Welcome to the very first Moreauvia novel. Moreauvia is not so much a place as a concept, or an alternate world. Moreauvia was conceived of and named by me, and developed with the author of this novel, Byron Starr. Originally I was going to co-author this book, but my input is really more editorial – Byron took this baby and ran with it, and I think we're all glad he did. But more on Moreauvia itself: Byron and I ran a limited 4-issue magazine called "Tales of Moreauvia" which was intended to celebrate alternative history and historical fiction, but also if possible to bring some awareness to our concept.

In Moreauvia, the digression with our own world is at a specific point in history, but also in what is scientifically known and correct. In Victorian times, there was a (much argued about and certainly not universal) belief in *élan vital*, or life essence, which was a possible cause for evolution as well as the driving force behind living creatures – and that it could be harvested and invested into machines. While the phrase was coined in 1907, there was certainly a similar belief in the essence of life being separate from an organism, and existing as an energy far prior – see our friend Dr. Frankenstein.

In the Moreauvian world, Charles Babbage's difference engine was completed and used, partly with the help of élan vital, and 19th century politicians and scientists took advantage of the advanced knowledge to help solve the moral issues of slavery and colonialism by creating worker animals – forcefully evolving domestic animals into more human-like forms to replace the morally reprehensible idea of human slavery.

1

Where does that leave us?

A number of different items in our own history are quite different in the Moreauvian cosmology – an abolition of slavery in the early 1800s meant no Civil War in the US, for one thing. The impact of the politics and economics of slavery in the colonial and even post-colonial eras can't be overstated, and the more Byron and I talked about historical points, the more fun we began to have. What if, instead of H.G. Welles writing *The Island of Dr. Moreau*, he wrote about a fictional vivisectionist in the south, and put forth the worst practices that actually existed in vivisectionist/evolutionist technologies – not a fantasy so much as a journalistic, but fictionalized account? *The Plantation of Master Moreau*? Champions of freedom for the beastmen started a movement, became known as Moreauvians?

I'll admit that my first ideas regarding a Moreauvian world first came simply from the fact that I played the (first edition!) *Gamma World* RPG in the 70s-80s as a kid, and really liked characters that were mutated animals with guns. I had a whole command team of a bear-man, goat-man, and dog-man. They were firearms, demolitions and science experts respectively, if I recall correctly. Then at some point in the 80s came a limited series comic book from Marvel called *Rocket Raccoon* – so awesome!

I probably shouldn't be admitting this in print, but my brother and sister and I never had dolls of the GI Joe or Barbie sort, but we did tend to collect stuffed animals – not sure whether that was intentional on my parents' part (probably – you can do a lot less damage beating someone with a stuffed leopard than with a plastic GI Joe) – though our animals did the things that normal kids' dolls would: drove Jeeps and Tonkas, or Kleenex box hovercraft, went to the bar (The Regal Beagle of course), had gang fights with the "bad" animals. You know, the usual… Anyway, Moreauvia came while I was recalling some of these great things, and I knew I wanted more – and if I had to wait for me to write them, it'd take forever. So I started the Moreauvia website (which may or may not yet be active as you read this – I had some issues with the ISP and lost the domain, and am in the process of getting it back) which explained the concept and invited some authors to play. If the site's back up, there will be more about Moreauvia and hopefully a couple stories we ran in the magazine set in Moreauvia from some of our other very talented author friends.

At any rate – *whew!* – there you go. There's probably more info than you need to actually enjoy this book. My immense thanks go to Byron for giving me some of the entertainment I was looking for, and to all the authors that contributed to *Tales of Moreauvia*, whether actual Moreauvian tales or not – I love historical fiction and alternate history, and every story was a treat.

—Pete S. Allen, editor/publisher/alpha weasel
Creative Guy Publishing

Chapter 1

COLONEL ROBERT COLE reclined in the desk chair, absently rubbing his thigh as he watched droplets of rain trickle down the windowpane. Through the smoky glass, he could just make out the expanse of the great Mississippi River beyond the end of the Burke property. His concentration on the raindrops was interrupted when his old dog gently thrust its head underneath the hand on his leg. He smiled and rubbed the dog's head as it nestled down, resting its head on Cole's sore thigh and staring up at him with baleful eyes. Cole looked around then, taking in the mostly empty room. The matron of the Burke household had deserted the place, moving her more valuable household artifacts to her house in Little Rock before leaving the Burke estate to Cole's troops.

A half-finished letter to the governor rested the on desk, dangerously close to the Colonel's smoldering pipe. Since the uprising had taken a turn for the worse, Governor Wheaton insisted on frequent reports; the problem was there was nothing to report. The Arkansas State Government had petitioned the Federal government in Washington for reinforcements, but the recent trouble with England meant all of the United States Regulars and most of the nation's militia were concentrated along the Canadian border. Cole believed that if President Stephen Douglas knew what was really going on up the White River they would send at least a brigade, maybe a full division. But the governor had been embarrassed by the turn of events and didn't want to admit how far gone the situation was.

Colonel Cole had seen copies of the governor's telegraphs to Washington, in which the governor said simply that there had been a slave uprising, and almost casually mentioned that the beastworkers were armed. However, he failed to give the details of the two standup fights where the so-called 'unorganized rabble' had bested the Arkansas militia. Sure, the engagements made the headlines around the nation, but what had really happened was entirely different than what was being told in the papers.

Cole ruffled Dog's ears and leaned back in his chair, wincing as pain shot down his left leg. It seemed he was always sore and sick these days. Since autumn it had gotten worse—he had lost so much weight that his clothes now hung on him. He looked like a broomstick scarecrow; everything fit loose or didn't fit at all. Lydia feared he had the cancer; he constantly told his wife not to worry, that the good Lord wasn't ready for him yet. But he knew she was right.

He pushed the letter to the governor aside placed a fresh piece of paper on the table. He dipped his quill into the inkwell and started a letter to his wife when a knock on the study's door interrupted him.

"Come in," the Colonel called out.

A small, scruffy man in a faded blue militia uniform entered the room. Three stripes on his shoulder identified the little man as a sergeant. "They here," he said, then gave a quick salute as though it was an afterthought.

"Who is here, sergeant?" Cole asked. He grabbed his hat and painfully rose to his feet.

"Federal boys, suh. Two big side-wheelers full of troops. They unloadin' now."

Cole was surprised. He had been watching out the window for at least an hour, but had somehow missed the steamers. They must have approached the docks from the north. He had expected the troops to come from the New Orleans garrison, but Washington must have pulled troops from the Canadian border. This was good news indeed; it meant they were probably regulars, and not the militia he had been expecting.

"Thank the Good Lord," Cole replied, walking toward the door. This was the first good news he'd heard in weeks. As he grabbed his overcoat from the coat rack he asked, "Has anyone contacted Major Thompson?"

"Already down at the docks," the sergeant said, helping the colonel put on his coat. "He helpin' em unload."

"These new troops, are they regulars?"

"I ain't been down to there yet, suh," the sergeant replied, shaking his head, "Soon as I heard the news, I run over here to let you know."

"That's quite all right, Sergeant," Cole said with a smile.

The colonel and the sergeant stepped out into the rain and started down toward the docks.

The clouds completely hid the moon and the stars. Beyond the hazy light coming from a few dim lanterns at the docks, it was pitch black. Occasionally, a forked tongue of lightning streaked across the sky. A pair of gangplanks ran between each of the two Army transports and the docks. The gangplank near the bow was steadily offloading troops while the gangplank to the stern was being used to offload supplies.

Two gunboats were tied off further down the dock. One was as big as the transports, though not nearly as tall. In fact, she was somewhat squatty and ugly compared to the tall, elegant transports with their fluted stacks and twin paddles mounted on each side. Like most of the larger river and coastal gunboats, she was a center-wheeler. Cole couldn't tell from this distance, but he imagined she might be one of the new ironclad warships. The other gunboat was smaller; she wasn't even half the size of her consort.

Colonel Cole stood on the hill overlooking the scene below. He had yet to go down to the docks and introduce himself to the commanding officer. For now he was content to enjoy the scene before him—reinforcements at last. Though the lantern light was hazy and dim, Cole could make out the bustle of activity below and it filled him with relief.

Joining him in surveying the scene below was a hawk-nosed captain in a dark blue uniform. For the last three months, Captain Reginald Jones had been one of the few members of the United States Army Regulars present to assist the Arkansas Militia. He had been visiting his family in Little Rock when he heard about the trouble along White River, and he quickly requested an extension of his leave and volunteered to help. Like Colonel Cole, he had missed the disaster at Clover Bend, but he had taken part in the engagement at Berkley. During the fight, Cole found Jones to be an energetic subordinate, whose love for battle seemed to be fueled by an extreme hatred of the creatures they were fighting.

Three silhouettes approached from the direction of the dock. Even though he could see but an outline, Cole could tell one of them was his Chief of Staff, Major Henry Thompson. Major Thompson tended to stand out; there weren't many one-armed men active in the military.

Thompson approached, saluted, and then introduced the officer commanding the new arrivals. "Colonel Cole, this is Colonel John Haiber."

Haiber was a tall, thin man with a narrow, youthful face. Even in his immaculate regular army officer's uniform he managed to somehow look awkward and clumsy. And he seemed far too young to be a colonel.

Haiber saluted then extended his hand, "It's a pleasure."

"It sure is," Cole said with an informal chuckle. He shook

Haiber's hand and was about to say more, but he noticed the other man who had accompanied Haiber and Thompson to the top of the hill. The man was a sergeant.

And he was black.

"Pardon my manners," Colonel Haiber said, and he turned to introduce the sergeant. "This is my Chief of Staff, Sergeant Marcus Parker."

Sergeant Parker saluted crisply.

Lightning flashed in the sky, followed by an awkward silence.

Haiber broke the silence, "I realize that it may seem odd to have a sergeant as a chief of staff, but current Army regulations prevent a Negro from advancing beyond the rank of regimental sergeant. I've found Sergeant Parker to be most qualified, and it certainly helps the morale of the troops to see one of their own serving in this capacity."

"A goddamn Colored regiment," Jones broke in. Without saluting, he turned and stalked off.

Another moment of awkward silence passed, broken only by a long peal of thunder from above.

Cole cleared his throat. "If you'll pardon me for saying, it appears the brass back in Washington is not taking the situation here in Arkansas seriously," Cole said in his smooth southern accent. His face was flushed, but his tone was even and calm. "We've got a slave uprising here. Have the powers that be considered that the last thing we need is a regiment made up of ex-slaves, who may or may not have their heart in the fight?"

Haiber seemed taken aback. His confusion made him seem even younger, but when he answered, his tone was West Point direct. "With all due respect, Colonel, my boys are fully trained soldiers—the equal of any regular unit. Furthermore, the slaves were freed two decades ago. I can assure you that every man in my regiment is either freeborn or they were freed at such a young age that they have no direct recollection of their shackled past. These are freemen, Colonel."

Colonel Cole sighed heavily. Five minutes ago he had felt as though he could finally see the light at the end of the tunnel. Now he once again felt the weight of the world settling down on his weary shoulders. "Perhaps we should meet in the morning when we've all had a night's rest." Cole turned away without waiting for a reply.

Major Thompson stood awkwardly for a second before turning to Colonel Haiber and saying, "I'm sorry, sir. The colonel's been under a lot of stress over the last few weeks."

"We all have," Haiber replied.

Thompson gave Haiber a quick salute then turned and followed Cole. The colonel didn't start up the hill toward the Burke House as Thompson expected—Cole was walking towards town.

Montgomery Point was a small community that served as little more than a stopping point at the intersection of the great highways that were the Mississippi and Arkansas Rivers. The Burke House was the only structure of any note near the docks, unless you counted a pair of dilapidated storehouses. Further inland, the community itself was little more than a handful of smaller homes centered around a lonely a dry goods store and a telegraph station.

The one-armed major jogged a few steps to catch up. "Sir, where are you going?"

"The telegraph station. I need to send a wire to Little Rock," Cole replied. He solemnly shook his head. "I hope I'm wrong, but this smells of politics."

"Perhaps you should wait until tomorrow," Thompson said, "I doubt you can reach the governor at this hour anyway. He's probably turned in for the night."

"Then I'll have someone wake him."

Thompson couldn't care less whether or not Governor Wheaton got a good night's sleep. He was, however, worried about Colonel Cole. The man had been under tremendous pressure for months now, and, while the old man tried to hide it, Thompson knew the colonel wasn't in the best of health. Cole was an experienced officer; in fact, he had been a bit of a hero in the French and Mexican War, but he was at the end of his rope. Thompson feared he might make a rash decision that he might regret in the long run.

"Are you sure you don't want to sleep on it?" Thompson ventured.

Cole didn't reply. He continued down the hill toward the station.

From atop the hill, Sergeant Parker watched the old colonel and the one-armed major make their way toward town.

Colonel Haiber turned to Parker and said, "Well, that didn't go very well."

"Better than I expected," Parker replied dryly.

Sergeant Parker liked his colonel, mostly. Haiber was certainly better than many whites, but he was still far from perfect. John Haiber was a rich boy from Massachusetts who proudly declared that he saw all blacks as equals. He was one of the last of the dying breed of Yankee idealists, men who preached equality for, and acceptance of Negroes. Unlike many of the idealists though, he went out of his way to be around blacks, even frequenting black churches in his spare time. Still, Parker often felt it was for show, that Haiber just wanted everyone to see what a great and noble idealist he was. And hypocrisy wasn't Haiber's only fault. Parker had serious doubts about the man's ability to command the regiment. He had a feeling that someday the colonel was going to get a lot of good people killed.

On the other hand, Haiber's quiet hypocrisy was certainly better than the outright hatred that radiated from other whites. Parker had much rather die following a man like Haiber than to live following someone who considered him little more than an animal.

"You lied to him, you know," Parker said suddenly.

"How so?"

"You got one ex-slave in your ranks who's old enough to remember the cotton fields."

"Sorry," Haiber said, wincing as if this minor slight pained him physically. "I forgot."

Sergeant Marcus Parker had been born into slavery on a plantation outside of Canton, Mississippi. He assumed there was a time when he had been too young to work in the fields, but he couldn't remember it. Then came freedom. His people didn't know about the advances in vivisection technology and how it had enabled the government to replace the slave population with evolved animals, and they certainly didn't know about the underhanded politics that had been just as important in bringing about their freedom. All they knew was one day they were working in the fields, and the next they were told to leave. With little more than the clothes on their backs, the newly freed slaves were herded into what the government chose to call 'Freelands.' Mississippi's version of Freeland was a worthless tract of swamp between the Yazoo and Mississippi rivers. The only crops that flourished in that godforsaken land were fields of wooden crosses that marked where the newly freed slaves buried their dead. Nearby plantation owners regularly sent wagons over the Yazoo and into the Freeland to pick up extra workers. Marcus could remember his father pushing and shoving his way into the crowds, trying to get a job, even if it was just for the day and only paid in cornmeal. One day he told his father that he didn't understand why he did it; that he'd rather starve than work for one of those arrogant bastards. His father replied that he himself would probably feel the same way if it was only his own belly he was worried about filling. At that point Marcus decided that he would never have a family.

Ten hard, lean years passed before the United States found itself at war with France over their colonial occupation of Mexico. Then came increasing tensions with England along the border of Canada; a war that if started would make the long and bloody French and Mexican War seem like a summertime military exercise. America needed cannon fodder, so they turned to the Freelands. Marcus was against signing up at first, but when so many of the younger boys enlisted, he decided to go with them so he could keep an eye on them. His age, along with the fact that many of the boys already knew and respected him, caused him to rise quickly in the ranks. Now, despite his best efforts to avoid any family ties, he found himself with a family that numbered just over one thousand.

Some thought that military life had taken some of the edge off of Marcus Parker; ten years ago he never would have taken an order from any white man. In truth, he may have learned to control his temper, but his bitterness and hatred still raged just beneath the surface.

The two men turned and walked back down the hill toward the dock.

As soon as the transports were unloaded, Colonel Haiber dismissed his chief of staff, returned onboard the *Anne Marie*, and retired to his stateroom. He undressed, washed his face in a metal basin, then dimmed the oil lamp hanging from the ceiling before finally climbing into his hammock. He was bone tired from the trip downriver, but he was too excited to sleep. A tiny spider was diligently weaving a web in a corner of the ceiling. Haiber watched as the spider gracefully connected each strand.

John Haiber was a long way from the wealthy Massachusetts estate where he had been raised. Twenty years ago, his grandfather, Whig Senator Charles Haiber had been one of the few men in Washington who struggled to free slaves for the right reasons. And, while he wasn't as renowned as Charles, John's father Paul Haiber was continuing the proud Haiber legacy of defending the weak.

The fifth of six children, John knew he would never inherit the Haiber political mantle. However, when he signed up at West Point, he hoped to help in his own way. As soon as he graduated, he requested that he be assigned to a Colored regiment. Since most officers viewed assignment to a Colored regiment a type of punishment, Haiber found that this choice, along with his political ties, gave him a fast trip up the chain of command. In fact, four months ago, he had become the youngest colonel in the United States Army and, since he had just entered West Point at the time of the conflict, he was the only active colonel who had not seen action in the French and Mexican War.

He had felt on top of the world when he first inspected his new command, the 13th Colored Regiment, but everything had been downhill from there on out. First, he found that he didn't get along well with the other white officers in the regiment. To a man they did not appreciate the fact they were serving under someone who was at least ten years younger than they were. Not only that, but most of them also resented the fact that they were assigned to a Colored regiment in the first place. Haiber used to tell himself that at least he had the respect of his soldiers, but there were times when he felt even his own chief of staff doubted his ability to lead.

He sighed heavily and reached over and turned the lamp out, leaving the spider to weave its magic in the dark.

Sergeant Parker stepped off the gangway and started toward the small village of tents situated in the mud, down near the end of the dock. Parker had been offered a small stateroom on one of the transports, but he had declined. Officers stayed in one place, enlisted men in another, it was the Army way. However, as an enlisted man holding an officer's position, Parker often felt himself caught in the middle, and when he felt this way, he always sided with his own.

He was almost to the edge of the tent village when he caught movement inland, near the base of the short cliff that rose up to the houses above. He squinted his eyes and made out four figures squatting and trying not to be seen.

Parker became uneasy. Haiber hadn't seen the need to set up pickets, and, to be honest, Parker really didn't see the need for them either, at least until now.

"Who's there?" Parker called out.

No answer. The figures slowly started making their way along the bottom of the cliff, still keeping to the shadows. What bothered Parker was the direction they were following along the cliff was bringing them toward, rather than away from the tents.

He drew his Army Colt and started toward the figures at a trot. "Stop! Stay right where you are!"

The figures stopped and raised their hands. "Damn, Sergeant Parker, don't shoot us. We just trying to stretch our legs a bit."

Parker breathed a sigh of relief and returned his pistol to its holster. He put his hands on his hips and said, "Okay, boys, step up so I can see who you are."

Although Parker wasn't a tall man, he was wide in the shoulders and his arms were thick and strong. The boys in the ranks respected him as they would their fathers, and, similarly, that respect often bordered on fear. Parker knew they feared him, too, and used this to his advantage. It had been years since he'd actually had to crack a head; the threat seemed to work just as well.

Four soldiers in dark blue uniforms stepped forward with their heads low. Parker recognized them immediately. He knew all of the soldiers in his regiment, but he knew these four particularly well. They were good boys for the most part, but they stayed in trouble, never anything serious, just enough to drive a regimental sergeant crazy, especially one who could see their potential.

"We awful sorry, Sergeant. We been cramped in that boat for three days. We just wanted to take a little walk, that's all."

"No one's going to be taking any walks. You ain't in Illinois anymore, boys. We're back in the South." Parker said, then he directly addressed the soldier who had spoken, "Eli, how long you had those corporal stripes? Three months? You supposed to be an example."

Eli lowered his head, "Sorry, sir."

"Sorry don't cut it. You boys just earned a week's worth of guard duty, and you'd be spending the night in the brig if we had one."

Seth and Joel groaned but accepted the punishment. However, Owen always had something to say. "It'd be dryer than the tents," he grumbled. "They got us camped in a damn mudhole."

"You'll do well to watch your mouth, Owen." Parker replied. "I'll see if I can't get us on some dryer ground tomorrow. Tonight you'll have to make do."

Chapter 2

THE DOGS WERE BARKING, but it wasn't an uncommon occurrence. Coons, possums, and even the occasional coyote or deer often wandered into town after dark—Little Rock had come a long way over the last few decades, but she still wasn't exactly Philadelphia.

Governor Ambrose Wheaton rolled onto his back and sighed as he stared at the semi-dark ceiling overhead.

Beside him his wife, Norma stirred. She rolled to face him. "Dogs keeping you up?" she asked.

"Yeah." In truth, his inability to sleep probably had as much to do with the thousands of two-legged dogs currently rebelling in the northeastern part of the state, but he didn't want to bother Norma with his troubles.

"Close the window," she suggested, then she rolled onto her side, facing away from him and away from the open window on his side of the bed.

Wheaton sighed again. He knew she was right, but the house got so stuffy when the windows were closed. He rolled his legs out of the bed, sat up and stretched his arms. Now that he was awake, he'd probably never get back to sleep.

"That settles it," he murmured. "I'm getting rid of that short-tail cur. He gets all riled up at anything that moves and that gets the others going."

"You won't do it."

"I most certainly will."

"That short-tail's your favorite."

"It don't matter," Wheaton said, then he stretched his mouth wide with a yawn. "Come sunrise, he's gone."

"M'kay," Norma muttered indifferently. Then her breath became heavy and even. She was already slipping back to sleep.

Moonlight shone through the open window, but not enough to allow Wheaton to see his house shoes; the governor sat at the edge of his bed, his feet searching the dark, cold hardwood floor.

Norma was right about the dog, Malcomb was his favorite. He knew he'd never be able to take the dog to the lake and throw it in with a rock tied to his neck; he'd never had the stomach for that method of disposal, even with his worst dogs, even the biters. There was no way he could do that to Malcomb. Maybe he could just give him to Simon Tibbons down the road. Surely old Tibbons would take him. The old man liked any dog that could tree a squirrel and the barking wouldn't matter since Tibbons was always so heavy into his jug by the time he went to bed he could sleep through any racket. Wheaton shook his head in the darkness. He knew he wouldn't even be able to give the dog to Tibbons. His sleep had been disturbed; he was angry. But tomorrow would be another story. He knew as soon as Malcomb bounded up with his little nub wagging tonight's transgression would be forgotten.

The tip of his toe brushed against the deerskin slippers. He slid his feet into their warmth. Just as he started to rise to his feet he thought he heard someone knocking at the mansion's front door—perhaps the dogs weren't just barking at a trespassing possum. He strained his ears, and the sound came again. This knocking was accompanied by the unmistakable sound of a man's voice, "Governor, sir!"

Norma was suddenly awake. "Who could it be at this hour?" she asked, her voice sounded perturbed at first, then it shifted to fear. "You don't think it's a thief." She paused. "Or one of those *beasts*."

Still sitting on the edge of the bed, Governor Wheaton chuckled. "No, I don't think it's either." The thought had crossed his mind when he first heard the knocks, but the voice that had called out was too clear not to be human. Besides, he doubted a beastman would have sense enough to knock on a door.

"Aren't you going to go see?" Norma asked, obviously still worried.

"Ella can take care of it," he said. "It's probably one of our good citizens, one with more liquor in their gullet than good sense in their head, here to complain about taxes or something. Wouldn't be the first time you know."

Norma grunted her disapproval.

The knocks came again, followed by the voice once again calling out. "Governor, sir! I have urgent business!" The voice didn't sound intoxicated.

Downstairs, Ella called out, "Hold your horses! I'm a comin'!"

The door was too far way for him to hear the exchange, but after a moment of silence passed Wheaton figured the interloper had been sent on his way, probably with a severe tongue lashing from Ella. He rose to his feet and started across the bedroom toward the open window.

Before he reached the window he heard footsteps on the stairs.

"Someone's coming," Norma said nervously.

"Just Ella."

A gentle rap came from the door.

"Yes?" Wheaton asked.

The door opened, letting the soft light of a solitary candle spill into the governor's bedroom. Ella poked her head into the room, her wrinkled, ebony face lit by the candle's glow. "Suh, I do so hate to be a bother at such an hour, but there's a man at the door who insists on seeing you."

"Ella, you know better. I most certainly do not entertain guests in the middle of the night."

When the blacks had been freed and moved to the Freelands two decades ago, an exception was made for the slave owners who required household servants. The beasts were considered acceptable replacements in the field, but they were not considered civilized enough to serve in the houses of refined Southern gentry. With few exceptions, the plantation owners and well-to-do business men took advantage of a clause that allowed them to keep household servants. Ella had served the Wheatons for almost three decades now. She was well-treated, but free in name only.

"I'm very sorry, sir, but he's from the telegraph station. He says he's got word from down river."

This changed everything. Wheaton grabbed a housecoat from atop the dresser, quickly put it on and followed Ella out of the bedroom and down the hall toward the front door.

When they made their way across the grand room, Wheaton could see a whiskered man in a military uniform in the doorway. Obviously a militiaman, his jacket was a dingy faded shade of blue, his mismatched blue-grey pants were wrinkled with a patch on one knee, and he sported a pair of blatantly non-regulation red suspenders. Worse yet, he didn't even bother to take his kepi off or salute in the presence of his governor.

"This had better be important," Wheaton grumbled as he approached. He already knew the message was probably urgent, but he was still peeved at having been roused out of bed.

"Just followin' orders," the militiaman said with a casual, unmilitary-like shrug.

"And just who in the blue blazes gave you orders to wake me at this hour?"

"Colonel Cole," the militiaman said, and he the telegram to the governor.

Wheaton grunted, glanced at the paper, then handed it back without reading it. "You'll have to read it to me; my reading glasses are on my nightstand."

Ella moved her candle close to the soldier so he could see. However, he didn't look at the telegraph. Still in a very unmilitary manner that Wheaton felt was awful close to disrespect, the militiaman simply told the governor the gist of what was said. "He says the reinforcements came in but all they sent was a couple of gunboats and one regiment. He wanted to know if you knew they sent a Colored regiment."

Wheaton sighed. "Wire him back and tell him I am aware of his situation and that I'll be dispatching Senator Pickering downriver to fill him in on the details." Wheaton stopped raised his eyebrows and gave the militiaman a curious stare. "Well?"

"Well what?"

"Aren't you going to write it down?"

"Naw, I got it. That all?"

Wheaton sighed. "Yes."

With that, the soldier turned and started back toward the telegraph station, still without giving so much as a salute or even a tip of his hat.

Wheaton turned to Ella. "Take the carriage and go over to Nathaniel Pickering's place. Tell him I need to speak with him tonight."

"Yes, sir."

Still clad in his housecoat and slippers but now wide awake, Governor Wheaton was sitting on his front porch when the carriage pulled back up the drive toward the house. Ella pulled the carriage up to the steps and Senator Pickering climbed out and made his way up to the porch.

Unlike the governor, Senator Pickering was fully dressed in a country gentleman's brown suit. In fact, walking up to porch with the casual smile on his face, he looked as though if he was about to ask for Wheaton's vote. No doubt about it; Nathaniel Pickering was a natural.

"Governor, sir," Pickering said, his smile widening as he ascended the stairs to the porch. "To what do I owe the honor?"

"You're certainly in better spirits than I was when they got me out of bed," Wheaton replied, rising to his feet.

"It's always a pleasure."

They shook hands, and Wheaton motioned to the front door. "Come inside and I'll explain."

Inside the house the grand room was dimly lit with a pair of lanterns resting on the mantle. Two chairs had been pulled up to the fireplace; although there was no fire, Wheaton figured it was the appropriate place for two gentlemen to meet and discuss important business.

As soon as they were seated Wheaton started filling the senator in. "Senator Haiber's son's regiment arrived this afternoon at Montgomery Point."

"Splendid," Pickering replied with a toothy grin.

"Yes, but, our dear Colonel Cole is not pleased."

"Colonel Cole? Pardon my ignorance of military matters, but I thought he was General Cole?"

"He is, sort of. You see, Cole is an old military hand. I'm sure he appreciates his current position as Commanding General of the Arkansas militia, but he prefers to be addressed by the rank he held during his active days in the Regular Army."

Pickering nodded in feigned agreement. Wheaton knew the concept of accepting a lesser rank as a matter of pride was alien to the ambitious young politician. The governor didn't see Pickering's ruthless ambition as a fault, however. They were on the same side here, and Pickering was an ally and he had the potential to be a tremendous asset to the party. In fact, many people in the Arkansas Democratic Party saw Nathaniel Pickering as Wheaton's heir apparent.

Before Wheaton could get started, Pickering thought of something else. "Please excuse me for interrupting again, but did you say Cole was upset? I thought he was aware of the situation."

"He left for Montgomery Point not long after I agreed to his expedition up the White River. He wasn't in Little Rock when we sent the message to Washington, and I didn't dare give him the details of the message to him on an open wire."

"I see."

"Besides, there are some details that I may not want him to know."

At this Pickering raised his eyebrows.

"Cole is an outstanding military leader. He was a hero at Palo Gaucho and there's little doubt he'd be commanding a corps on the Canadian border if it wasn't for his fragile constitution. But Cole isn't politically savvy, if you get my drift."

Pickering's grin widened. "I do indeed."

Wheaton reached over and gave Pickering a friendly slap on the leg. He smiled and said, "And that, my friend, brings us to the reason I had you dragged out of bed at this late hour. I'm sending you downriver to Montgomery Point. You will be accompanying the colonel on the expedition up the White. I know it's quite sudden, but I'm afraid you'll have to leave for Montgomery Point tomorrow morning."

It was almost impossible to catch a man like Nathaniel Pickering off guard and, for a moment, Wheaton thought he had managed to do so. Surely the young politician hadn't expected to find himself shipped downriver for a military expedition with less than a day's notice. However, Pickering's smile never faltered and after only a brief moment of silence the senator replied. "It's always a privilege to be of service—anything I can do to help the party."

Wheaton was pleased by his protégé's reaction, but he found himself oddly disappointed at not having at least surprised the young buck. Still, he had one more card up his sleeve.

"There's another reason I'm sending you with Cole."

"Oh?"

"Remember those two beastmen that were captured just outside the city last week?"

"Yes."

"We questioned them quite thoroughly, and you won't believe what they told us. They claimed they were delivering a message from Longtooth. They said he wants to negotiate."

This time Pickering was surprised. He sat up in his chair, "Really now? Do you suppose those savage beasts were telling the truth?"

Wheaton pretended to clear his throat. Actually the pause was so he could savor his protégé's surprise. There were times when Pickering seemed to be too confident, too controlled, too much the perfect politician. Wheaton enjoyed seeing the chinks in the young man's armor from time to time, no matter how insignificant they might be.

"I don't know; I can't be certain," Wheaton finally said, "But whatever the truth, we can't let the Whigs get wind of this. Using Senator Haiber's son on the expedition may keep them from voicing any opposition to our methods of putting down the uprising, but if they hear the rebels attempted to negotiate, rest assured, they will use it to their advantage."

Pickering nodded in agreement.

"That's one reason I want you with them. If Longtooth makes any attempt to contact anyone on the expedition, I want you to go through the motions. Don't put yourself at risk, but agree to the meeting. Just be damn sure the negotiations fall through, and when they do, I want you to use this opportunity to capture Longtooth."

"How much of this should I tell Cole?"

"It's probably best that we explain what we're doing with Haiber and why we requested his regiment, but I don't think he needs to know about the possibility of Longtooth contacting him. That's a political issue."

Pickering was about to reply when a crash came from the hallway behind them. Both men spun around.

"Norma? Ella?" Wheaton asked.

"Sorry, suh," Ella's voice replied. "I knocked Mrs. Norma's vase off the table in the hall here. I'm very sorry, I'll clean it right up."

"Well, what in the blue blazes were you doing traipsing around the house in the dark?"

"Eavesdropping, I'll wager," Pickering muttered.

Wheaton shook his head, "Ella knows better."

"My candle went out," Ella said, poking her head around the corner.

"What were you doing in the hallway? You've given our respected guest the impression that I can't even keep a servant who minds her own business."

"I'm very sorry, suh. I's just coming to see if y'all needed anything. When my candle went out I stumbled into the table."

"The good senator and I are fine, thank you very much. Go to bed and leave us be."

"I got to clean this mess up."

"Clean it in the morning. My guest and I have important business to attend to."

"Yes, sir. Sorry, sir."

Wheaton turned to Pickering and said, "I'm terribly sorry for the interruption. You were saying?"

Pickering tilted his head like a dog deciphering a peculiar sound. He listened as Ella's footfalls dissipated down the hall and didn't say a word until he could no longer here them. "I agree. Cole seems to know his profession well enough, but it's best to leave the political decisions to the people's chosen representatives."

Wheaton nodded in agreement.

"One thing, though. You mentioned that I was not to place myself in any danger. What if the beastmen don't agree to meet under our terms? What if they want to meet at a neutral location. Should I go with the party?"

"Heavens, no. They might decide to use you as a hostage."

"Then who should I send in my stead?"

"There's a Captain Reginald Jones with Cole at Montgomery Point. Jones is a regular army officer who was on leave when the trouble started. He volunteered to go along on the expedition. He is not a member of the militia and therefore has no direct ties with Colonel Cole. I met with Captain Jones before he left for Montgomery Point, and I believe him to be a very reliable officer. I feel you can take him into confidence."

"Very good." Pickering said. He sat up and moved to the edge of his seat. "What time shall I depart?"

"One of Cole's steamers arrived yesterday for supplies. I want you to be on it when it starts back downriver at daybreak. I'll wire Cole; he'll be expecting you."

Pickering rose to his feet. "I'd better start packing."

Ella's heart was still hammering from the close call when she heard the front door shut. She waited until she heard Governor Wheaton's footfalls on the stairs before she dared to set foot out of her bed. There were few pieces of furniture in her tiny servant's room near the kitchen; just a small rickety bed and chair and writing table. She moved across the small room and took a seat at the table.

Ella sat in the dark for a little while longer, making sure the master was asleep. Then she took out a tinderbox and carefully lit her candle. She took a piece of paper and a quill and inkwell out of her writing table. The Wheaton family had moved the old writing table into her room mostly for looks and so Ella could use the drawers to store her clothes; they had no idea that their longtime servant could read and write. She had learned before she moved into the house, back when she was a slave in the fields. It was illegal then and she had never really found much use for it until now.

Her hand trembled as she did her best to write down everything she heard. Her handwriting sloppy and her spelling was crude at best; still, it was good enough to convey meaning. She had missed the last part of the conversation, but she knew what she had heard was of the utmost importance.

As soon as she was finished Ella blew out the candle and made her way out the door and down the dark hall toward the kitchen. This time she was extra careful not to bump into anything. Once she was in the kitchen Ella removed several pieces of dried meat from a jar on the counter.

When Ella opened the back door three dogs greeted her with wagging tails. "Hush," Ella said sharply, before they could start yapping. She handed a piece of dried meat to each dog. One by one they took the treat and then they pranced off to enjoy their bribe.

Ella tucked the rest of the dried meat into a small sack and started toward the woods. She took several glances behind her as she made her way across the pasture half expecting to see a light in the master bedroom window. She knew if she was caught this time there would be no talking her way out of it.

Ambrose Wheaton was no fool.

Once she was at the edge of the woods, Ella took the dried meat out of her sack, then she cupped her mouth and hooted like a night owl. She knew if the Nell didn't hear the signal, she would smell the meat.

There was no answer at first. Ella took another cautious look over her shoulder, then turned back to the woods and hooted once more.

Then she heard movement in the brush ahead.

"Nell?" she called out in a whisper, "That you?"

No answer.

"Nell, come on out. You know I can't see you in the dark."

More movement in the brush, then a shape began to form. Finally she stepped into the moonlight where Ella could see her. Nell was a small dogbreed, probably less than five feet tall. And she appeared even smaller since, like so many of her kind, she tended to walk with a stoop. She looked bad, like she was nothing more than loose skin draped over a bony frame.

"Got something for you, sweetie," Ella said, holding the meat in her outstretched hand.

Nell inched forward.

"You know I ain't gonna hurt you, so why you got to be like this every time?"

"Sorry," Nell murmured and she gingerly took one of the pieces of dried meat from Ella's hand. Nevertheless, she took a cautious step back before cramming it into her mouth.

Nell hadn't looked this rough three months ago when she had first started serving as a messenger between Ella and the rebels. But she had been told to stay in the woods behind the house, and not to stray. She had to live off whatever Ella could manage to sneak out to her, and Ella could only make the trip to the woods once or twice a week for fear of rousing suspicion.

Ella cast another cautious glance over her shoulder at the dark house behind her, then she held out the folder piece of paper. "Nell, get this to Longtooth. It's very important."

Nodded, took the paper, then held her hand out for another piece of meat.

Ella handed her the whole bag. "When you finish the meat, put the letter in this. It may rain and we don't want that letter getting wet."

"Okay," Nell said then she took the bag, and started devouring the strips of meat.

Nell didn't know it, but there was something else in the letter as well. Ella had watched Nell's health deteriorate over the last few months and she just couldn't bring herself to stand idly by and watch the creature she now considered her friend wither away and die. In her letter, she had suggested that Nell had done enough for the cause. She asked Longtooth to send someone else.

Ella started to leave, then she stopped and turned to the hunched creature who looked so much like a human yet so much like beaten mongrel. "Nell, you take care, you hear."

Nell stopped eating long enough to reply.

"You, too."

Ella turned and started back to the house.

Chapter 3

THE STORM HAD PASSED during the night and the rain petered out by daybreak. Thompson sat on the couch in the Burke House with the newspaper, the *Little Rock Trumpet*, spread out before him on the coffee table. Occasionally he would glance up from his reading to check on Colonel Cole, who was once again sitting at a small writing table near the window.

Henry Thompson had served as the IV Corps cartographer during the drive on Mexico City. At the battle of Palo Gaucho, where the United States Army had soundly defeated the French Colonial Army under Charles de Lorencez, a shell had exploded among the IV Corps staff, mortally wounding the commander of the corps, General John Reynolds. Thompson was also wounded in the explosion, but he didn't realize how bad it was until later in the hospital. In fact, he didn't even realize he was going to lose his arm until the surgeon reached for the bone saw. There was never any discussion that he could remember. One minute the surgeon was picking shell fragments out of his arm and the next minute he apparently changed his mind and reached for the saw. He could still remember the fear he felt when he realized what was about to happen, and the nauseating horror five minutes later when he saw his own bloody arm tossed into a pile of discarded limbs.

Thompson often considered it God's cruel joke that he lost his left arm. The surgeon was the first of many who would tell him, *be glad it wasn't your right*. More often than not, Thompson just smiled and agreed, never bothering to tell them that he had been left-handed.

Even in these trying times, the loss of an arm had been enough to keep Thompson out of active military service; however, it hadn't prevented Colonel Cole from asking him to serve as his Chief of Staff when the revolt began, and this request made Thompson feel indebted to the old colonel. Although they had only worked together for three months, Thompson already felt a strong tie to Colonel Cole. Cole was the one man who hadn't seen the crippled cartographer as just another name on the Invalid Reserves roster.

Last night, as soon as Cole had left the company of Colonel Haiber, he had gone directly to the telegraph station and sent an urgent telegram to the governor, informing him of what had transpired. The reply had been delivered first this morning and much to his, and Cole's, surprise, Governor Wheaton already knew about the developments. Wheaton then informed him that he would be dispatching Senator Nathaniel Pickering to act as a liaison representing the governor's interests.

Thompson knew this news was yet another blow to Colonel Cole's flagging morale; now he was going to have to play nursemaid to a politician.

Thompson looked up from his paper and said, "Colonel, it's already half past nine. Don't you think we should call on Colonel Haiber?

Cole seemed to think about this for a moment then he said, "Yes, I guess we'd better."

Thompson folded his paper and rose from his seat.

Cole started to rise, then glanced out the window. "Never mind," he said, "Looks like Haiber got tired of waiting. He's coming up the hill now."

Like most colonels, Cole didn't require a large staff, just an officer to serve as chief of staff, a quartermaster, and a couple of messengers who would only be attached during combat or drill. This meant that in most circumstances, Thompson served in every role the colonel needed. At times he was even a butler.

"How many guests, sir?" Thompson asked.

"Three," Cole replied still looking out the window, "A naval officer seems to be accompanying the colonel and his Negro today."

"Would you like to meet with them at the table, sir? It's a little early for dinner, but I can find something in the pantry."

Cole rose slowly out of his chair. "No need. I'm sure they've already had breakfast."

"We should at least offer them something."

"Stop fretting," Cole said with a rough smile, "I do declare, Thompson, sometimes you carry on like an old woman."

Three sharp knocks sounded on the door.

"Come in," Cole answered.

The two officers entered first, followed by Sergeant Parker. Haiber entered the room somewhat sheepishly, hat in hand. The naval officer strode forward like he was boarding an enemy ship. He seemed friendly enough, in fact he was all smiles, but he dominated the room in seconds.

"Good day, colonel," the tall officer trumpeted in a deep Southern accent, "the name's Captain Jeremiah T. Morison, United States Navy."

"It's a pleasure," Cole said genuinely pleased. And perhaps he was pleased to meet this overbearing captain. At least he was another Southerner.

"I hope you don't mind us barging in unannounced," Haiber said apologetically.

"Not at all," Cole replied.

"We just thought it might be a good idea to—" Haiber started.

"Old Widow Burke," Morison interrupted, as he gazed

around the room, as if sizing it up for prize court. "Is she still around?"

"She's been ill of late," Cole replied. "She's been staying with relatives in Little Rock for some time now. The good lady was kind enough to give us full run of her house."

"Well, I guess you'd better update us on the situation," Morison said as he moved over to the dinner table and took a seat. Cole and Haiber followed his cue and sat as well. Thompson followed them to the table but remained standing. Parker remained by the door.

"Would y'all like anything to drink?" Thompson asked. "We've got whiskey. I also found a bottle of imported scotch hidden behind the bread box."

"I don't drink, son," Morison boomed with an overbearing voice that was accompanied by a friendly grin, "Abstinence is holiness."

"No, thank you," Haiber said.

Cole shook his head then said, "Have a seat, Major."

Thompson glanced over to where Parker stood by the door, at rigid attention. He motioned toward a chair, but either Parker didn't see him or he chose to ignore the offer.

Cole cleared his throat and started the story from the beginning:

"It started on a farm in northeast Arkansas, close to Smithville, around two years ago. It was a small farm with no more than six hands, all dog-breeds, five males and a bitch. The farmer had a reputation for being heavy handed with his slaves—he had a riding crop and didn't mind using it. Now y'all know as well as I do that the dog-breeds are generally loyal, but there's always a limit.

"Story has it that one day the farmer got in the liquor and went to beating on the bitch and ended up killing her; but that wasn't all. Let's just say he did some terrible things that turned even this old veteran's stomach. Anyway, his hands found out what he had done and they killed him.

"When word got back to town, the sheriff at Batesville rounded up a handful of volunteers, and went out to the farm to capture the dog-men. He brought in four, but one got away. The next thing you know, the whole area's in an uproar. Most of the people wanted the dogs hanged immediately but there was some outcry about how these dogs had been treated. Sure, they're animals, but even animals deserve better than that poor bitch got. Well, the issue was settled when a group of plantation owners led a mob to the jail. They bribed the jailer then took the dogs outside and let the mob have them.

"Somehow word got around to the slaves all over the northeastern portion of the State, and they started causing a little disorder here and there. Some refused to work, a few even turned destructive, but not too many. The militia was called out and we put them back to work without much trouble. It wasn't a violent uprising like this one. I think there was something like three deaths throughout the whole affair.

"The whole time this is going on, the dogbreed who escaped was starting to become a bit of a legend among the slaves. He even took a name that I guess he figured sounded more like a dog. He started calling himself Longtooth.

"Anyway, after the uprising the plantation owners became far stricter. Harsh, even. They believed a lack of discipline to be the root of the problem. And it didn't make matters any better that the state put such a large bounty on the renegade dogbreed's pelt. It seemed every month we had some bounty hunter killing an innocent slave just because they thought they could pass their hide off as belonging to Longtooth.

"All things considered, I'm surprised it took as long as it did for all hell to break loose. The slaves had their Spartacus and the plantation owners seemed hell bent on pushing their workers to the breaking point. Finally, when it did happen, it happened all of a sudden, like it had been planned from within. Thousands of slaves in the Northeastern part of the State simply disappeared into the night. Soon word came that an army some thirty thousand strong was camped in the woods near Gainesville.

"Now you may think you've heard what happened next because it's been all over the papers for four months now, but let me tell you what really happened. The governor called up the militia. I was to take command in Little Rock, then move north. However, Senator Silas Pruitt proved he had the Devil's ambition. Despite not having any military background he said he would 'lead an army of the righteous in a crusade against the unholy beasts that have risen among us.' I believe that's what he said word for word.

"He gathered volunteers in Batesville, then, and without any government sanction he set out with one of the three Arkansas militia regiments and about three thousand armed volunteers from all over northern Arkansas and southern Missouri— about four thousand effectives. When they camped at Clover Bend, they thought the rebels were several days away. They didn't even bother to put out pickets. The beasts fell on them at night. I imagine the rebels couldn't have had more than two hundred, maybe four hundred firearms, mostly old shotguns and muskets they had taken when they robbed their masters the night they disappeared. The papers said they used their claws and fangs, but I've interview several witnesses who say that those who didn't have guns used farming instruments or sharpened sticks. Pruitt's little army was completely routed. The volunteers, and even the militia, dropped their guns and ran.

"You can imagine my reaction when I arrived in Batesville.

This buffoon had just hand delivered several thousand rifles and muskets to the enemy. Pruitt survived the attack and returned to Batesville, but he decided to cheat the hangman and put a bullet in his own forehead.

"After the disaster at Clover Bend, the rebels became bold and moved south. As they approached Elizabeth the residents fled, leaving the town in their hands. I thought that this would be their undoing and set out with my two regiments, hoping to catch them unorganized while in the act of looting the town. However, Longtooth was sharper than I anticipated. He tried another night attack near Berkley, but, unlike Pruitt, I had pickets out. We had just enough warning to draw into a line. And let me tell you, for a group of unorganized rebels, they fought like the devil. They pushed back both of my flanks and even managed to isolate and destroy two companies that had become separated from the main line. The only thing that kept my men from making a headlong retreat was the fear that if they broke formation they would be at the mercy of the beasts. And they were probably right, judging from the stories the survivors of Clover Bend were telling.

"The next morning I collected the wounded and withdrew from the field. I returned to Little Rock and tried to convince the governor to call for Federal troops right then, but he insisted we could put down the rebellion ourselves. Since our militia is mostly armed with muskets and older rifles and a few antique field pieces, he decided to borrow weapons rather than men from the Federal government. Washington agreed and a steamer was dispatched from the Saint Louis Armory carrying one thousand new Springfield rifles, two six-pounder and four twelve-pounder field guns, and a pair of twenty-four-pounder naval pieces that we were going to place on a steamer to enable us to patrol up the White River.

"Apparently the steamer delivering the arms was ambushed

on the Arkansas River. At the time, we thought the rebels were still much farther north so when the ship didn't arrive we assumed there had been an accident, but after several more steamers were attacked we realized that they had moved down to the mouth of the White River."

Morison leaned forward in his seat. "At least the beasts won't be able to make use of the cannons," he said.

"That's what we thought, too," Cole replied. "We believe the ships that have been captured, three in all, were taken by subterfuge. They probably used small boats and boarded under the cover of fog. But lately they've taken to using the six-pounders to fire at ships from the banks."

"Reckon how they learned to use the guns?"

"We're not sure," Cole replied, "but there was a Colored regiment that hailed from Western Tennessee that was recently disbanded for disciplinary problems—the 5th Colored Regiment, I believe. Some of them may have got across the Mississippi River to help the rebels."

"Um, no, that couldn't be the case," Haiber spoke up, "the 5th was like the 13th in that it didn't have an artillery battery directly attached, so it wouldn't have artillerists. Besides the 5th wasn't actually disbanded for—"

"How did they know a steamer was coming carrying arms? And how did they know when it was coming?" Morison asked, interrupting Haiber. It seemed he didn't mind sharing the stage with an old military man like Cole, but when the younger pup spoke, he inevitably found something more interesting to say.

"We don't know, but we assume somebody's helping them."

"Who would do that?" Morison asked, "The English?"

Cole shrugged. "I don't know how they could have made contact with the rebels, but an English spy is a possibility."

"Something else I noticed," Morison said slyly as he leaned forward over the table like he had a dark secret that he was just dying to tell, "The way you told the story, you've got me to thinkin' that you may hold a little sympathy for the rebels."

Cole tensed at first, perhaps he thought Morison was accusing him of treason. The expression passed as sudden as it came on; the old colonel relaxed and replied, "When I put down that uprising two years ago, the beasts were as docile as cattle. Hell, they were downright friendly, despite the fact my boys was forcing them back to their owners at gunpoint. Then the plantation owners start treatin' them like they did."

"Come on, Cole," Morison said, his teeth still bared in a sly smile. "They're just animals."

"I know they're animals," Cole replied, then he motioned to his dog, who had just laid his head on his master's foot, "but I wouldn't go and treat ol' Dog half as bad as they was treatin' their slaves."

With the sly smile still on his face, Morison leaned back in his chair.

"Even then the rebels didn't get out of hand until Clover Bend," Cole continued, "You see, not all the beasts joined Longtooth. Some were still with their masters when Pruitt's little holy army came through. Pruitt's men killed beastmen wherever they went, whether they had taken part in the rebellion or not. I heard from a good source that on the way to find Longtooth they took fourteen innocent workers out of their quarters, tied them up, and burned them alive while Pruitt stood before them reading out of the Holy Scripture. That's what caused them to get so damn worked up at Clover Bend, that's why they fought so hard at Berkley, and that's why I'm not going to be able to convince them to go home this time."

"I see," Morison said, his teeth still showing.

"Now, don't get me wrong. I'm a soldier. It's my duty to see that this insurrection is put down, and I will do just that."

"Bully for you," Morison thundered with a grin. He slammed his hand down on the table, causing Haiber to jump. "A good soldier always sees to his duty."

Thompson wondered if this was the only bit of knowledge the Captain had gleaned from Cole's story. In fact, he wondered if Captain Morison had been listening at all.

Another knock came from the door, and without waiting for an answer, two more officers entered the room, Captain Jones and Colonel Cole's Quartermaster, Captain A. J. Baxter. Baxter made his way over to the table, but Jones stopped as soon as he entered the room and glared at Parker.

Parker remained rigid as if at attention.

"Looks like someone left the door open and look what wandered inside," Jones said, then without taking his piercing eyes from Parker he said spoke to Cole, "Colonel, I doubt a fine lady like Widow Burke would approve of a Colored in her house."

"Actually, her servant's black," Thompson commented, but his polite attempt to ease the situation only added fuel to the fire.

"Yeah, that's what they're good for," Jones took a step closer to Parker. "Say, *boy*, why don't you fetch me something to drink."

"That's quite enough, Captain," Cole said. "Come have a seat. I just briefed out newcomers on the situation and we were about to start discussing our options."

Jones glared at Parker for another second, then walked over to the table. As he sat down he cast a cold glance across the table at Haiber, who turned red but said nothing.

Cole waited until everyone was seated before starting again, "The draft drained many of the able-bodied men out of the State. When the uprising started we only had three regiments of infantry, each with its own company of cavalry attached.

The disaster at Clover Bend all but wiped out the 2nd Regiment and, to make matters worse, I had detached the other two cavalry companies and sent them ahead of my column. They joined Pruitt and suffered heavily at Clover Bend. The 1st and 3rd Regiments were both banged up at Berkley, and afterwards many of the militiamen decided that they'd had enough and went home. The governor called for more volunteers, but was unable to come up with enough to fill out two regiments." Cole nodded to his quartermaster, "Baxter, you can fill in the rest."

"Yes, suh," the red-haired, freckle-faced boy said then he started rattling off the details of the Arkansas militia regiment in an odd Southern drawl that was spoken remarkably fast, "We only got one regiment but it's a strong one—twelve full companies instead of ten. What we lack is good arms. Company A, commanded by Captain Jones here, has Springfields but the other eleven companies just got a mix of old rifles and muskets. We ain't got cavalry horses, lost all of those at Clover Bend, but we got enough tack and untrained mounts to equip a mounted company. So far we ain't done it, beings as we gonna be in swamp and woodlands, infantry will do fine and we won't have to worry about horse fodder."

"We've got twelve hundred militia and the 13th Colored brings that up to about twenty-two hundred," Colonel Cole said. "Not quite as many as I had hoped, but I believe it will be enough if we move fast." Cole turned to Thompson, "I need your map."

"Yes, sir."

As Thompson got up to retrieve the map, Cole turned to Morison, "The White is running high on her banks this year. A local pilot said even the shallows on the way to Elizabeth will be around six and a half to seven feet for another month. I'm kind of worried about that big gunboat. Will your ships be able to make the trip up river?"

"With ease, sir." Morison said grandly, "The *Baton Rouge* draws about five and a half feet and the *Marmora* could float on this table if we spilled water on it; she only draws two feet. We're more likely to have trouble with the Army's transports; they draw right at six feet."

"The state chartered three smaller steamers to carry our troops," Cole said, "two are already here, and another is on the way. I can't recall their draft, but they won't have a problem up the river."

Thompson returned to the room and unrolled a thoroughly detailed map of the lower half of the White River and the surrounding area.

"After Berkley, Longtooth's followers seemed to scatter throughout the region. We hoped that the casualties he'd suffered had caused the beasts' unity to collapse. It was wishful thinking. The beasts are more organized now than ever before. Their main base of operations is on the east bank of the White River, somewhere south of Elizabeth." Cole used a kitchen knife to trace a line down the first twenty miles of river south of Elizabeth, "But they've got small outposts all over the area, covering all of the roads and major trails leading to Elizabeth." Again using the knife, Cole pointed at several locations on the roads where Thompson had marked the map with small Xs. "If we move on them by land, they'll be alerted well ahead of time. They'll be able to gather forces and hit us at night again. Last time we barely held on long enough to withdraw, next time we may not be so lucky."

"These Xs are approximate locations, correct?" Haiber asked.

"Actually, I feel certain they're accurate. I've got a scout who's been reconnoitering the area. He's yet to lead me astray."

Thompson cringed at the mention of this scout—the man

who called himself Hunter. The major's mother had raised him with the conviction that there's some good in everyone. But he imagined his mother had never met a man like Hunter. Thompson knew Cole didn't like the scout either, but so far every bit of information this devil of a man brought them had been well worth the gold he demanded.

"My plan is simple," Cole continued. "We take the steamers up the White River. We'll be fighting the current, but we'll still make twice the time we would make if we traveled by land, even if we forced marched night and day. We'll be able to reach their main camp before all of their outlying positions can be called in. We then unload and with cover fire from the gunboats and destroy the main portion of their army. From that point it will just be a case of hunting down small bands."

"A bold plan!" Morison bellowed, again slapping the table. "When do we sail?"

"Probably in about a week. I'm supposed to meet with my scout at the mouth of the White two days from today. I have one more assignment for him. After that I'll give him a couple more days to complete his mission, then we head up river." Cole rose from the table, "I guess that's everything for now. If you'll excuse me I'm expecting a telegraph at the station."

The officers rose to their feet as they dismissed the meeting.

Parker cleared his throat, "If I may, Colonel Cole."

Jones muttered, but Cole said, "Go ahead, sergeant."

"The 13th is camped at the end of the docks. I would like to request on behalf of the troops that we be moved to dryer ground."

"By all means, sergeant," Cole replied. He turned to Thompson. "Major, would you see that a suitable site is located?"

"Right away, sir."

As the guests made their way to the door, Morison continued to demand attention with his loud, jovial comments and observations. Haiber, on the other hand, quietly thanked Colonel Cole for his hospitality then made his way to the door in silence.

Captain Morison continued the loud one-sided conversation as the three soldiers descended the hill. This was the second time this morning the Captain had told them of his exploits off the Yucatan Coast during the French and Mexican War. Morison seemed to like the sound of his own voice, especially when it was loudly proclaiming his glory days as the First Mate on a United States sloop of war during the conflict.

Haiber nodded every now and then, but remained silent. At least Haiber feigned interest; Parker didn't even go that far. He walked on in stony silence. Of course he imagined Morison wasn't as interested in impressing a sergeant, especially a black one.

When the trio finally came to the gangplank leading to the *Baton Rouge*, Morison grasped Haiber by shoulder in an overtly friendly gesture that was probably more of an effort to keep the colonel from leaving before his tale of glory was over. Parker stood near the edge of the walkway, dutifully waiting for his commanding officer.

Minutes passed and finally Parker finally spoke up, "Begging your pardon, sir, I need to return to the camp and see that my boys are ready to break camp."

Although Parker spoke to Haiber, it was Morison who answered, "Of course, please carry on."

Parker remained in place, waiting for his superior officer to grant him leave.

Instead, Haiber spoke to Morison, "Duty beckons me as well, captain. Perhaps we can pick up the conversation later this afternoon."

"Certainly," Morison loudly proclaimed, "You can call on me any time."

Haiber and Parker continued down the walkway for a few more feet before Haiber muttered, "Likes to talk, doesn't he?"

"Yes, sir," Parker replied.

The regimental camp was scattered all along the Army's portion of the dock area, with tents coming right up to the board walkway. When the two soldiers came to the gangway that led to the first Army transport, the point that normally marked their parting of ways, Parker turned to walk away into the camp area.

"Wait," Haiber said.

Parker turned but said nothing. Haiber's face was flushed and he appeared awkward and uneasy.

"I hadn't forgotten," Haiber said, "I was going to ask Colonel Cole for permission to move the campsite."

"I apologize if I overstepped my bounds, sir."

Haiber shook his head, "That's not the point. I just want you to know it had not escaped my mind."

Parker nodded, "Yes, sir."

For a moment Haiber seemed as if he had something else to say then he just said, "Carry on."

Without a word Parker turned on his heels and continued into the tents.

Chapter 4

MAJOR THOMPSON STOOD beside Colonel Cole on the dock.

The *Isabella*, the last of the three chartered steamers, arrived late that afternoon. She had been a graceful little steamer before the State of Arkansas got its hands on her two weeks ago. Now planks had been added around her walkway and thin iron plating added to her pilot house, to protect her crew and the militiamen from marksmen. An antique bronze four-pounder on a field carriage was situated on the front deck of vessel. A few practice rounds had revealed that, even with wedges blocking the wheels, the light gun jumped halfway across the wooden deck when it was fired, but there wasn't enough time to construct a proper naval carriage.

There were no troops on the *Isabella* during her trip down the Arkansas from Little Rock. She carried the last of the essential supplies, mostly flour and perishables. In addition, she carried one important passenger—Arkansas State Senator Nathaniel Pickering.

Pickering stopped at the top of the gangplank and glanced up and down the deck. The politician smiled as he walked down the plank. His teeth were small and numerous. Thompson thought he looked like a possum who had decided that playing dead wasn't working, so it was time to show some teeth.

Pickering handed his suitcase to Thompson, "Thank you, my good man." He then turned his possum-grin to Cole and extended his hand. "It's a pleasure to finally make your acquaintance. Little Rock is singing the praises of Arkansas' own Napoleon."

"Don't know that I would go that far," Cole replied.

"Truly, I have heard nothing but glorious tales regarding your experience in the war and your capacity as a commander. It is truly an honor to meet you."

Cole hated politicians, but he knew how to play the game. He smiled and replied, "Likewise, your reputation precedes you, senator. We have an extra room at the Burke House. We'd be honored to have you as our guest."

"Splendid," Pickering replied happily.

Once they had completed the required political posturing, Pickering became serious. "Is there somewhere we can talk in private?"

"Right this way."

Cole led the way up the hill to the Burke house.

Cole and Pickering sat at the dinning table alone. The sun had already begun to set in the west, casting the grand front room of Burke House, with its east facing windows, into a gloomy darkness. A solitary lantern hung by the front door, casting long shadows about the room.

"I suppose you've heard about the division in the party," Pickering said in a hushed voice.

"I can't say that I have. A good soldier leaves the politics to the politicians," Cole replied. He said it in a friendly manner, but Pickering gave him a questioning glance as if he was trying to determine whether or not he had been insulted. The senator wasn't a military man; perhaps he was unaware that, in some circles, it was taboo for a professional soldier to become involved in politics. In fact, many of the older, more traditional, officers didn't even vote, much less publicly display any political affiliation.

And Cole was certainly an older, more traditional officer.

"It seems that you may have no choice in the matter,"

Pickering said cautiously. "What happens here is of the utmost importance to the well-being of the Democratic Party and therefore important to overall well-being of these United States of America. Governor Wheaton gave me specific instructions to confide in you as to the true nature of the operation."

"Very well then. You have my ear."

Pickering took a sip of imported scotch from his glass before proceeding. "Since our solution to the slavery issue, our party has had full control over both the house and the senate, and every presidential election has been a landslide. The Whigs have become little more than a nuisance, losing support across the nation with the exception of a few districts scattered about the New England states. However, we've recently found that the use of Negroes in the military has caused a division in our own ranks."

Pickering paused to take another drink from his glass.

While Cole never followed the chaotic ups and downs of the political world, he did know more about the overall situation than he let on. He knew the southern states had largely profited during the slavery experiment by sending their black population to Freelands, which were little more than overpopulated reservations. These states had seen their political power rise considerably since these ex-slaves now counted as a full body, rather than just three-fifths when counting the population of a state for determining representation in the U. S. Congress. Of course, underhanded tactics such as intimidation and ballot stuffing were used to make sure the Freelanders either voted the way their one-time masters wanted them to, or to see that they didn't vote at all. It seemed like the perfect setup, until the chronic poverty of the poorly supervised and critically overcrowded Freelands began to cause widespread criminal activity. Negro raids in and out of the Freelands became common and an all-out uprising had been brutally suppressed in Georgia's Freeland back in 'fifty-nine. Soon the Southern Democrats were protesting the Freelands they themselves had established. The sole exception was Texas and Arkansas, not because of any true loyalty to the old party, but simply due to the fact that these two states had sent their freed blacks into Indian Territory and therefore they had no Freeland within their borders. In protesting the Freelands, the Southern Democrats had also found themselves against the use of Colored regiments, fearing that the act of setting up Negro military units was tantamount to giving arms to future revolutionaries.

Pickering swished the scotch around in his mouth before swallowing. "Good stuff," he commented.

Cole nodded. In truth he had yet to try the scotch. He assumed since the bottle had been hidden the Widow Burke had not intended it to be found, much less drunk. Apparently Pickering had no such qualms.

Pickering continued. "A little over one third of the party, mostly in the South, have aligned themselves with John Breckinridge, who we fear is considering starting a third party or perhaps even siding with the Whigs. Governor Wheaton is one of the few loyal Democrats in the South who realize the benefits of raising Colored regiments, but the current crisis has marred his reputation and were it not for Pruitt's blunder at Clover Bend, I would say his reelection was all but lost. Still, even with his chief rival disgraced, dead and buried, this uprising has been a stain on the great solution put forth by the Democratic Party. Nevertheless, party leaders have realized a way that this operation can be transformed into the greatest political boon since Andrew Jackson. It may well be the prefect opportunity to show the value of the Colored regiments, and with that, the loyalty of the blacks in the Freelands." Pickering said, "We have a fine battle with southern soldiers fighting alongside Negroes, putting down a slave uprising. It will make for perfect headlines in all of the major papers."

"I see," Cole replied with only marginal interest.

The senator picked up one of Widow Burke's silver knives from the place setting and used it to check his teeth in the reflection. He set the knife down and said, "I assume you've met the Colonel of the 13th Colored Regiment."

"I have," Cole replied. "Though I can't say I was impressed."

"He'll have to do. His regiment was chosen for a reason. His father is Paul Haiber, son of Charles Haiber. Charles was one of the most influential Whigs of the last decade and his son Paul appears to be cut from the same timber. As it just so happens, the Whigs are also stumping against the use of the Negro regiments, but for an entirely different reason." Wrinkling his nose in disgust, Pickering continued, "They see that they've bet on a losing horse so they're determined to handicap the race. They undermine our slavery solution by pointing to the supposed mismanagement of the Freelands, and now that we have backed the use of Negro regiments, they're trying to say that they too are mismanaged. So, you see, by having the son of one of their most prominent leaders in command of a regiment that takes part in the battle, we have affectively clipped their wings. They will be unable to darken the victory without bringing insult to one of the most powerful Whig families in the nation. Furthermore, it will also bring to light their duplicity on the issue."

"With all due respect," the old colonel said, his words hinting at sarcasm but his voice sincere, "I wish only to fulfill my duty as a soldier. I have my orders and, while I am overjoyed that you stand to benefit from the success of our expedition, it makes no difference to me."

Pickering's Southern charm flattened for a second, giving

way to a dark scowl. He grasped his glass and roughly tossed down the rest of the scotch. When his lips returned from the glass, his smile had returned, albeit half-heartedly.

For a moment Cole thought he might have gone too far. He didn't like politicians, but he also knew they made for dangerous enemies. "More scotch?" Cole added with his own half-hearted smile.

"I appreciate your hospitality, but I believe I've had enough for tonight." Pickering replied, his smile now tight and strained, obviously forced, "I believe I'll call it a day."

Pickering stood and made his way to the stairs at the back of the room.

Chapter 5

HEY! YOU AIN'T SUPPOSED to be up here." a voice called out sharply.

Parker turned and saw that he had been joined on the upper walkway by one of the steamer's crewmen. A tall, bony man with bad teeth stood near the stairs, his hands balled into fists. He was quickly joined by a short gotch-eyed man with greasy black hair. The men's clothes were filthy with grime and soot—obviously these were coalmen from the engine room.

"Yes, I am," Parker replied bluntly.

"Says who?"

"Captain Webster."

At first the two men seemed taken aback by this, then the taller man's smile widened, revealing more rotten teeth. He took one step further onto the deck, then reached to his waist and patted the handle of a knife that was tucked into his belt. "Captain may be fine with it, but I don't take too kindly to your kind nosing around on our ship."

How stupid could this man be? Parker thought. He casually patted the Colt at his side and said, "I don't care."

The rusty gears began to turn in the man's head and his smile faded.

"Hey, you two!" a voice called out from below. "Get off the walkway this instant."

The shorter of the two men turned said, "Damn, it's the mate. Let's go before he busts us good."

The taller man didn't take his eyes off Parker at first, but when the mate called out again he didn't have much of a choice. He spit at Parker before turning away. Luckily the spittle missed the mark and landed on the floor at Parker's feet. Parker didn't want to cause a scene, but there was only so much he could take.

Parker continued along the walkway, inspecting where planks had been added, transforming the simple walkway railing into four to five inches of makeshift wooden armor.

He looked to shore and saw Colonel Haiber making his way along the docks.

"Colonel, sir!" he called out.

Haiber looked up and gave the sergeant a lighthearted smile. "Did you get lost? Our ships are over there," he said, pointing down the dock at the big Army steamers.

"I'll be right down," Parker said. He turned and made his way down the stairs and then down the gangplank, joining Haiber on the docks. "Have you been on board those steamers, sir?" He said as he approached.

"No. Why?"

"Well, sir," Parker said, turning to the ship and motioning to the extra planking along the walkways, "they nailed those boards to the side to protect their boys from rifle fire when they go up the river. I was thinking maybe we ought to do the same."

"I don't know," Haiber said hesitantly.

"If we don't do anything our boys will be exposed through the whole trip upriver," Parker said, now finding himself getting agitated at his leader's usual lack of decisiveness. "Those transports ain't made for fightin'. I'll bet a bullet could pass right through the walls and kill someone inside if it hit just right."

"I suppose we could ask Captain Morison."

Parker shook his head. "It's not his concern. Those are *Army* steamers, and they were placed under *your* command."

"I guess so, but I still can't do anything without consulting the ships' captains."

Parker sighed.

"I just can't do it without going through the proper channel, you know that," Haiber said, his voice whiny and giving no hint of an officer's authority.

"All right, then." Parker said. "Let's go see the captains."

Captain Fergusson leaned on the rail, his stern deep-set eyes bouncing back and forth between Haiber and Parker as if he was trying to figure out if this was some sort of joke.

Fergusson was an Army Captain, so he was three grades down in rank from a Naval Captain which was the equivalent of a Colonel in the Army. However, Fergusson was a firm believer in the old Naval tradition that when they were onboard *his* ship, no man outranked him. If the President of the United States decided to grace the *Anne Marie's* planked decks, he'd damn well better salute the captain before he left the gangway. This was one reason Haiber and Parker had gone to Captain Letney first. They figured Letney would be more likely to agree with alteration to his ship, and if they had one commander on their side it might be easier to convince Ferguson. But Letney told them that since Fergusson had seniority they had better ask him; Letney said he would agree to whatever Fergusson said.

"Now let me get this straight. You want to add planks to the side of my ship?"

Haiber paused, almost as if he was expecting Sergeant Parker to do the talking. Finally he said, "Yes, captain. We believe that it would protect the soldiers while we ascended the White River."

"You do realize that both transports draw close to six feet and that the extra weight would increase her draft to the point that they might become stuck in the shallows."

This time Parker did speak. "I was thinking we could remove planks from the bow and stern and maybe remove the cover over the upper walkway to lighten the load."

Fergusson snorted in contempt. "You want to take my ship apart and put it back together, is that what you're saying?"

"No, that's not what we're saying at all," Haiber said.

"It damn sure sounds like it."

"I assure you it is not," then Haiber slipped into his formal West Point mode. "Captain, sir, I believe reinforcing the walkways is crucial to our current endeavor. The protection of our soldiers while they are in transit is of utmost importance. I strongly suggest that you assist us in preparing your steamer to meet the task at hand."

Fergusson arched one of his bushy eyebrows, "Shall I consider this a direct order?"

Parker was hopeful. Maybe Haiber would actually come through this time.

But Haiber seemed stumped. He hesitated, then finally said, "No, but this request will go in my report."

Fergusson shook his head. "I'm afraid you'll just have to write it in your report, because I won't be a part of dismantling my own ship."

Parker felt his face burning. "We can't go upriver without some sort of protection for the men. You heard how the beasts been shooting at steamers on the Arkansas River, think about how rough it'll get once we're up the White within a few miles of their camp. The White ain't near as wide as the Arkansas. They'll be right on top of us. It'll be like shootin' rats in a barrel." Parker turned to Haiber. Bordering close to outright insubordination, he thrust his finger out at his colonel and said, "I want that to go in the report. If my boys get shot all to hell while sitting in an unprotected steamer, I want it written down that I tried to get you two to do something about it."

Haiber was speechless.

Fergusson snorted contemptuously again. "We're not going to meet that kind of resistance."

"But what if we do?"

Fergusson rubbed the whiskers on this chin then said, "I'll tell you what; you can do it, but I'm not going to be held responsible. You can't use my men and you damn sure can't use my carpenters. But rest assured, if I think that you're not doing it right I'll have my men take down everything you've put up. So you'd best find yourself some experienced carpenters for the job."

Parker sat on a crate near the edge of the dock, looking up at the tall, defenseless transports. He had never been one to give up, especially on something that seemed so important, but he had exhausted all of his options. Where the hell was he going to find experienced carpenters? And not just any carpenters would do. He knew Fergusson was right about the ship's draft. They had to add the planks to the steamers in a way that wouldn't increase their weight, and they had to keep the weight evenly distributed as well. What Parker really needed was carpenters who had experience working on steamers.

After gaining a partial success with Fergusson, Parker had tried just about every option he could think of. He approached Captain Morison, but found that the captain considered the transports the Army's problem, not the Navy's; borrowing his carpenters was out of the question. Colonel Haiber was lost and out of his depth—of little help, and, truth be known, the rest of the officers in the 13th Colored Regiment couldn't care less if their troops were exposed, so long as they themselves were safe in the staterooms. Parker even ran into opposition when he tried the simple task of acquiring the extra planks they would need; he found that the local sawmill was unwilling to deal with a Negro.

Frustrated at every turn, Parker now found himself sitting at the dock, hoping for a miracle.

"Hey, um, you Parker?" a voice asked from behind him.

Parker turned and instantly recognized Captain A. J. Baxter, Colonel Cole's quartermaster. "Yeah, that's me," Parker replied.

"Colonel Cole sent me down here to give you a hand," the red-headed young man said.

"He did?" Parker said, perking up somewhat.

"Yes, sir, me and the carpenters from the Arkansas steamers."

Parker sprang to his feet.

"We ain't got but five carpenters, all told; so we'll have to use your men for most of the labor, if that's all right with you."

"Of course it's all right."

"Colonel talked to a mill on down the road a piece. He told them that the State will foot the bill for the timber."

"Thank the good Lord," Parker said.

He then found himself wondering if he hadn't misjudged Cole. Maybe there was at least one Southerner who wasn't all that bad. Then he realized that Cole was probably just doing his duty. Protecting the soldiers until they reached the battlefield was a high priority for any commander. It proved Cole was a wise officer, but it didn't exactly make him a saint. Still, Parker found himself wishing his own commander was more like Cole.

"When can we get started?" Parker asked.

"The carpenters had to collect their tools, but shouldn't be far behind me. The first load of timber probably won't be here for another hour, though."

"I'll go fetch my boys."

Chapter 6

AT FIRST GLANCE, the camp on the bank of the White looked in complete disarray, like it had been laid out haphazardly with no thought whatsoever of organization. Makeshift tents and a few simple, windowless log structures dotted the muddy ground near the water. The soft ground had turned to mud after only a few days and now, after several weeks, it was a virtual quagmire. Still, there was some underlying structure to this city of refugees. Latrines had been dug near the river, downstream and well away from the water supply. Guard duties and hunting forays were regularly scheduled. Woodcutting teams took shifts in the forest, while laborers used the fallen trees to build structures and even fortifications. Everyone knew their role in the new community.

Longtooth walked the length of a small hill that ran along the edge of the river, just south of the camp. He was an ordinary-looking beastman with short brownish hair, and ears that were somewhere between pointed and floppy. The only thing that made him stand out from the rest of the beastmen was a dark blue United States officer's overcoat—a trophy from the battle at Berkley.

Longtooth preferred to be by himself when he could, but his moments of solitude were far and few in between. Even now, as he walked along the hill, trying to gather his thoughts, he was not alone. Further along the hill, a team of laborers were digging entrenchments along the crest, and just down the hill, on the opposite side as the camp, woodcutters were clearing the trees along the river's edge.

And, of course, Dillon and Gregory were never far. They

were currently about fifty yards down hill, both trying to give Longtooth some time to himself while still staying at his beck and call.

Dillon sat on a stump, reading his tattered Bible. The big swinebreed was a true oddity. For one thing, he stuck out simply because he was a swinebreed, since dogbreeds made up the vast majority of the beastmen in the United States. It was also quite unheard of for a beastman to know how to read. But what made Dillon really unique was his undying faith. Dillon never seemed to notice the irony that his religion specifically excluded animals from the promises of heaven; the original writers of the Bible had apparently not foreseen walking and talking—and, more importantly, self-aware—animals. Dillon knew the Bible better than most human preachers; he used the parts he liked to suit his needs. Not on purpose, mind you; Dillon truly believed his own rhetoric. He saw Longtooth as a sort of savior sent to save the beastmen; not quite the second coming of Jesus, but something close to it. As a result, the massive pigman had taken it upon himself to serve as his savior's personal bodyguard. Longtooth didn't particularly care for his role as a savior in Dillon's eyes, but as long as Dillon refrained from using it in his frequent sermons, he kept his feelings to himself. He knew Dillon meant well and he didn't want to injure the big fellow's pride.

Gregory, or rather Gregory McMillan as he often introduced himself, was another story altogether. The tall, hound-looking dogbreed stood out from the common beastmen for an entirely different reason. Unlike the others, he was well-mannered, and despite the fact that he had been living in the same muddy camp as the others for weeks now, he still managed to appear clean and well-dressed at all times. Although dogbreeds were generally gentle and loyal, Longtooth had noticed that once they tasted freedom, their animalistic side often combined with their force-evolved human-like side, to give them a bit of a harsh violent streak. Not so with Gregory McMillan. He was refined and adamantly non-violent. Unlike most beastman slaves who had labored in the fields from sunup until sundown, then were locked away in crude shelters for the night, Gregory had been the household servant for a well-known doctor just outside of Little Rock. He had been so much a part of the doctor's family that they had even given him their last name—McMillan. However, Gregory's soft heart prevented him from overlooking the plight of the beastmen owned by the plantation owners, and when the call went out for an open rebellion he had slipped away to join them. He didn't believe in violence, but he believed in their cause and he was going to do what he could to help them. In a way, Gregory hated himself for leaving the doctor's family, especially their young son Timothy. As a result, it was only natural that he attach himself to Longtooth in much the same way he had been attached to Doctor McMillan—Gregory basically saw himself as Longtooth's personal butler. In truth Gregory needed to serve more than Longtooth needed the service. Longtooth would never turn Gregory away, though. In fact, he saw the tall, often depressed, dogbreed as the one shining example of how humans and beastmen could live together in harmony.

"Longtooth!" a voice called out form the direction of camp. Longtooth immediately recognized the voice as belonging to Sid, his unofficial second-in-command.

The stern grey-coated dogbreed stood at the foot of the hill. Although dogbreeds are created from larger specimens of dogs, mostly curs, hounds, and the occasional thick-coated dog from farther north, Sid looked more like a wire-haired terrier. His demeanor had none of a terrier's usual playfulness, though. Sid was always all business.

"Yeah?" Longtooth answered.

"We got a message from Little Rock," Sid said, holding a folded piece of paper over his head.

"Bring it on up," Longtooth called out.

Sid started up the hill, no doubt grumbling under his breath about having to make the climb. Sid grumbled a lot, but he was loyal. And more important, he was very intelligent. Longtooth was a realist when it came to his people's intelligence. Although he knew little about the science surrounding the process, he knew that when a vivisectionist took an animal and created a beastman increasing the brain-size and therefore the intelligence was one of the highest priorities of the operation. However, it was still a hit and miss science. He and Sid had been lucky. They were intelligent even by human standards. There were others, including Gregory and Dillon, who were intelligent in their own way, and even compared favorably to humans in some areas, but he and Sid were the only two that he felt could truly match the wits of the humans facing them and stand a chance of coming out on top.

Once Sid reached the top of the hill he handed over the letter. Sid had just started learning to read and write. He was making progress but he was easily frustrated, so he usually didn't read unless he had to.

Longtooth unfolded the note and read it. When he finished he looked up at Sid. "They know we want to talk, but they don't want to listen. They're going to try to capture me if I try to negotiate."

Sid grunted his displeasure, but otherwise didn't say a word.

"She also mentions that they will start upriver soon, probably in a week or two."

"Then we should move the camp inland," Sid said.

Longtooth shook his head. "We can't keep running from them. We've got to stand and fight."

"We already fought them, twice. They keep coming. We can't keep fighting their fight. They'll eventually win and it'll all be over."

Longtooth often found that Sid's intelligence was more of a liability than an asset. In a way, Sid was right. But in another way, he was terribly wrong. "We've been over this," Longtooth said, cautiously. He wanted to make his point, but he didn't want to rub Sid the wrong way. "If we run off and hide in the swamp, they'll just hunt us down and kill us there, and no one will ever know our story. But if we keep taking the fight to them, fighting their fight, as you say, people will hear about us and some day they may see things the way we do."

"Some day," Sid snorted, "I have a feeling some day's going to come too late for us and everyone with us."

"If they make it upriver I plan on getting the women and the children out of here before they arrive," Longtooth said, he always referred to them as such rather than calling them *bitches and pups* like the humans did. "I'll also let any man go who wants to."

Longtooth could immediately tell Sid took the comment the wrong way. Sid's ears lowered to his scalp and his tail lowered a touch. His voice was deeper, almost to a growl when he replied. "I ain't going to leave you. We may disagree, but when I told you I'd follow you to the gates of hell, I damn well meant it."

"I didn't mean you, Sid. You know that."

Sid didn't reply, but he didn't have to. His ears perked up a touch, and his tail rose somewhat. He was still miffed, but not angry.

"Gregory!" Longtooth called out, "Send for Mouser!"

Sid grumbled.

Sid was unaware of the slight growl that escaped his own lips when he saw Mouser heading their way.

Mouser was panting happily, his tail wagging behind him as he strode up the hill toward where Longtooth and Sid stood. Despite the name, there was nothing feline about Mouser. Mouser was all dog. In fact, in some ways his happy, excited and overeager demeanor personified the expectations that humans had for their canine companions. Mouser wore a blue soldier's kepi on his head, tilted slightly to the left, with a soft black feather sticking out of the band. The hat was a trophy of war; the feather had been stolen from a discarded maid's feather duster.

Life was fun for Mouser. He was fairly intelligent as dogbreeds went and extremely quick-witted, but he had a knack for not taking anything seriously.

Sid hated him. He couldn't understand why Longtooth insisted on using this puppy in a dog's body as their chief scout.

Once he was at the top of the hill, Mouser removed his hat and bowed dramatically to his two superiors. "It's a pleasure."

"Same here," Longtooth replied in his casual manner.

Sid barely restrained a growl.

"Mouser, the humans'll be coming upriver soon." Longtooth explained. "I want you to gather your scouts and go downriver to meet them. Make 'em bleed. If you get the opportunity to get on one of the transports, do so at night, but don't get drawn into a heavy fight. If you try to board them once, don't try it again. They'll be ready for you the second time. We're going to need your scouts for the final battle."

"You can count on me," Mouser said eagerly.

"Take the two smaller guns with you." Longtooth added. "Be careful with them. They're the only guns we've got that can be moved around easily."

"I'll treat them like they're from my own litter," he said with a happy pant. "I'll nurse them if I have to, though I fear my tits may be dry."

Sid had heard enough. "This is serious, Mouser," he growled.

Mouser's tail wagged furiously. He patted Sid on the shoulder, "I'm just funning around." Mouser was so happy-go-lucky that he was completely oblivious to the fact that Sid couldn't stand him.

Longtooth ignored the exchange. "Take the boats downriver, but be sure and pull them into the woods," he said.

"Will do," Mouser said, happily. "That all?"

"I believe so."

"Good, I'll get my scouts. We'll be halfway to the Mississippi before you can mark a tree." Mouser turned and practically ran back down the hill.

Sid turned to Longtooth, "One day he's going to get us in trouble."

"I admit, he's too excitable, but he's a fine scout. And don't forget what he did at Clover Bend."

"Yeah, Clover Bend," Sid said, again with a growl, almost as if he was growling at the very name of their greatest victory. "He was lucky and you know it."

Longtooth didn't reply.

Sid could tell Longtooth didn't want to argue. Sid wanted to press the issue, but he held his tongue. Longtooth hated arguing. This was one of the strange ironies of their current situation. Longtooth hated confrontation, but he was bound and determined to fight a battle that Sid felt was all but impossible to win.

Of course while Sid disagreed with Longtooth's decision to stay and fight, he had to admit that if they did manage to win it would be a huge blow and might even cause the uprising to spread throughout the Southern states. And was the coming fight really all that impossible? Longtooth certainly had a few tricks up his sleeves.

Contrary to the popular saying, when it came to beastmen, one often *could* judge a book by its cover—at least when it came to intelligence. As a rule, the vivisectionist who took the time to see that his creations had proper posture, workable hands, were able to speak properly, and had few, if any deformities, were the same vivisectionists who paid particular attention to the growth and therefore the capacity of their creation's brain. Longtooth, Sid, Mouser, Gregory, and even to a lesser extent Dillon were all obvious examples. They stood upright, their hands were well-formed, their larynx functioned almost as well as any human's, and they were fairly attractive specimens when compared to the garden-variety beastman.

Cooney was an exception to this rule. His back was stooped, his left leg was a good three inches shorter than his right, his hands were gnarled and twisted and even his face seemed to have somehow become warped and ruined during his alteration—the left side of his face was numb and frozen in a perpetual snarl. All of this was an illusion, however. Cooney was extremely intelligent and his twisted body hid the fact that he was actually quiet agile and dexterous. But the greatest illusion involved his twisted, angry face. This couldn't be farther from the truth. Cooney was actually one of the most laid back beastmen in the camp.

Cooney stood near the edge of the river, gazing out at his new pride and joy, a massive United States Army transport that was tied alongside the camp. A smaller steamer was tied behind the first, but this little sternwheeler didn't hold near the place in Cooney's heart. Hammers could be heard ringing from within the steamer and Cooney knew he should be joining them, but he took his time at the water's edge, admiring the steamer like a young pup admiring the love of his life.

Months ago the *Empress of Saint Louis* had been a large Army transport which had been used to transport Southern regiments north on the Mississippi so they could unload near the Canadian border. When she had been ordered to return south to deliver supplies and munitions to Little Rock no one had expected her to come under attack, so she had no soldiers or marines on board. She fell without a fight. Mouser's scouts got carried away and killed all the members of her small crew. As much as Longtooth hated such massacres, no one could deny that this one atrocity was a blessing in disguise. With the crew dead, there would be no witnesses to report that the beastmen had actually captured the steamer rather than sunk it. And of course the humans never imagined the beastmen could operate a machine as complex as a steam engine, much less pilot a steamer, so the presence of this ship would be a complete surprise.

After the *Empress of Saint Louis* was captured, the beastmen managed to capture another steamer on the river and they also took one that had been tied at the docks in Elizabeth when they overran the town. The former was taken downriver and sunk as an obstruction, while the latter was currently resting behind the *Empress of Saint Louis*. The big army steamer now had a new name, a new mission, and a new captain. Cooney had renamed her *Big Dog* as soon as he had laid eyes on her; he felt it was a simple, yet appropriate name. Her new mission was to protect the beastman. Her new captain was Cooney. Although she was nominally no one's property, Cooney had been placed in charge of her and he felt a certain benevolent ownership over the vessel.

Prior to the uprising, Cooney had been one of about a dozen dogbreeds shoveling coal in a steamer that plied the Mississippi. They had been docked at Memphis when the uprising broke out. Cooney had always been the unspoken leader of the bunch and when he suggested they steal a skiff, cross the Mississippi and join the rebels, they had all agreed. It had taken them some time to find Longtooth; he and his party finally met up with the rebels at Elizabeth.

When the *Empress of Saint Louis* had been captured, Longtooth quickly found a use for Cooney and his little group of coal shovelers. They were asked to put their experience working on a steamer to use and help get the steamer upriver. Once this job was completed, Cooney was asked to do what he could to turn the ship into a warship. With all of the captured cannons being used ashore, Cooney had focused his efforts on strengthening the steamer's bow, transforming the transport into a ram. The grand steamer's topside was trimmed away, her stacks shortened, and her pilothouse transformed from a spacious roomy workplace to an open air station that was little more than a wheel on top of the whole structure. All of this had been done to lighten her load so the excess wood could be used to strengthen her body.

Her previous captain probably would have been ashamed of the transformation. No doubt he would believe his graceful steamer had been ruined in her transformation to such a squatty, ugly vessel. But Cooney didn't see it that way. He thought she was beautiful.

As he stood near the water's edge he wondered if perhaps he had been the noble captain of such a vessel in a past life— or perhaps the captain of graceful oceangoing clipper, with billowing white sails harnessing the wind. A light smile creased the good side of his face at this thought. It was utter nonsense, and he knew it. The best he could hope for in a past life was that he had been someone's prize birddog. Now he *was* the captain of a ship, not in some past life, but in this one.

Chapter 7

COLE AND THOMPSON STOOD on the muddy bank of the White River waiting patiently, as they had been for the last two hours. One of the chartered steamers, the *Gabriel Hastings* or '*Gabby*' as she was called by her crew, was anchored in the river behind them. They were only a few miles up the White; the rebels were supposed to be miles upstream, but Cole wasn't taking any chances. A company of militia had accompanied the steamer on its short trip upriver; they had been ordered to form a picket line along the edge of the woods to prevent a possible ambush.

Dog darted back and forth along the edge of the water, marking rocks and shrubs along the bank. After the water's edge was sufficiently surveyed, Dog headed inland and started marking the trees at the edge of the woods.

Cole shifted his cane from his left to his right hand then shifted his weight from one leg to another. Thompson knew that, despite the cane, the long wait was bound to be painful for the old man.

"I could get a chair from the ship," Thompson ventured, although he already knew the answer. It had taken quite some time just to convince the colonel to use the cane.

"No, thank you. I'm quite all right," Cole replied predictably. He shifted his weight once more then took his watch from his pocket and checked the time.

"Reckon they finally caught him?" asked Thompson.

"Hope not," Cole said, although Thompson suspected he had mixed emotions on the subject.

Near the edge of the woods Dog suddenly stopped and froze,

ears perked and nose to the wind. He let out a shrill sound that was somewhere between a yelp and a bark then returned to his master at a run.

The wind shifted and Thompson smelled something dead.

Private Lawton sniffed the air, but his partner on the picket line spoke first.

"What's 'at smell?" Private Saunders said as he pinched his nose.

"Somethin' died, that's for sure," Lawton replied.

Then they heard movement in the brush—something was slowly heading their way. It didn't take long for them to realize that as the sound got louder, the smell grew stronger.

Lawton shouldered his musket, but kept the barrel down. Without taking his eyes away from the woods before him he called out, "Hey, Sergeant! Over here! Somethin's a comin'!"

Saunders continued pinching his nose in disgust, but Lawton was slightly more accustomed to the smell. He and his brothers used to make extra money digging graves back home in Lanark.

They heard Sergeant Gogan crashing through the brush behind them, but he didn't arrive before the newcomer stepped out of the brush, a scrawny mule trailing behind him. The man was so filthy it was impossible to tell the color of his skin; it wasn't until he took several more steps that Lawton realized he was a white man. The stranger was stocky and stoop-shouldered, and at first glance appeared oafish, but as he drew nearer Lawton noticed that though his posture was poor, his stride was smooth and fluid. He didn't make a sound as he moved through the underbrush; they never would have heard him coming if it hadn't been for the mule. He wore a wolf pelt on his shoulders and over his head, not unlike the ones that the Plains Indians wore while hunting buffalo, only this pelt was much larger, covering the big man like a cloak. To his horror, Lawton suddenly realized that the wolf pelt was actually the skin of a dogbreed.

Lawton assumed that the terrible dead smell came from this dirty newcomer, but then he noticed the carcasses of small dead animals draped over the mule. Several squirrels, rabbits and possums were tethered together with rope so that they hung down the sides of the poor scrawny mule; the varmints were in various stages of decomposition.

The newcomer was well-armed: among the dead critters, a Spencer carbine hung from the mule's saddlebags, next to it, a heavy blade that looked like some sort of meat cleaver. A Bowie knife was strapped to one of the stranger's thick legs and a Navy Colt was tucked into his pants.

Lawton raised his musket and took aim. "Why don't you stay right there, friend."

The newcomer stopped and smiled. Every tooth in his head was as rotten and as black as his soul. "Ah ain't ya friend."

Despite the fact that the newcomer had stopped, Lawton felt threatened.

The tense silence was broken only by the droning cloud of thick green flies circling the poor mule.

"Jus' stay, there." Lawton said, almost sheepishly.

Beside him, Saunders started to shoulder his musket, then he started retching. After three retches, he dropped his gun, hugged a nearby pine and lost his morning grits behind the tree.

Sergeant Gogan came up behind Lawton, but stopped as soon as the newcomer came into view. "Jesus wept," he said, then gagged once but managed to keep his food down.

"You boys gonna take me to Cole?" The stranger drawled, "Or you all gonna stand there and piss yer pants?"

"You Hunter?" Gogan finally asked.

"Yup."

"Um, well, come on," he said hesitantly, "Colonel's waitin'."

Lawton lowered his musket.

Hunter left his mule and started toward the three soldiers. Gogan turned to lead the way and Lawton stepped aside, wanting to stay as far away from the filthy man as he could.

Shoulders stooped, Hunter walked by.

Suddenly Hunter's arm shot out and grasped Lawton by the hair. With a swift, powerful tug he pulled Lawton's face to within an inch of his own. Lawton felt something cold on his throat and realized it was a knife.

The big man's breath was fetid, almost as bad as the odor emitting from his mule.

"Ah don' like folks a pointin' guns at me," he whispered hoarsely.

The coldness at Lawton's neck intensified, becoming pain as Hunter slowly pulled the blade across his skin, just hard enough to cut but not hard enough to slit his throat.

"Cole payin' me good. He payin' me gold," Hunter whispered, "Ah like gold." The pain grew more intense. "Almos' as much as ah like killin'."

"Hey, stop that," Gogan said, his voice weak and laden with fear.

Hunter turned and looked at Gogan. The sergeant had drawn his pistol but dared not take aim. The big fiend turned back to Lawton and said, "You lucky he payin' a lot a gold."

Hunter let go. Lawton staggered back against a tree. He clasped his hand to his throat and felt blood, not a lot, but enough to unnerve him.

The stoop-shouldered demon of a man put his Bowie back in its sheath and walked toward the river bank.

Dog growled low in his throat as he cowered behind Cole's legs.

Thompson sympathized. He wished he was anywhere but on this stretch of muddy bank with this vile human. Even though the mule had been left in the woods, the smell of rotten death was still strong about its owner.

"They ain't got but a little under two-thousand at da main camp Dat's all," Hunter said, "They took a beatin' at Berkley. More'n we thought. And some ain't with Longtoof no more. They left to hide in da swamp."

"You reckon Longtooth's grip on his army is beginning to slip?" Cole asked.

Hunter's brow furrowed. "No, they leavin' was his doin. Ah don't know why though. Even da dogs don' know why."

"Have you actually seen this camp of theirs?"

"No, too many dogs there."

"If you haven't seen the camp, how do you know how many are with Longtooth?"

"Ah catch me one and he tell me, he tell me a lot 'fore I kill 'em," Hunter paused in his story long enough to hock up a fair amount of phlegm. He spat and continued, "They don' know much; they know enough to tell me what I needs to know." Hunter's eyes turned from Cole to Thompson. "You wanna know how ah do it, doncha?"

"Excuse me?" Thompson asked.

"They gots this," Hunter said, pointing at his nose. "I gots this," he said, pointing to his head.

Thompson desperately wanted to take a step back—hell, part of him wanted to turn and run—but he stood his ground.

Hunter, however seemed to realize he was intimidating the one-armed lieutenant and he relished the thought. He took a step forward and pressed on, "Wanna know how ah make 'em talk?" Not waiting for a reply, he drew his knife and held it before his eyes. "Ah slowly peel off they skin. They yap like puppies when they hurtin', but when they hurtin' real bad, they scream just like injuns do."

Thompson noticed a necklace hanging from Hunter's neck made from over a dozen large canine teeth. It came to him that these teeth had probably been removed before their previous owners were dead.

"Hunter," Cole snapped. "I need you to reconnoiter their camp."

Hunter turned back to Cole. Perhaps he didn't like being interrupted because he seemed angry. His knife still before his face, his knuckles became white as he squeezed the handle, but Cole didn't back down.

"Can you do it?" Cole asked sharply.

"They camp is gonna be a tough one," Hunter said as he returned his knife to its scabbard, "It gonna cost ya."

"I realize you don't work for free."

"What you pay?"

Cole took a pouch out from his pocket and held it before Hunter's face. He bobbed the pouch, making it jingle.

Hunter's hands greedily reached for the sack, but Cole pulled it away.

"This is the pay for your work thus far. Meet me up the White River across from Chickasaw Bluffs a week from today with information on their camp and I'll pay double."

"Dat not much time," Hunter said, musing, but Thompson could tell the man had already decided to take the job.

"It should be plenty."

Hunter nodded, "Ah do it. Now gimme my gold."

Cole handed the pouch to Hunter.

When Hunter's hand moved toward his master, Dog came from behind Cole's legs, growling and snapping.

Hunter regarded him with a black-toothed grin and said,

"Ain't that a sight. That dog *know* I can kill him; he still wanna fight. They all dumb like that."

Chapter 8

ELLA REINED THE CARRIAGE in at the front of the governor's house and stopped.

"Thank you, Ella," Governor Wheaton said as he stepped to the ground.

Ella nodded in the way of a reply. It had been a long day in which the governor seemed to need to be everywhere at the same time. She was tired, the horse was tired, and the governor was tired. Of course the horse was about to be put up for the night and the governor was about to kick back to smoke his pipe, but she still had to make supper.

She was about to crack the reins and take the carriage around back when someone called out from down the road.

"Governor, sir!" a thin man called out. He was well-dressed, even wearing those small wire glasses that were so popular among the upper class these days. "A packet steamer just arrived with an important message," the man said. Running at a trot, he was holding his glasses to his nose with one hand while hold the letter over his head with the other.

Ella recognized Postmaster Richard Britt. She imagined it had to be something important to send Mr. Britt running down the streets of Little Rock like the seat of his pants was ablaze. She laid the reins down, and got out of the carriage and made like she was inspecting the horse's harness.

Wheaton laughed. "Calm down, Richard."

Postmaster Britt kept on coming, still waving the letter as he ran, "It's from the President."

"It's still nothing to go and have fit over," Wheaton said.

The postmaster ran up to the governor, his breath coming in

77

pants, he barely managed to draw enough air to say, "I figured it's important, being's we got all that trouble upstate."

Wheaton took the letter, smiled and patted Britt on the shoulder, "You know you probably would've got here just as quick if you'd taken the time to get on a horse."

"I didn't think about that," then he defensively added, "You know, it's not every day a packet steamer arrives with a letter from the President."

"Wonder why they didn't send a wire?" Wheaton said as he inspected the letter, paying particular attention the elaborate wax seal.

"Don't know," Britt gasped, "Must be pretty important."

"Well, if our good President thought it was important enough to send a packet steamer and our own postmaster thought it was important enough to run halfway across creation, I guess I'll go ahead and read it."

He broke the seal and unfolded the letter. As he read the message, his face lost most of its humor and became cold and serious. Ella didn't care for that look.

When he finished he folded the letter and placed it back in the envelope.

"This certainly changes everything," he muttered.

His smile returned, albeit halfheartedly, "Please come in, Richard. I've got to prepare a telegram to send down to Montgomery Point. Since the station is on your way, I was hoping you'd drop it by on your way back."

"It would be my pleasure."

When the two men turned to go inside, and Ella swung herself back into the seat. She hoped she could make it around the house and put up the horse in time to get inside the house and eavesdrop on the men. However, her hopes were dashed when Wheaton said, "Ella, would you please wait for Postmaster Britt? I don't think he could manage the run back to town."

"Yes, sir."

Ella waited until she was sure the master was in bed before she came out of her room and made her way through the dark halls of the Wheaton house, past the master bedroom on her way to the governor's study. She quietly opened the door and made her way over to his desk. There was just enough light in the room for her to make out the various papers scattered about the surface. Some were letters and from various Arkansas politicians, but most were just simple notes the governor wrote to himself to help his memory. She rifled through the papers on the top of the desk, but didn't find the letter from the president. Next she started looking through the drawers. She knew Mr. Wheaton would never discard a letter from the president, but she couldn't find it anywhere.

Finally, just as she was about to give up, she spotted a bit of white sticking out of his coat pocket—of course, he was going to take it with him to the capital building tomorrow.

Ella removed the letter from the coat pocket, took it out of the envelope and held it up so she could read it by the moonlight. However, she found it was a long letter and she didn't have enough time to decipher it. Instead, she decided to steal the letter. Tomorrow, when the governor would be looking for it, she could help convince him that he lost it.

Still moving as quietly as possible, Ella made her way down the stairs and on to the kitchen where she found strips of meat to bribe the dogs and to feed the beastman she hoped would be in the woods behind her house. Two days ago a beastman had been captured nearby. Ella had been worried that this had been Nell, or perhaps her replacement. But there was no use in worrying now; there was nothing she could do about it one way or the other.

She fed the three dogs their treats, then, with the letter gripped tight in her hand, she took off across the pasture. Her heart raced as it always did, but this time she didn't take as many glances behind her.

Once she reached the edge of the woods she took the dried meat out of her pouch, held it aloft and softly called out, "Nell?" then she realized that if a beastman was out there it probably wasn't Nell. "Anyone there?" She asked.

No answer.

"Hello?" she called out softly, but still received no answer.

She nervously gripped the letter so tight, it crumpled in her hand. She knew how important this letter had to be, but what if there was no one to give it to? She felt tears well in her eyes. "Hello?" she tried again, this time a little louder.

No answer.

She hazarded a look back toward the house. The lights were still off.

"Please, Lord, please help a poor soul," she whispered, then she stamped her foot in frustration and tried one more time. "Hello? Anyone there?"

After a few more tries, she finally gave up. She tucked the letter into the bag with the dried meat and started back across the pasture. She was out of the pasture and halfway across the backyard when she noticed the back door was open. Someone was standing in the doorway.

Her pulse quickened. She stopped in her tracks and hid the bag behind her back.

"Ella, just what do you think you're doing?" Governor Wheaton asked.

She let the bag fall to the ground behind her, then she casually took one step backward. Bringing her foot down on the bag, she pressed it down into the damp ground.

"I asked you a question," the governor demanded.

Ella's mind raced. What if the beastman they had captured was her contact? What if he had told them about her? She it would mean the hangman's noose for her. Ella was speechless, all should could manage was to say, "Sir?"

"You heard me, Ella. What are you doing up and about this time of night?"

"I's just taking a walk, that's all. Fresh air does a soul right, you know."

"Taking a walk? At this hour?"

"Yes, suh," she said, "The stars is out; I figured I'd take a walk."

"You know, Norma's been saying she thought she heard you coming and going at all hours of the night, but I thought she was hearing things," Wheaton stepped out of the doorway. She could see him better now. There were bags under his eyes.

"I just been having trouble sleepin', dat's all. We got all this trouble going on and I just been worried. I don't want those beasts to come and get us," she wished she hadn't said it as soon as it was out of her mouth.

Governor Wheaton smiled slyly, "You don't want the beastmen to get you so you go walking at night by yourself?" He shook his head, "Ella, I thought I knew you better."

She hung her head and didn't say a word.

"Who is it?" he asked.

"Suh?" she asked, genuinely confused.

"Don't play coy with me," he said, his smile widening, "You've got yourself a beau, don't you? I figured you's too old to go courtin', but maybe not."

Ella brought her hand to her face. She hoped he would see the gesture as an attempt to hide a blush, not one to hide a smirk. "Sorry, suh. I guess you caught me."

First thing the next morning, Ella went back outside to

retrieve the bag. However as soon as she opened the door she knew something was wrong. Two of her master's dogs had each end of the bag she had carried to the woods yesterday. Or rather, they had what was left of the little sack. It was torn to shreds.

Tiny bits of paper were also scattered about the yard. Ella ran out and gather the paper, but found that the damp air, combined with no small amount of dog slobber, had caused the ink to run. The only part she could make out was a portion of the letterhead.

Ella disposed of the bits of paper and tried to tell her the message hadn't been that important. However, deep down inside, she knew she was wrong.

Chapter 9

THE SOUND OF SAWS and hammers echoed from the docks below. Sergeant Parker wiped the sweat off his brow with a red handkerchief, then grabbed one end of the last plank in the buckboard wagon. Like the soldier on the other end of the plank, he was stripped to the waist. After a nod from Parker, they heaved the plank out of the wagon and tossed it down, where two more shirtless soldiers picked it up and started down to the docks.

Parker stood up and stretched his sore muscles, causing his head to swim. Not enough to make him lose his balance, but enough to tell him he needed a drink of water.

When he looked down, getting ready to jump out of the wagon, he noticed something. His chest and arms were still as thick as they'd ever been, but his stomach now poked out over his belt.

When did that happen? Parker thought.

He turned and glanced at Corporal Cooper, who had been on the other end of the plank. Cooper's waist was trim, like his used to be.

"You okay, Sarge?" Cooper asked.

"Yeah, I just need a drink of water." Parker got out of the wagon, and walked over to where a group of his men were taking a break under the shade of a majestic old oak tree. He took a canteen down from a tree limb and took a long swig.

"How many more loads y'all need?" A white man in a dirty farmer's slouch hat asked from his seat in the front of the buckboard wagon.

Parker brought the canteen down from his lips and said,

"Keep 'em coming. I'll tell you when we've got enough."

The man in the slouch hat grunted by way of reply then turned and popped the reins, setting his mules into motion. Parker couldn't help but take a grim satisfaction in telling the white man what to do, and in his reaction.

He turned to the scene below him. His men were swarming all over the two Army steamers like fire ants on a dead possum. Yesterday had been the first day they had been able to work on the steamers but it was already obvious that progress was being made. Still, Parker couldn't help but feel somewhat bitter as he watched the white carpenters boss his men about. The whole scene reminded him of his youth, and he didn't like that one bit.

But then there was Captain Baxter.

"Hey, uh, Parker, sir," Baxter called out as he hurried up the hill.

"Here come ya boy, Sergeant Parker," one of the soldiers under the tree said, bringing laughter from the others.

"That's enough," Parker said sternly and the soldiers subsided—mostly. He could still hear a couple of chuckles coming from that way.

"Sir, the carpenters workin' on the *Anne Marie*'s stern want to get started on the rear planking," Baxter said with his usual boyish enthusiasm, his rapid-fire chatter tempered with a soft southern accent, "but there ain't enough wood to keep the stern and midsection crews both workin'. We're low, even with that last wagonload."

"Split the wood between both groups. If they run out they can take a break until the next load comes in."

"Well..." Baxter regularly hesitated to give his opinion, driving Parker a little bit crazier each time the boy spoke.

"Go ahead, what is it?" Parker asked.

"Sir, if we keep packin' timber on her stern we're gonna run into some trouble down the road. I mean we got to protect those boilers, and that's gonna weigh down the rear even more. She'll be running with her nose all up in the air and her ass draggin' bottom." Baxter briefly bit his bottom lip then added, "Well, maybe not that bad, but you see what I'm gettin' at, sir."

"Tell the carpenters working on the stern go ahead and start strengthening the pilothouse."

"Yes, sir, that would work," Baxter said hesitantly.

"But?"

"Well, I was thinkin' they could go ahead and start on the boilers. I mean, that's where a lot of the extra weight'll go. Once the planking's in place there we'll have a better idea what we got to work with."

"Okay, do that."

Parker had never met anyone like Baxter. The young redhead was a strange combination of two extremes. On one hand he was incredibly naïve, almost childlike; on the other, he was amazingly intelligent. In fact, when it came to numbers, the boy was downright brilliant. It was like having a ten-year-old engineer supervising the operation, rather than a twenty-four-year-old farmer's son.

Baxter turned to leave, but Parker grasped his arm.

"Sir?" Baxter asked.

"Come here," Parker led him a few steps away from the troops under the tree. "You got to quit calling me 'sir,'" Parker explained in a whisper.

"Why?"

"You're an officer. I'm a sergeant. *I* call *you* sir."

"Oh, I just, I mean, you're older, so I thought..." Baxter paused when he saw the look on Parker's face, "I don't mean you're *old* or anything, sir, I mean, sergeant."

Parker sighed then bluntly said, "Get down there and tell

those carpenters to start on the boilers."

"Yes, sir."

After Baxter turned and started down the hill, the men under the tree saw something that happened so rarely that most of Parker's men believed it was a myth—the rough old sergeant cracked a smile.

On the hill, a gathering of forty officers, a few mounted on horses, most standing, overlooked the work at the docks. Officers from both regiments were present. In fact, of the twenty-two captains and forty-four lieutenants that made up the upper command of the two regiments' individual companies, more than half were present.

Although he was only a captain, Reginald Jones carried himself among the others with the bearing of a general among his staff.

"At least they know how to work," he grumbled. "They oughta be armed with hammers, not rifles."

Several of the officers grumbled in agreement.

Even the majority of the officers of the 13th sided with Jones. Only the handful of company commanders who actually believed in their troops were absent from this group. Those present were the officers who had been placed in the Colored regiment due to low grades or too many demerits in military school or perhaps as punishment for insubordination in their previous command. A vague sense of duty and perhaps the last vestiges of a guilty conscience had kept these malcontents from open insubordination until now, but in Jones they had found someone who spoke aloud what had been preoccupying their minds for years. Jones' hatred was pure and incandescent, and they were drawn to him like moths.

One of the few officers to have a mount on board the transports, Lieutenant-Colonel Anthony Santiago sat in the saddle near Jones. Although he tended to agree with the captain, he wasn't filled with the same burning hatred that the other officers possessed. When he graduated out of Virginia Military Institute seven years ago, he had requested to be deployed to a Colored regiment. Santiago was neither Whig nor idealist, he just felt that the Colored regiments offered a faster track to promotion—put very simply, he could start out as a third lieutenant in a regular regiment or a first lieutenant in a Colored regiment. Santiago was often surprised that more officers hadn't overlooked their prejudices and taken advantage of the opportunity. As he expected, Santiago was propelled through the ranks, at least at first. Much to his surprise though, he had recently been passed over in favor of Haiber, a West Pointer with connections. The experience of this disappointment was fresh in Santiago. In truth he was indifferent to the plight of the soldiers; the target of his wrath was his commanding officer, Colonel John Haiber. Santiago's hatred was different than that of his companions, but it was hatred nonetheless.

"Excuse me," a voice called out from behind the party. "Excuse me, please."

Wearing his brown suit and possum grin, state representative Nathaniel Pickering made his way through the men and horses. He walked up to the head of the group, glanced down at the scene below them for a second, before turning his winning smile up towards Jones. "If I may, I'd like to have a word with you."

"Shoot."

"In private."

With a shrug, Jones dismounted and followed the politician away from the officers.

Santiago watched as they spoke under a nearby tree. At first the two men were rigid and formal, but after a few minutes they were laughing and shaking hands like old pals.

For some reason, seeing this made Santiago uneasy.

Colonel Haiber sat on a rock near the edge of the cliff, watching the work going on at the dock. While the ship was undergoing its drastic reconfiguration, his quarters had been temporarily moved to one of the bedrooms in the spacious Burke House. However, he wasn't comfortable there, especially not since Pickering had moved into the house. Haiber had never been at home around politicians, including his own father and his famous grandfather.

For the time being, Haiber just wanted to be alone, but solitude was a rarity in the military. It had taken him some time, but he finally located an isolated spot inside a stand of short trees, where he could watch the work, but where no one would see him.

Every now and then he would hazard a look over at the hill to his right where a throng of officers gathered around Captain Jones. He didn't like how the officers were beginning to flock to this hate-filled captain, but what could he do? If he put his foot down and demanded that they assist in strengthening the transports, their quiet disrespect might turn to outright insubordination. He had enough on his mind without worrying about a possible mutiny among his officers less than two weeks before he took his regiment into battle.

Haiber placed his elbows on his knees and his head in his hands. He sat in this position for some time before getting to his feet. His first thought was that he would go back to his room and compose his weekly report. However as he stood on the cliff watching the men working below he began to wonder what they would say if he walked down there, took off his own shirt and joined them. He turned to the gathering of officers on the hill and wondered what they would say as well.

Haiber turned away and started back down the trail that ran just behind the cliff. He continued on until he reached the wagon track that would lead him down to the docks. He stood there for quite some time, before he sighed heavily and started across the tracks in the direction of the Burke House.

Chapter 10

THE MORNING FOG LIFTED EARLY, giving the pilots an unobstructed view of the river as the steamers left their moorings and made their way to their designated spots in the line. The sun was shining brightly overhead by the time everything was in order for the expedition up the White River. The *Mamora* led the way, followed by Morison's flagship, the ironclad gunboat *Baton Rouge*. The three Arkansas steamers came next, carrying the Arkansas militia, followed by the recently modified Army steamers, which carried Haiber's regiment.

Colonel Cole stood on the upper deck of the *Gabby*, which was first of the three Arkansas steamers in line. Now that the operation was underway, his staff was no longer the skeleton crew it had been: three additional lieutenants had been attached from the companies, as well as a surgeon and his assistant, both of whom had been sent down from Little Rock just in time to catch the expedition before they departed. Thompson and Baxter had both received brevet promotions to Lieutenant-Colonel and Major, respectively. Cole had also received a brevet promotion from Brigadier General of the Arkansas Militia to Major General of the militia, but he still preferred to be addressed by his Regular Army rank of Colonel.

Pickering joined Cole at the rail. Cole reached up and touched the brim of his kepi in the way of a greeting, but said nothing. He was enjoying the silence of the morning and hoped the politician wouldn't ruin it.

"Fine day," the politician said with a smile.

Cole turned his eyes from the steamers and gazed into the distance. Just over the trees in the west he could see menacing black clouds threatening to overtake the otherwise clear blue sky.

"It won't last," Cole replied. "Storm's coming."

Mouser yipped with joy as he moved gracefully along the edge of the river. Several miles downriver a small group of his skirmishers had fired on the last transport, then, just as he had planned, they disappeared into the woods and leapfrogged upriver past another small detachment of scouts. The process had repeated itself until the scouts were now arriving at his position where he was planning a full blown attack.

The scouts were the best the rebels had to offer—the pick of the litter, as Mouser liked to say. There were only around three hundred of them, but they were all as stealthy as their leader and they were all tremendous shots. They also seemed to share their leader's enthusiasm. The Scouts were proud of their role in the coming fight. They took pride in the fact that, unlike the others, they weren't expected to and wait for the enemy to come to them; instead, they were going to take the fight to the enemy.

Mouser had been Longtooth's primary scout since the beginning and it hadn't taken the charismatic dogbreed long to develop quite a following of his own. Not only that, but while Mouser wasn't as intelligent as Longtooth or Sid, he was extremely quick-witted. And sometimes in the heat of battle, quick wits are far more important than a sound mind. The beastmen had been unorganized and largely unarmed when Pruitt's army had tried to catch them. Nevertheless, Longtooth had gone on the offensive at Clover Bend and his bold attack had worked. However, the battle would not have been near the rout it had been if it wasn't for Mouser's quick thinking.

Longtooth had ordered Mouser to use his scouts to take out the enemy's pickets. However, when it was found that Pruitt had failed to post pickets, Mouser had improvised. He and his scouts slipped into the sleeping camp and stole many of the enemy's weapons, which were neatly stacked near the tents. When the signal was given to attack, the humans stumbled out of their tents to find their rifles in the hands of the enemy. As a result, there were those among the scouts who felt that Mouser was the real hero of Clover Bend.

Mouser stopped and glanced up and down the river. Night had fallen, but his keen vision could still make out the shapes of his scouts hiding in the brush—most of them anyway, some of his scouts were so good he even had trouble finding them once they were in place.

Up ahead a group of dogbeeds were busy covering a skiff with brush near the edge of the water. They saw Mouser look their way, stopped what they were doing and waved.

Mouser out from the brush so he was sure they could see him, then swept his hat off and bowed grandly.

"How much longer?" one of the dogbreeds asked in a voice that was little more than a whisper, but was still easily heard by Mouser's sharp ears.

"They're still some way downriver," Mouser replied in like tone, "It'll be a couple more hours before we see them, and that's just fine and dandy 'cause I got a few more surprises in store for them before they get here."

"If they still a few hours downriver why we whispering?" another dogbreed asked, his voice still hushed.

"Practice," Mouser said with a toothy smile. He wasn't sure if they saw the smile, but he heard the laughter of his scouts and it warmed his heart.

Mouser continued on his way, passing two more hidden skiffs before he came to another hidden treasure. He patted the black barrel of the little iron cannon, and turned to the crew. "They won't be able to see you until they round that corner. Don't shoot unless I tell you to. We're going to take them by surprise so if everything goes well, we'll take the ship without you ever even firing a shot."

Cline, a scruffy bulldog-looking dogbreed who served as head of the gun's crew, motioned to the scouts who were positioned near the skiff and said, "Why they get to have all the fun?"

Mouser feigned a look of concern. "Don't you worry your ugly little head about that, this is just the first of many surprises I have in store for them."

"Where the other gun?" another member of the crew asked.

"Y'all sure are full of questions tonight," Mouser said, "It's downriver."

"Aw, they gets to shoot first," yet another crewman complained.

"But y'all are part of the big show. Trust me, they'll hate they missed this one," Mouser said. He reached out and patted Cline on the shoulder. "Look alive. Tonight's our night. It'll be just like Clover Bend."

Mouser turned away and grabbed a low tree limb that hung out over the water. Holding the limb with one hand, he swung himself out so that his body hung over the water while his feet still rested on dry land. He removed his kepi and waved it as he called out, "Clover Bend!"

Beastmen all along the edge of the river let out a yell; it was a sound that seemed more like the yipping and barked of dogs than any human cheer.

While the scouts hooted and howled, Mouser turned to the river. He raised his nose to the air and smelled rain.

Lightning lit up the night sky as strong gusts of wind pushed the rain, causing it to cascade down in waves. Most of the men on the Army transports had taken refuge inside the superstructure, but for those who wouldn't fit inside, the upper deck provided barely adequate cover for those huddling together on the lower deck. The wind swept the rain in under the deck, drenching those below. Most of the unlucky souls crowded outside the steamer took refuge on the starboard side of the ship, where the superstructure blocked the worst of the wind and rain that was sweeping in from the West. Still, the soldiers on the lower deck faired much better than their comrades overhead. The most miserable soldiers on the ships were the watches stationed topside—with no shelter over their heads, they had no choice but to weather the storm.

Up ahead, the two Navy gunboats were leading the way, followed by the militia's three chartered steamers. Next came the *Anne Marie*, under the direct command of Colonel Haiber. Last came the *John F. Roe*; Lieutenant-Colonel Santiago and Sergeant Parker were in joint command of this vessel as it brought up the rear.

Parker walked along the upper deck, hand raised to shield his face against the driving rain. There had been a roof over the walk two weeks ago, but in an effort to lighten the steamer they had removed the roof and used the excess timber to further strengthen the rails that ran alongside the walkways. It seemed like a good idea at the time, but right now Parker was beginning to second-guess his opinion concerning Baxter's supposed genius.

"How's it going, Sarge?" a private asked.

"I've seen better days," Parker said, then he noticed another private down the walk who was sitting with his back to the plank-reinforced railing. "Hey," he called out, picking up his pace. "You supposed to stand watch, not—"

His voice was drowned when a flash of lightning was quickly followed by a loud peal of thunder. Suddenly a soldier collapsed nearby.

At first Parker didn't realize what had happened, then he saw the blood. The soldier lay on the wet plank floor with his head propped against the superstructure, his eyes wide as he watched his life pulse out of his chest in a thick red crimson.

"Oh sweet Jesus; please no sweet Jesus," the soldier muttered, then his breath stopped but his eyes continued to stare.

Nearby, other soldiers realized what had happened—it wasn't the first time a bushwhacker had used the sound of thunder to conceal the report of his rifle. Scattered rifle shots rang out from all around the *Roe* as soldiers took pot shots into the dark.

"Hold your fire!" Parker shouted.

Lieutenant-Colonel Santiago came out of the pilothouse and started down the walkway toward Parker. "What happened?"

"Bushwhackers again, sir," Parker said.

"You may not have noticed, but they're picking off the sentries, sergeant. Tell the men to keep their damn heads down."

"Sir, I don't—"

"Damn it, Parker," Santiago said, "That's an order, not open for discussion. Tell men on the decks to keep down. We can see all the way around the ship from the pilothouse."

"Yes, sir," Parker said.

Santiago turned and walked back to the pilothouse. He had just opened the door when an explosion erupted on the deck below.

Parker ran to the stairs then bounded down, taking four steps at a time. Even before he made it to the lower deck he could hear the sound of someone screaming.

One of the beastmen's six-pounders had been hidden in a

masked position. It had lain in wait while the gunboats and the other steamers passed by, before firing at the *Roe*. Having fired once, its crew hauled the light cannon back into the woods.

The shell had hit the planking on the starboard side of the ship. The six inch timbers had just managed stop the shell, but when it exploded, it spread iron fragments and wooden shards across the deck. One soldier lay on his face, unmoving. Judging by the pool of blood under him, he was either dead or dying. Another man, the one Parker heard scream, was lying on his back, both of his legs shredded by the explosion, and another man had a shard of wood as long as a forearm wedged into his shoulder.

It could have been worse, though. If the extra planking hadn't been there, that shell would have passed right through the ship's thin walls and exploded inside the packed superstructure.

Santiago appeared at the top of the stairs. He seemed at a loss for words.

"Sir, they're targeting the *Roe*," Parker said, "They ain't hit any of the other ships yet. We're last in line and they keep hitting us. I think they're up to something. We need to keep lookouts posted."

Santiago seemed to consider this. When he finally did speak, he wasn't quite as blunt and forceful as he had been before. "Tomorrow morning I'll contact Morison and see if we can't have the *Marmora* bring up the rear. For the time being we need to keep our heads down and ride out the storm."

"Yes, sir,"

Santiago returned to the pilothouse and Parker saw that the wounded were cared for. The sergeant then made his rounds, telling all of the soldiers to keep their heads down and instructing the lookouts to rejoin their companies. The lookouts were relieved, but Parker couldn't shake the feeling that they were making a big mistake.

The cotton was high this season. This meant more profit for the master, but all it meant for the slaves was more work. Still, little Marcus Parker couldn't help but be swept away by the marvelous height of the cotton plants this year.

"Now, Marcus, you stay outta the way," his older brother Jerod said.

"Ah wanna help," Marcus said.

For some reason Jerod found this extremely funny. And when Jerod laughed, he always did so with his entire body. He cocked his head back, put one hand on his hip and slapped his knee with his other hand. His entire bony body shaking as he whooped and hooted.

"What so funny?" Marcus asked. "I'm old enough to help."

Still chuckling, Jerod lowered himself so that he was perched on his heels. He looked into Marcus's eyes and said, "Remember when I was sick?"

At first he didn't, but then Marcus remembered. They were in the Freeland and Jerod caught pneumonia. But that couldn't be right, Marcus was only seven; they wouldn't be moved to the Freeland for another three years.

"Yeah, I remember." Marcus said, the memory now becoming painful. "You died."

"When I was sick daddy told you not to go in my room, but you did anyway. You got sick. But you didn't die."

Marcus suddenly felt guilty; he had lived but his beloved brother Jerod had died. Jerod had always been such a warm and loving young man, always able to see the good in any person or any situation, yet little Marcus had grown up cold and hard. It seemed wrong that someone so full of love was cut down so young while someone driven by hate lived on. Marcus lowered his head.

Jerod gently placed his hand under Marcus's chin and raised his head so their eyes met. "You strong. Always have been." Jerod moved his hand and placed it over Marcus' heart. "You always been stronger here than any man I ever knowed."

His movements were now slow and gentle, more like Marcus' mother. Jerod had always been the type who squeezed hard when he hugged; it always burned a little whenever Jerod patted Marcus' back. Right now Marcus wanted nothing more than to run into his brother's arms and feel that strong loving squeeze, but he stood there.

Just like a little soldier.

Jerod drew his hand away and smiled. "You strong, but you can't fight the world alone."

"I don't understand," Marcus said, trying to be strong but fighting back tears.

"Fog's rollin' in." Jerod said.

"Huh?"

"Sir, the fog's rollin in." Jerod repeated, but this time the voice didn't sound at all like Jerod.

Sergeant Parker's eyes fluttered as he slowly came out of his dream and into reality. He was sitting on the upper deck with his coat over his head as shelter from the rain, which had now slowed to a drizzle. Sergeant Roland was kneeling before him.

"Truth be known, the fog's already here," the company sergeant said, a little embarrassed and perhaps a touch guilty, "I'd got you up sooner, but I guess I dozed off m'self."

Parker rubbed his eyes and sat up. "Better tell the boys to keep one eye on the river. I've got a bad feeling about the way they've been targeting the *Roe*."

Roland and Parker rose to their feet. Three shots rang out. One bullet hit the planking right beside the two sergeants, the other bullet slammed into Roland's chest with a sickening thump and the third one passed so close that Parker heard it crack like a whip as it passed right before his face.

Parker dropped to the ground, but before he did he glanced in the direction the shots had come. The fog was so thick he could barely make out the trees at the edge of the river. When he hit the ground he realized he had seen something else— shapes on the water.

Boats.

He started to call out, but apparently other soldiers had also made the discovery. Rifle fire sputtered all along the starboard side of the steamer and was answered from the boats in the river.

Parker drew his pistol as he rose to his feet and ran for the stairs. As he ran, he saw that there were at least a dozen boats, some of which were actually alongside the *Roe*. On the deck below he could hear the grunting and swearing of melee.

When he reached the stairs he found a lone figure ascending. It was dark, but he could make out a muzzle and pointed ears on an upright body. The creature held a pistol in its right hand and a hatchet in its left. The beast lunged up the stairs, taking aim with its pistol and raising its hatchet overhead.

Parker fired first. The bullet hit the dogbreed in the upper chest. Staggered, the beast missed a step and fell sideways into the railing. Wounded, but still fighting, it took aim and fired. Splinters flew as the bullet buried itself in the wood next to Parker's head. Parker pulled the trigger three more times. The first shot was a misfire, probably caused by damp powder, but the next two rang loudly, hitting the dogbreed in the head with at least one of the shots.

Continuing down the stairs to the lower floor, Parker found that while only a handful of the creatures had managed to get onboard the *Roe*, they were putting up one hell of a fight. He tried to pick out an enemy, but in the darkness and the confusion of the melee it was hard to tell friend from foe.

However, it was soon evident that the superiority of numbers was quickly turning the melee to his boys' favor.

He heard heavy splashes as the few remaining beastmen dove into the river to attempt escape rather than risk capture.

"Shoot them!" a lieutenant called out.

Soldiers lined the railing, firing into the water. Most of the soldiers were reloading when the hidden cannon opened fire from the shore, showering the lower deck with a blast of canister. The big 24-pounder at the *Roe's* bow roared a reply into the darkness.

It was all but over, yet for several more minutes the men continued to fire into the water and at the bank of the river. The *Roe's* big gun fired two more blasts in the direction from which the beastmen's gun had been fired. Up ahead, the *Anne Marie* fired one shot from her gun as well, but this was more a gesture of solidarity than any real attempt to take out an actual target.

Seeing that the boarding attempt had been thwarted, Parker turned and started back up the stairs to get the surgeon. Halfway up, he noticed the body of the beastman he had killed. The short-nosed bulldoggish beast lay to one side of the pathway, stretched out under the handrail, with half its body hanging off the stairs. Even in death the pistol and the hatchet were still gripped firmly in its hands.

"What's going on?" Colonel Cole asked as he came out of his stateroom. With the *Gabriel Hastings* four boats ahead of the *John F. Roe*, and the sound muffled by the humid air, Cole hadn't heard the gunfire. He did, however, feel the rumbling under his feet stop when the engines stopped.

"Don't know, sir," a sergeant replied as he hurried down the hall.

Cole hurried toward the pilothouse as fast as his aching legs would carry him.

Colonel Cole was halfway down the walkway, when Lieutenant-Colonel Thompson came out of the pilothouse and started his way, probably on his way to get him.

"Why have we stopped?" Cole asked.

"The *Roe* is under attack."

"They been taking pot shots at her all night, why stop now?" Cole asked, a little agitated.

"It wasn't just a few shots from the bushes this time," Thompson replied, "As far as we can tell, the enemy tried to use the fog to cover a boarding attempt."

Behind them they heard the muffled boom of the beastmen's 6-pounder. Due to the weather, the shot sounded as if it was much further down the river than it really was. This shot was followed by a louder blast from the *Roe*'s 24-pounder.

Cole then began to rethink what had transpired that night. It had appeared as if the beastmen had been taking potshots at the *Roe* just to make sure the sentries weren't watching, and then they launched their full-out attack. Were they that organized?

Mouser ran down the muddy river bank, just inside the trees.

"Fall back into the woods!" he called out, "Fall back!"

The big steamer had moved further upriver and was all but concealed in the fog. Still, the occasional rifle shot rang out from her upper deck. These shots were more than likely blind potshots, but there was little sense in risking lives unnecessarily.

He passed several beastmen as he ran along the bank, many of them soaking wet from an impromptu swim in the White River and some of them wounded. Almost all of the scouts who came out of the water were without weapons. They had been forced to drop them in order to swim. This startled Mouser more than anything.

"Cline?" he called out, "Where's Cline?"

"That'a way" a beastman replied, pointing toward a position frighteningly close to the same position the gun held at the beginning of the engagement..

Mouser's mind raced. Cline was in charge of the gun they had used in the ambush; why was he still so close to the river's edge? That gun should have been withdrawn as soon as it fired a shot to cover the retreat.

"Mouser, over here," Cline called out form the darkness.

Mouser stopped and tried to adjust his sight, but the foliage in the area was too dense to allow more than a few rays of starlight into the woods. He could see much farther than a human could in such darkness, but not quite far enough. He raised his nose to the air, but the smell of gunpowder was too strong.

"Over here!" Cline called out again.

"I can't see you," Mouser said, but then he found he could make out the outline of four beastmen frantically waving their hands over their heads. "Wait, there you are," Mouser said, and he started his way.

When Mouser reached Cline he saw something that made his heart fall to his stomach. The six-pounder was lying on its side in a shallow ravine. One wheel was completely shattered and the cannon itself was half buried in the soft mud.

"I'm awful sorry," Cline explained. "We was pulling back after firing one shot just like you told us to, but we got too close to this here ravine and it slipped in. Broke a wheel on the way down. We been tryin' to get her out, but she stuck good."

One of the other members of the crew whined softly and another said, "We sorry."

Mouser knew Longtooth wouldn't be pleased, but it was going to take more than this one mishap to break his spirit. "Don't worry y'all's ugly heads about it," he said cheerily, "We got another one."

The other three crewmen seemed to perk up, but Cline's head was still down and his tail was low.

"Really, it's all right," Mouser said, giving him a playful slap on the shoulder, "Now see if you can't find yourselves some rifles. This ain't over. Not by a long shot."

Chapter 11

CAPTAIN MORISON STOOD on the deck of the *Baton Rouge* with his coat pulled tight around him. There was no wind, thunder or lightning, but the rain was once again coming down in buckets. A small skiff came along side. Sailors pulled the boat up to the warship and helped the smaller vessel's occupants climb onboard.

"Welcome to the *Baton Rouge*!" Morison boomed as Haiber set foot on the deck.

Haiber didn't reply. He wasn't in the mood for Morison's showmanship.

"Right this way, Colonel" Morison said, and he turned on his heels and led the way into the gunboat's casemate.

Once inside, Haiber and Parker were led to the officers' mess. In stark contrast to what they would expect from the large and loud captain of the ship, the room was small and plain. A few detailed maps and charts of the Mississippi River and her tributaries hung here and there and a solitary painting of a sloop of war, probably the one Morison had served on during the French and Mexican War, hung behind the captain's chair. Colonel Cole, Lt-Colonel Thompson, Senator Pickering and Alexander Stewart, the 13th Colored Regiment's chief surgeon were already seated at the small table. Once Morison, Haiber and Parker joined them, it was elbow to elbow.

With a long skinny body and a face that consisted of deep-set eyes and hollow cheeks, Alexander Stewart looked more like a corpse than a surgeon. Haiber liked him, though. He was one of the only true-blooded Whigs in the regiment and as such he was there for the right reasons.

Stewart started the meeting by saying, "It was a short fight, but a bloody one. There were eighteen killed and thirty-one wounded in this morning's engagement. Of the wounded, fourteen are severe. We never expected to have this many casualties so early in the expedition. We do not have the means necessary to treat the severely wounded. We need to send them back downriver to Montgomery Point. From there they can be offloaded and taken to the hospital in Memphis."

"I'm not so sure that's possible," Cole said, "The rain has the river running a lot faster than we anticipated. We're already behind schedule. If we return down river to drop off the wounded we could lose as much as two weeks."

"Begging your pardon, sir, but we need to get these boys to a hospital," Stewart said politely but emphatically, "They're going to need more care than we have available here."

"I agree with Stewart," Haiber said. On the way over, he had made up his mind he wasn't going to be pushed around this time, not by Morison, not by Cole. This time he was going to stand his ground early and stick to his guns. "I've been over to the *Roe*. Some of those boys aren't going to make it if we don't send them back down the river."

Cole was shook his head. "This expedition depends on speed. It's apparent they know we're coming, but that doesn't mean they've had time to gather their forces. It's imperative that we get up river as quickly as possible."

Now Thompson broke in, "Colonel, why don't we load the wounded onto one of the smaller vessels like the *Isabella*? Our excess troops could transfer over to the *Roe*."

"That's a great idea," Haiber said, "The Army transports are designed to carry more than five hundred, so we could accommodate the extra soldiers without any problem."

"It would take too long to transfer the men and ammunition. We'd be giving them an extra day to prepare for us," Cole said, now obviously becoming frustrated. "At least a day, maybe more."

"Send the *Marmora*," Morison said, "The *Baton Rouge* can do anything she can do."

"We need the *Marmora* for scouting," Cole said.

"There's not enough room on the gunboat anyway," Stewart said.

"We need to send one of the transports back with the wounded. That's all there is to it," Haiber said emphatically, now feeling quite proud of himself.

Then his feet were swept out from under him from the last person he would have expected.

"I agree with Colonel Cole," Parker said.

Everyone present seemed shocked to silence. They all turned their eyes to the black non-commissioned officer.

"I checked on the boys before we left the ship. Three of them won't live to see tomorrow no matter what we do and four more probably won't survive the trip downriver anyway. So we're talking about sending back one of the steamers, along with enough troops to guard against possible attack, all for the lives of seven soldiers."

Haiber was downright confused. He couldn't believe the turn of events. However, Stewart quickly turned on Parker. He thrust a bony finger at Parker and said, "Those seven soldiers have a right to live, sergeant,"

"Don't lecture me! I knew these boys when they was kids," Parker snapped. "But last night we saw what a handful of those creatures can do. We're about to face thousands of them. We need to have every soldier possible in the line."

That settled it. Parker had spoken his piece and remained silent through the rest of the meeting, but what he said had sown doubt in Haiber's mind and perhaps the minds of everyone else present. Stewart continued to argue, but one by one the rest of the men present switched sides and before they left, Cole had his way. They would press on.

On the way back to the Army Steamers, Parker sat in the back of the skiff by himself. Stewart was still fuming, and Haiber still seemed confused. The rain had died to a drizzle. Parker watched the droplets fall into the river and he began to wonder whether he had made the right choice. Despite his good intentions, he felt as though he had just killed those seven boys. He might as well have put a pistol to their heads and pulled the trigger; they didn't stand a chance now.

He was intently watching the water when someone patted his knee.

It was Haiber. The colonel had scooted to the back of the skiff. Parker suddenly wished the boat was longer so he could scoot further into the back; the last thing he wanted to do right now was talk about their recent disagreement.

Much to his relief, and disbelief, Haiber didn't bring up the subject.

They sat in silence for a while before Haiber said, "How did the men handle themselves last night?"

"They did fine. Casualties were high for such a brief engagement, but they gave as good as they got."

Haiber nodded, but Parker could tell something else was bothering him. Haiber glanced out at the trees then asked the real question, the one that had probably been bothering him all morning. "What about the enemy? How did they fight?"

"Like demons."

Chapter 12

ALTHOUGH SUNSET WOULDN'T COME for another two hours, the black clouds had blanketed the sun, casting the woods into a sea of darkness. The big man moved silently through the woods, steadily approaching the river. The dead animals were so far away from the river that Hunter couldn't smell them at all. The rain would hinder the dawgs sense of smell as well, not to mention the fact that the river was flowing rapidly meaning the dawgs on the other side would have an even harder time catching his scent. However, Hunter was thorough. He set them out anyway as a precaution.

Hunter had learned his latest trick from the Comanche. They would rub a dead carcass on their bodies before approaching a buffalo herd. The buffalo wouldn't smell a human, they would smell a dead animal. They would suspect nothing until the Indian was close enough to strike. Hunter was no fool, though. He knew the dogs, as he called the beastmen, were smarter than buffalo, so he altered his tactic. He would wait until the wind was right then move in and place a few animal carcasses in the area, so that if the wind shifted the scent of rotten varmints would overpower his own scent. And even if the dogs went to investigate the smell, they wouldn't find him. They would only find dead animals.

During the last few interrogations, he learned that the dogs had a name for him. They called him The Disease. That's exactly what they thought it was when he first started moving among them; they thought it was a disease that killed small creatures and advanced their decomposition. Of course, just like when he hunted Indians, he couldn't bring himself to stop with just interrogating a one or two dogs then hiding the body. He was having too much fun. Soon the dogs weren't only finding dead animals, they were finding his victims tortured to death. Now he placed the carcasses further away, because if the dogs smelled them they would know he was in the area. However, he still needed them to throw them off if they got on his trail. Hunter hadn't made it this far in life living carelessly.

Hunter, stopped and checked the wind as he neared the river. The wind was light, blowing in from the west, toward the probable location of the dog's camp. But the rain was coming down hard once more and that would help hide his scent.

He listened and could hear the rushing water; he was close. In fact, if the last dog he questioned was correct—and how could someone lie when they were under that much pain?— the main camp should be right across the river.

He moved forward, his footsteps making hardly a sound.

Through the trees, he saw the flicker of a few torches and lanterns before he reached the river, not as many as one would expect from a camp of thousands, but, then again, the dogs didn't need as much light as people. Hunter took his time as he approached the river, carefully watching for lookouts. The camp was supposed to be on the other side of the river, but that didn't mean guards wouldn't be posted on this side. When he reached the edge of the woods, he peered across the river and saw the beastman camp for the first time. The camp was roughly what he expected, an Indian-like village only with lean-tos and makeshift tents rather than tee-pees. It was even roughly the size he had expected, probably a population of around two thousand. He was somewhat surprised to see that the camp was moderately fortified.

However, he noticed something in the river itself that took his breath away. His mouth fell open and he stood for several minutes trying to take in what he was seeing. Two steamers sat in the river, moored alongside the camp. There was simply no way the dogs had learned how to operate the steam engines, but, on the other hand, there was no denying their presence.

Across the river, a pair of pups were playfully splashing each other in the water near the opposite bank. Suddenly one of them stopped and looked his way.

Damn those dogs and their sharp eyesight!

He slowly moved back into the woods, hoping he could disappear before an alarm was raised. However, as he backed away one of the pups leapt out of the water and ran back to the camp shouting, "The Disease has returned! The Disease is here!"

Hunter turned and started back the way he came in a hurry. Behind him he could hear yapping and barking as the dogs piled into the boats and starting across the river.

His legs weary from miles of running, Hunter stopped and slumped against a tree. His breath was coming in pants and his side was killing him. He had his carbine in his right hand, but he had left his mule behind. They had been after him all night and they were steadily gaining ground. The rain, along with his decoys had been more than enough to throw off the dog's noses, but Hunter hadn't counted on them getting onto his trail so soon; they were following him too close. Constantly on the run, he hadn't been able to stop and cover his tracks. The dogs were simply following footprints in the mud that any amateur could track.

Still, he had a chance. He had run all night and now he realized he was going to make it to the beach across from Chickasaw Bluffs in time to meet Colonel Cole. The colonel would be there with his soldiers.

And with his gold.

Even with his life on the line, it was the thought of all that gold that caused Hunter to pick up his pace. He loved gold. Gold and killin'.

Fifteen years ago Hunter had been known by his given name, Ronald Eldridge, but names don't make a difference—the way he saw it, he had always been Hunter. He had killed his first man when he was only a boy, had knifed him for his gold watch. It was his first kill and his first taste of gold. For the rest of his life the two ran hand in hand. Little more than a second rate thief and sometimes murderer along the Ohio River, it wasn't until he moved west that Ronald Eldridge came into his own. He had traveled west to the Colorado Territory when he heard that Wells Fargo was paying a reward for the scalps of Comanche braves. They had paid their bounties in gold. He quickly found that the railroad people couldn't tell a woman's or child's scalp from an Indian warrior's—either that or they didn't care. After a few months he discovered that they couldn't tell an Indian scalp from a white's. He seemed to have an endless supply of gold; then someone discovered what he was doing. He had to leave the territory and change his identity. His mama, the whore, had chosen the name Ronald Eldridge; he chose the name Hunter. Yes, he had always been Hunter. Just like he had always been The Disease.

Hunter left the woods and stumbled onto the short beach that ran along the edge of the river. He had made it. The tree-lined bluffs ran along the other side, but there were no steamers in the river. Cole wasn't there. The big man ran along the beach, hoping against all hope that a steamer would round the corner, but none did.

He stopped and regarded the rushing water. He wouldn't be able to survive in the fast current even if he did know how to swim.

Five figures stepped onto the beach about one-hundred yards away; even in the darkness he recognized one as none other than Longtooth. Hunter turned to run, but three more figures appeared on the beach in the opposite direction. His eyes couldn't part the darkness well enough to see into the woods beside him, but his ears told him all he needed to know—he was surrounded.

Desperation grabbed him. He threw his carbine to his shoulder and took aim, but when he saw they were armed and aiming back he stayed his trigger finger. Why weren't they shooting? With their guns ready, the dogs slowly approached him. This gave him just enough time to come up with a plan. Moving slowly, he made sure they saw him put his carbine down on the muddy beach. He then drew his pistol and put it on the ground as well. He drew his knife, but he didn't place it on the ground. He held it out so they could see, slowly turning it so the moonlight would reflect off its bloodstained blade.

No one could best him with his Bowie. If he could trick Longtooth into a duel he could grab the dog then hold the others at bay by threatening to kill him.

He turned to Longtooth. "Longtoof! You wanna fight, we fight!"

The four rifle-armed dogs stopped, and Longtooth stepped forward, away from them.

Hunter began to smile as Longtooth approached when the dog was within ten feet he stopped.

"The Disease," Longtooth growled.

Hunter nodded, "Yeah, that me. I kill dogs, pups, and bitches. I don't give a damn. If it got fur, I kill it."

Longtooth stood in silence. Hunter sized him up. He'd seen the wanted posters, and he'd glimpsed him from afar once, but this was the first time they had actually met and it was a bit of a disappointment; Longtooth wasn't as big as he expected. This was going to be a lot easier than he first thought.

Hunter motioned with his free hand, "Come on, Longtoof.

We fight. Unlessen you yeller?"

Longtooth showed his teeth. Hunter wasn't sure if he was smiling or growling, but when Longtooth reached down to his belt he knew the fight was on.

Then he realized Longtooth was grabbing a pistol.

"We fight with knives!" Hunter shouted, "Settle this like men!"

"I ain't no man," Longtooth said. He took aim. "And I'm damn proud of it."

"No!" Hunter shouted, trying to charge forward.

The pistol barked twice, both bullets slamming into his chest. The first shot stopped his charge and the second sent him staggering. The pistol rang out three more times, each shot hitting Hunter in the chest as he fell backwards.

He spun as he went down, landing facedown in the wet sand. His breath was pained and short. He tasted blood and bile in his mouth. He tried to rise, but found that there was no strength in his arms.

A booted foot rolled him onto his back and he was staring down the barrel of a pistol. He couldn't believe they aimed to kill him like a common animal.

The muzzle flashed but he never heard the shot.

Chapter 13

I CAN'T BELIEVE you're going to do this," Sid snarled. "If they going to try to arrest you, why go talk to them? They ain't going to listen."

Longtooth remained silent. He looked down at the dead body at his feet, then turned to where Gregory stood near the edge of the woods. Gregory's head was low, causing his droopy jowls to droop even further. Longtooth couldn't understand how Gregory could mourn the death of a savage human such as The Disease—the one known to men as Hunter. But, in a way, Longtooth envied Gregory. Sure, he had come a long way since his days his days as a ruthless, murdering brigand, but he wished he could see the world through Gregory's eyes, to see some good in all living things.

Longtooth turned to another nearby dogbreed and said, "Send a message to Mouser."

Sid threw his hands in the air. "Great, now he's ignoring me."

Longtooth continued giving orders to the messenger. "Tell him to cross over to the west bank with about fifty of his scouts and meet us across from Chickasaw Bluffs." He turned to another beastman and said, "Go back to camp and get David. Hurry back, but don't forget he can't run very far without gettin' tired. You may have to carry him, but he ain't heavy."

Then Longtooth turned back to Sid, "I ain't ignoring you, Sid. But I ain't going to argue with you either. I've made up my mind."

"It just don't make any sense. You know they ain't wanting to talk, so why talk?"

"I got reasons."

The problem was, Longtooth knew he would never be able to explain his reasons to his loyal yet outspoken second-in-command. Sid tended to see things in black and white with no grey, and his decision to contact the humans despite the fact they planned on using the meeting as a trap certainly resided in a grey area somewhere in between two extremes.

"I'm taking Gregory and Dillon with me, we'll use Mouser and his scouts for escorts when they get here," Longtooth said to Sid, "I need someone to stay behind and lead in case they do take me prisoner. I was thinking…"

Sid interrupted, "Hell, no. I'm going with you."

"Who will lead if something happens to me?"

"You know as well as I do if something happens to you they'll fall apart. They ain't gonna follow me or no one else but you." Sid nodded toward the big boar, who was reading his Bible beside the river. "They all just as bad as Dillon. They worship you. That's why I don't want you to go and do something stupid. If something happens to you, it's over."

"I'm sorry, but it's something I got to do."

Sid grumbled. He turned to Longtooth and snapped, "I can't talk you out of it?"

"I'm sorry, but no."

Sid sighed, shook his head and walked away. Maybe he was trying to tell himself to give up the argument, but Longtooth knew he hadn't heard the last of it. Sid was just as headstrong as he was.

Gregory moved away from the beach as soon as the beastmen started stringing up The Disease's body. He couldn't understand why they had to go that far; he couldn't believe Longtooth would order something so barbaric.

He stepped further into the wood. When he started feeling

the tears building in his eyes he hid his face in his hands just in case someone happened to see him. He was so out of place here. And he was so terribly homesick. He missed the warm home and the good meals, but most of all he missed the warm hearts of his old family.

Most of all, he missed Timothy. Every night the young boy seemed to haunt his dreams. In those dreams he would often look up at Gregory with tears streaming down his cheeks and ask, *Why did you leave us, Gregory?* All Gregory can do in the dreams is say *I'm Sorry*, but he was never able to bring himself to explain because he knew the boy wouldn't understand. And, to him, that was the real tragedy. Timothy never would understand.

Gregory smelled a presence and removed his hands from his face. A scraggly dogbreed was only a few feet away, staring up at him with a cruel grin that looked more human than beast. Gregory knew that there had to be others in the camp who were like him, but if there was, they always kept to themselves. The wicked ones weren't shy at all though. They made themselves known. The fight at Clover Bend brought out the beast in many of Longtooth's followers, and Longtooth made the worst offenders leave. But he didn't get rid of all of them. He couldn't. There were just too many of them.

"You don't like it, do you?" the beastman said, walking up to Gregory with his tail high and his shackles raised.

He was a small ratty-looking beastman, probably half Gregory's size, but the wicked ones were always bold when they knew someone wasn't going to hurt them and it was common knowledge that Gregory McMillan wouldn't hurt a fly.

Gregory tried to turn away, but the little dogbreed caught him by the arm.

"He killed my friend, skinned him while he was still alive," the beastman said, his tail lowering as he spoke and his voice

117

changing to a low growl. "He killed Jacob's bitch, too. Did you know Hannah?"

Gregory remained silent.

"Did you?" the beastman growled, his grip growing tighter.

"No," Gregory said, his voice barely a hoarse whisper.

"She was a sweet thang, like you," he said with a sneer, "She wasn't doing nothing but taking water out to Jacob while he was on watch. When Jacob found her, she was still alive. But she didn't live long, not with what The Disease had done to her."

"Leave me alone," Gregory said, closing his eyes.

The dogbreed didn't. In fact, he took a step close so he could look up into Gregory's face while he spoke. "That's why I don't give a damn about him or any other humans. They all can die for all I care, and I hope I can make 'em hurt like Hannah did before they go."

Gregory opened his eyes. He nodded toward where Hunter dangled from a tree near the edge of the woods and said, "What could you possibly gain by becoming what he was?"

The beastman's eyes grew wide and the growl that escaped his throat was all animal. He was about to attack, when another beastman came from around Gregory and seized him by the arms.

"What you think you doing?" the newcomer asked the ratty little beastman.

At first there was no response, Gregory's aggressor pulled against the newcomer. Finally the enraged beastman sputtered, "Let me go! I want him!"

"No!" the other beastman said, struggling to control his friend. "Don't do it!"

"I'm going to tear him apart!"

"You know what Longtooth would do to you if you hurt Gregory? He'd hang you up beside to The Disease, that's what he'd do."

"No, he wouldn't," Gregory said, sobbing as he spoke, but he felt joy in his heart knowing that he was right. Longtooth would never do such a thing, because he was better than that.

Chapter 14

THE RAIN HAD FINALLY LET UP by the time the column of steamers reached the bluffs. Colonel Cole watched the long, thin beach from the pilothouse as they came around the bend. He saw the sailors on the two gunboats ahead excitedly pointing at the beach, but they weren't far enough around for him to see what they were pointing at.

Then it came into view.

Hunter's body was hanging from a limb over the beach, his head to his chest and his tongue bloated.

"Damn," Cole muttered. He wasn't concerned over the loss of Hunter; he just knew that this meant he wouldn't have the information he needed concerning the enemy's camp.

"What the hell?" Baxter said, "Who's that?"

Cole's attention had been so focused on the dangling corpse that he missed an even stranger sight not much farther down the beach. A man stood near the edge of the water. It was a tall, gaunt, shoeless old man with a wispy beard. He held a stick in his hand with a white handkerchief tied to the end.

"What do you make of that?" Thompson asked Cole.

"Looks like someone wants to talk," Cole replied.

David Donovan sat in his chair with his bony knees together and his long, arthritic fingers resting casually on his lap. His clothes were tattered and his thin hair was in disarray, but he was not an unclean man. He seemed to have a pious air about him. Not the aggressive self-righteousness of a man who thinks he is better than everyone, but the calm demeanor of a humble man who knows he is as good as anyone.

He sat in his chair with two uniformed Colonels and a well-dressed politician standing before him, yet somehow he seemed untroubled and at ease. On the other hand, the two soldiers and the politician seemed nervous.

"And you were with them of your own free will?" Cole asked for the third time of the meeting. He simply couldn't believe this was the case.

"Yes, I was." Donovan said in a smooth, soft voice, one that sounded as if it should be reading bedtime stories to grandchildren rather than answering questions in a military interrogation. "I'm a member of the Liberty Society. I happened to be in the area when the slaves walked out. I decided to go with them. Many of them already knew me so they gladly accepted me as one of their own."

"You're a member of what?" Cole asked.

"The Liberty Society," Haiber answered for him. The young colonel relaxed noticeably and smiled. "It's a group founded by Frederick Douglass; my grandfather played an important role in its early years. They sponsor schools for the beastmen throughout the north."

"It's an illegal group of rabble-rousers that's what it is," Pickering said with venom in his voice, yet somehow he still managed to keep his politician's smile. "They teach the beasts to read and help runaways."

"There are no federal laws against the teaching of beastmen to read." Donovan said calmly, "and only nine states currently have laws against it."

"Including Arkansas," Pickering said sharply. Then he pressed on with his own questions. "Why were you here in the first place? Did you have a hand in starting this revolt?"

"I was sent by the Society to report on the well-being of the slaves in Arkansas. We heard rumors and planned on making a formal complaint before Congress."

Pickering grumbled and his smile faltered a little.

"Why did the beastmen send you as their messenger?" Cole asked.

"Because if they sent one of their own there's a good chance someone would have shot him before he was given a chance to speak."

"True," Haiber said.

"What do you expect?" Cole asked, "They left my spy's corpse dangling on the same beach they left their messenger."

"If that monster was in your employment, you should be ashamed of yourself." Donovan said, scolding without losing his calm demeanor.

Cole ignored the comment. "If you're a messenger, what is your message?" He asked.

"Longtooth wants to talk. He wants to see if we can settle this without further bloodshed."

When Pickering heard this his smile returned in force, but it wasn't the smile of a man who wanted to avoid bloodshed. It was the smile of a man who had secrets.

Cole noticed the smile. He turned to Pickering and asked, "You're for this parley?"

"Why of course," Pickering said, with his Southern charm suddenly returning in force. "Any way we can lessen the bloodshed is fine with me."

Donovan seemed to notice the sudden change as well; he gazed at the Southern politician with untrusting eyes.

Haiber asked. "How does he plan on going about this meeting?"

"There's an abandoned cabin about a mile inland. He told me to give you directions then I shall remain here as a hostage."

Cole and Haiber glanced at each other. Pickering kept on smiling.

"How will he know we agreed to the parley?" Cole asked.

"Fire three shots from your cannons and he will be waiting for you."

"I don't know," Thompson said, "It sounds like a trap, or at the very least they're trying to buy time."

They were gathered in the *Baton Rouge*'s officer's mess again. Cole, Haiber, Morison, Thompson, Parker, Pickering and Jones were present. It was the same group that had met after the attack on the *Roe*, except the surgeon had been replaced by Captain Jones.

"The importance of our endeavor compels me. I believe it's an opportunity that is well worth the risks," Pickering said.

"I agree," Cole said. "He must know that he's fighting an impossible battle and killing a party sent under a flag of truce will only make it worse on his own people when the revolt is put down."

"What if he just wants hostages?" Thompson asked.

"I admit that would complicate matters, but it wouldn't change the outcome."

"Besides, I think Mr. Donovan is telling the truth," Haiber said.

"Of course you do," Jones growled.

Haiber shot Jones a cold glare but didn't say anything.

"Mr. Donovan said they want us to send a small party," Cole said, "I say we send an officer and twelve handpicked men."

"We need someone who represents both Arkansas and the United States government," Pickering said, "Captain Jones is an Arkansas native with a Regular Army commission. I say we send him."

"You got to be out of your mind," Parker said.

Jones rose to his feet, "I don't take that kind insolence from a white man, and I damn sure don't take it from your kind, boy!"

Parker also rose to his feet. "You call me boy one more time and I'm gonna forget you an officer!"

"There will be none of this hullabaloo on board my ship!" Captain Morison bellowed as he too sprang to his feet.

Everybody shuffled nervously. Parker and Jones continued to glare at each other across the table, while Morison cast angry looks back and forth between them.

"Gentlemen, please be seated. This is not the time or the place," Cole said calmly.

Slowly Parker and Jones returned to their seats, followed by Morison. The tension was still thick in the room as they continued to cut stern glances at each other, but it was apparent that the physical confrontation had been avoided.

As soon as it was apparent that order had been restored, Thompson spoke up. "Let me go," he said quietly, almost apologetic. He too felt that Jones was a poor choice, but he didn't want to rouse the anger of the volatile captain.

Cole lowered his head and unconsciously drummed his fingers on the table once. When his head rose from his chest all eyes were on him. "I believe Captain Jones is the best choice for the mission."

Parker turned his eyes toward Cole in disbelief. Although they said nothing, the looks on Haiber's and Thompson's readily showed their disapproval. Pickering's smile seemed to broaden a touch.

"The good colonel's right," Morison said, in his loud voice, "There's a strong chance this stew may sour; we may need a man of Jones's strong character in command."

"You send Jones and your little *stew* is gonna go rotten," Parker said.

"You forget your place, *sergeant*!" Morison bellowed.

"That sergeant is my chief of staff," Haiber said, actually sounding forceful for once.

"And this is my ship, young man," Morison said, "Control your chief of staff or I'll have you both removed."

"Gentlemen, please," Cole said calmly. "Why don't Morison, Haiber, Pickering and I discuss this in private."

"Agreed," Morison said.

Jones grunted his displeasure as he got out of his chair and started toward the door. Thompson was right behind him. However, Parker lagged behind a little and when he walked behind his Colonel's chair on the way out he firmly grasped Haiber by the upper arm and whispered, "You know as well as I do what's gonna happen if that bastard goes to the parley. If you can't talk them into sending someone else, at least talk them into sending someone with them who can keep an eye on him."

"Like who?" Haiber replied, also in a whisper. "Most of our officers seem to worship him."

"Send me."

With that, Parker excused himself from the room.

Haiber sat in the skiff with his face was still aflame from the meeting. Morison and Pickering had insisted that Jones should lead the parley, and every time Haiber had tried to rationalize with them, Morison would interrupt with some loud exclamation and then Pickering would launch into lofty dissertation on the importance of having strong men in strong positions. The latter of which seemed ludicrous; if Jones was such a man of iron, why did he always feel compelled to better himself by berating and bullying those around him? The most infuriating part of the whole episode was how Colonel Cole agreed with them. Haiber had begun to respect the old colonel, but now he found himself thinking of the old man just as he had thought when they first met—another ignorant Southern bigot.

When the skiff pulled alongside the *Anne Marie*, Haiber was met by an unlikely pair—Lieutenant-Colonel Santiago and First Sergeant Parker.

"How did it go?" Parker asked.

Haiber just shook his head as he pulled himself out of the skiff and onto the deck of the boat. When his feet were firmly planted on the deck he said, "I thought I might win Cole over when I suggested Lieutenant-Colonel Thompson, but he seemed to have his heart set on Jones. In two hours Jones will pick twelve men and they'll be off to meet Longtooth."

"It'll be a disaster," Parked said.

"I talked them into letting you tag along, but I'm not sure that's such a good idea."

"It is a bad idea," Santiago said, "that's why I would like to go as well."

Haiber glanced back and forth between the two. This was an unexpected, yet welcome occurrence.

Santiago continued, "You don't understand how bad this man is. He'll pick a dozen men like himself and once they're in the woods, they're likely to kill Sergeant Parker. In fact, I have no doubt they will."

"If you go with them, what's to keep them from killing you?"

Santiago shrugged, "I guess they could, but if they come back missing a black sergeant it looks suspicious but it will probably be overlooked. If they come back and a lieutenant-colonel is missing, Jones's court marshal will be inevitable."

"What makes you think they'll agree to send you along? It was all I could do to get them to allow Parker to go."

"Cole's in charge of the expedition." Santiago said, "Officially he has rank, but he's still a retired officer, so that makes you the ranking active officer present."

"Even if he is retired, his regular Army rank is Colonel and he has years of seniority over me," Haiber replied.

"I'm not suggesting you try to pull rank. All you have to do is tell him that you would like to have an active regular officer present as an observer. Remember, Jones is officially on extended leave; he's here as a volunteer."

Haiber nodded. "Good idea. I'll do it." Then he asked, "Mind if I ask what brought this on? I thought you were on his side."

Santiago shrugged. "A man can only take so much hate."

For the first time since they left the Mississippi, the sky was clear overhead. The twelve handpicked men from Jones' Company A walked down the gangplank onto the beach, each of them glaring at Parker as they strode past him. Black smoke still wafted low over the water from the three cannon blasts from the *Baton Rouge*'s big guns.

Captain Jones was the last to walk down the plank. He stood at the railing of the ship with Pickering by his side. The two spoke briefly. Pickering's ever-present smile was absent; he was dead serious about whatever they were discussing. Jones nodded, his expression also cold and serious; he then turned and walked down the plank.

"Did you see that?" Parker asked Santiago. The two still weren't exactly chummy, but the grim reality that they were about to put their lives on the line and only had each other to fall back on had worn down most of the old animosity.

"Yes I did," Santiago said, "This whole expedition is looking uglier by the minute."

Jones walked past Parker and Santiago, giving both of them a cold glare.

Donovan stood at the railing of the steamer. "Longtooth said he will mark the way with white strips of cloth tied to tree limbs," he called out. "You should be able to see the first one from the beach."

"Ah see it," one of the soldiers called out pointing into the woods.

"Let's go then," Jones said.

There was no trail, they had to push their way into the brush in a single file line to reach the strip of cloth, but, sure enough, once they reached that reference point, they could see another piece of cloth further in the woods.

Long after the small party of men disappeared from sight Colonel Cole stood on the upper deck of the *Gabby*, gazing into the Arkansas wilderness as if he could part the trees by sheer willpower. His legs ached, but he had refused when Thompson had offered to bring a chair topside.

Everything seemed to be unraveling. The swift expedition upriver had turned into a slow trudge against a strong current, and now this little parley had delayed progress even more. At Palo Gaucho everything had happened so fast. He had been hailed a hero for his split second initiative. That had been only six years ago, but it seemed like a lifetime. There was little left of the man who had two horses shot out from under him that fateful day. It had been easy to order hundreds to march to their deaths with bugles blowing and bullets flying; it was different now.

Cole had rather be left alone, but privacy was in short supply. Lt-Colonel Thompson knew his colonel's moods well enough to remain quite some distance away, remaining available but not underfoot. He was the exception, though. Pickering had obviously decided that it would probably help his political prospects if he was seen standing next to the commanding officer as much as possible; he was like an infection that just wouldn't go away. Captain Morison had also come over from the *Baton Rouge*, but at least he was uncharacteristically quiet for the time being.

Haiber was present as well. He had decided to return to the *Gabby* to see his two men off and had yet to return to his own ship. Cole had mixed emotions about the young colonel. He was glad the boy was finally showing some backbone; he just wished he didn't have to be the target of this newfound aggressiveness.

Haiber nervously glanced at the sun. "Surely they will be back before nightfall."

"It won't take long," Cole said.

In a way, Cole wanted to tell Haiber about the real reason for the parley. It's not like the young colonel could do anything about it now. However, Cole knew it would cause another disagreement, and this one wouldn't be behind closed doors; it would be in full view of the soldiers, and that would be bad for morale.

"I'm curious," Haiber said, "If they return with Longtooth's demands, how will we get back to them with our counteroffer? Surely you don't mean for Jones to handle the negotiations."

"There won't be any negotiations," Pickering said, and suddenly Cole had no choice in the matter. It looked like Haiber was about to find out about the real mission.

"No negotiations?"

Cole turned to Haiber. "We've ordered Jones to arrest Longtooth and bring him and his party back to us."

"What?" Haiber shouted. "Why wasn't I informed of this?"

"Because the decision had already been made," Cole said. "We knew this might not be a popular decision, so we kept it to ourselves."

Thompson walked over and joined the crowd. Cole wasn't surprised to see even his loyal chief of staff's face flushed with anger.

"The decision had already been made?" Haiber said, his voice was suddenly high pitched as his temper went from controlled anger to borderline rage. "Who made this decision?"

"The governor of Arkansas gave specific instructions before we left Montgomery Point—if Longtooth contacts us in an attempt to make negotiations he is to be captured and taken back to Little Rock in chains." Cole said.

"Sir, you may answer to the governor of Arkansas," Haiber shot back, "but I answer to the President of the United States."

"I assure you," Pickering said, "the President is well aware of our intentions."

"Did you know about this?" Haiber asked Morison.

Morison nodded, "We discussed the matter after you left to return to the *Anne Marie*."

Haiber shot a cold glance back to Cole.

Cole said, "I assure you, there was no concerted effort to keep you in the dark."

"I should have been told," Haiber said. "You may take sending men off to die lightly but I'll be damned if any of my boys are going to get killed on some political errand."

Cole understood Haiber's position, but this didn't mean he would stand for outright insubordination. "You forget your place, Colonel." Cole shot back, "I am the commander of this operation, and it is I, and I alone, who decides whether or not to hold a council of war. You were assigned to my command for this expedition and you will follow my orders whether you like them or not. And as far as sending your boys, if you will recall I was against sending any of your men on this mission."

Haiber was furious. He turned and started to tromp off the deck, then turned back and thrust a finger in Cole's face and said. "You'd better hope they make it back from this little errand of yours."

"Young man!" Morison boomed, ending his brief bout

of relative silence, "I'll see you before a court marshal for threatening your commanding officer!"

Haiber withdrew the finger, but not the threatening glare. Cole continued to fume as well, and Morison was about to belt out another declaration when Thompson butted in, "Gentlemen, please," he said, "The men are watching."

Haiber once again turned to leave.

As he turned, Cole's voice softened somewhat and said, "They'll be all right. The beasts won't hurt them if they've got Longtooth as a prisoner."

Then Pickering spoke, "They won't have Longtooth when they come back."

Haiber stopped once more. Everybody turned to Pickering. The politician's smile actually widened; he seemed to feed off their attention.

"What do you mean?" Cole asked.

"I received a telegram from the Governor just before we started up river. He said that he had received a letter from the President that changed our position on capturing Longtooth. You see, there are those in the party who fear that the Whigs will try to use the rebel leader as a political puppet to attack our policy of using of the beasts as laborers. Longtooth is to be shot on sight. I instructed Captain Jones to carry out these orders just before he left."

Parker hated Jones like he'd hated no other man. However, he did have to grudgingly admit that the man had a sharp tactical mind.

Four soldiers in blue darted across through the waist-high grass and took up positions near a small outbuilding. After surveying the house before them, they signaled back towards the woods. Four more men darted from the woods and moved to a brush covered position that covered the house from another angle. As soon as the second group was in place, Jones took the last four soldiers with him and they hurried toward the main door. He never said a word to Parker or Santiago, so they followed along behind the last group.

They were almost to the door when it opened.

The four men stopped and took aim. Jones drew his pistol.

A large dogbreed that looked like some sort of shaggy hound mix stepped into the doorway. "Did you really have to go through all that trouble? We were well aware you were coming." The beastman said in a voice that surprisingly clear, and sounded even somewhat educated.

Parker knew the beastmen could speak, but it was still strange to hear words coming from the mouth of such an alien creature.

No human spoke, so the beastman continued, "Please, put the guns down. There's been enough blood. Let's sit and talk. No killing today."

"You Longtooth?" Jones asked.

"No, I'm afraid not. The name's Gregory McMillan."

"I'm supposed to meet Longtooth."

"He's inside."

The men started cautiously moving forward.

"Leave the guns out here," Gregory said.

"Like hell," Jones replied. "We're bringing our guns with us. I know what you did to the men who tried to surrender at Clover Bend."

Gregory started to say something else, but a voice from inside the house said, "It's okay."

When Gregory turned to lead the way into the house, Jones turned the two other groups of men and, using hand signals, he ordered one group to watch the front door and the other to go around back. Parker thought it was somewhat strange to cover the back door if they were only here to negotiate;

however, he imagined Jones was just being cautious just in case this turned out to be a trap.

Parker and Santiago followed Jones and the four soldiers inside the cabin.

The inside of the cabin was more spacious than it looked outside, largely due to the fact the entire interior was made up of one room. The place looked to have been ransacked after it had been abandoned, but judging by the nests of shredded paper in the corner and the tiny tracks in the dirt floor the culprits were probably rats and raccoons rather than beastmen. A makeshift table, a door resting on a pair of wooden kegs, sat in the center of the room. Six more kegs surrounded the table, serving as chairs.

Aside from Gregory, three more beastmen were in the room; all of them appeared unarmed. Two beastmen sat at the table and another stood behind them. The one standing was an obese swinebreed holding a Bible. However, while he was pink and rotund like a domesticated pig, there was a wild gleam in his tiny eyes that said he was as deadly as a razorback. The two sitting were dogbreeds. One was shorthaired, with grey fur and stern expression.

The other dogbreed was Longtooth. Parker had never seen any of the wanted posters, nor had he read any descriptions. Still, he knew full well which one was Longtooth as soon as they entered the room. His brown-and-black medium length fur could best be described as nondescript, and his ears seemed too perky to be described as floppy, but they sagged too much to be called pointed. Nothing was peculiar about his teeth; Parker had half expected some fiendish freak with dagger sized teeth, but there was no hint as to why the dogbreed chose to call himself Longtooth. Aside from a relatively nice officer's long coat his clothes were also quite simple. Yet Longtooth still managed to stand out. Perhaps it was his calm demeanor or the way he held himself, but Parker had no doubt that this man—or rather, this dog—was a born leader.

Jones, however, had no similar feeling of recognition.

"You Longtooth?" he asked the grey dogbreed.

Without a word, this dogbreed nodded toward the dogbreed sitting next to him.

Longtooth rose from his chair and extended his hand. "I'm Longtooth."

Much to Parker's surprise, Johnson drew his pistol and the other four soldiers leveled their rifles at the beastmen. The pigman surged forward but Longtooth held up his hand and calmly said, "No, Dillon. It's okay."

Dillon stopped. His pig stout hissed as he furiously inhaled and exhaled.

"What's going on?" Parker asked no one in particular and received no answer. He did notice, judging from Santiago's blank expression, that he was just as stunned by this turn of events.

"First you will remove that coat," Jones said. "You ain't fit to wear the coat of an officer in the United States Army and you damn sure ain't fit to die in one."

Longtooth slowly removed his coat. He reached out to hand it to Gregory, but Jones cuffed him with his pistol first. Longtooth went to his hands and knees and the coat fell to the floor.

"What the hell is going on here?" Parker asked, now with some authority in his voice.

Jones turned to Parker, "I have orders to execute this dog on sight."

"By whose authority?" Parker asked.

Jones didn't even honor that with a reply. Longtooth looked up from the ground and Jones placed the barrel between his eyes.

Parker drew his pistol and aimed it at Jones. This in turn caused two of the soldiers to turn their rifles from the beastmen and aim them at Parker. The sergeant didn't seem to notice. "The United States Army does not execute prisoners without a trail."

"He's not a prisoner; he's an animal. It's like putting down a dog that's gone rabid."

Parker glanced down at the dogbreed on the ground. He noticed the long thick scars along his back and remembered similar scars along his father's back. *They called us animals, too.* He though.

"Put your gun down or I will shoot you," Parker said, his voice calm and dead serious.

"What did you say?" Cole asked.

"The Governor gave me specific instructions. He said the President wanted to avoid the order becoming part of any official report so he suggested that handle the matter discretely." The politician managed to somehow seem earnest and sincere without slacking his smile in the least. "I trust you all will refrain from any mention of this conversation. He'd prefer if the death looked like an escape attempt."

"You mean to tell me that you gave someone under my command orders to execute a prisoner without a proper trial?" Cole said.

"We both receive our orders from the same place," Pickering said with a casual shrug. Then he grinned his most earnest grin, "We're on the same side here."

The smile didn't have the effect Pickering had hoped for. Cole was furious. He turned to Thompson, "Major, would you be so kind as to place Mister Pickering under arrest?"

In that instant Pickering's smile shattered and collapsed into a sagging frown. "Y-you can't do that."

"The hell I can't." Cole said. "I have never stood for the execution of prisoners and I never will."

"Now wait just a second," Morison chimed in. His voice loud as usual, but somewhat pleasant and more than a little condescending. "Aren't you overacting a little here? I understand that the good citizen here has overstepped his authority somewhat, but this hardly warrants the arrest of an elected official."

Cole was in no mood to be patronized. "Captain, I had no idea the Navy condoned the execution of prisoners."

Morison gave a hearty laugh, ignored the insult, and tried another angle. "These beastmen, they're just animals, Colonel."

Cole ignored the remark. He turned to Thompson, "Confine the prisoner to his quarters. Post a guard and see that he does not come out for the duration of the expedition. Understand?"

"Yes, sir."

Cole turned to Haiber, who had remained silent during the exchange. "This was not my doing."

Without a word, Haiber turned and walked away. Morison, too, left the deck without another word.

With everyone gone, Cole reached down and ruffled Dog's ears.

Jones didn't seem scared. Not that he seemed to doubt Parker's resolve, he just didn't seem to care that he was about to die. In fact, he almost seemed excited by the prospect. Parker was beginning to think he was going to have to shoot the man, which meant he would in turn be gunned down by the two soldiers, but he found that he too was without fear.

"Wait just a minute," Santiago finally said, coming out of his initial shock. "Did Cole give the order to do this?"

"Yeah," Jones said, but he didn't say it with his usual brash confidence.

"He ordered you to execute Longtooth?" Santiago pressed.

Jones' didn't answer immediately. His eyebrows knitted into a scowl and after a few seconds he said, "It's not important who gave the orders. What is important is that I have been ordered to kill this dog."

"It *is* important who gave the order, soldier." Santiago snapped.

Again Jones paused. "Pickering," he finally said. "And his orders came straight from the governor."

"Pickering has no authority," Santiago said, "He's here as a civilian observer, nothing more."

"His orders came straight from the governor," Jones repeated.

"What were the orders Cole gave you?"

"He didn't know about the governor's order."

"That doesn't matter and you know it," Santiago snapped. "You take orders from your commanding officer, not from some civilian who may or may not represent the wishes of our government."

Jones was becoming frustrated and therefore angry. He turned to Santiago and shouted, "But the governor—"

"If the governor went outside of the chain of command then he is at fault as well," Santiago yelled back, "Now, what were the orders given to you by Colonel Cole?"

Jones turned away from Santiago and swore under his breath.

"What were your orders, Captain?"

Finally Jones reluctantly said, "Cole told me to bring Longtooth and his party back as prisoners."

Santiago's face was flushed from the heated exchange, but he managed to calm himself and reply in an even tone. "Then,

Captain, I believe those are your orders."

Jones scowled. He glanced at the soldiers and for a moment he seemed to contemplate ordering them to shoot Santiago and Parker. They would have done it too; Jones's company had only served under him for a few months, but they were quite loyal to their hate-filled yet charismatic leader. However, Jones turned back to Longtooth and spit in his face, then put his pistol in his holster.

Parker slowly lowered his pistol.

"When he's hung, I get his pelt," Jones said, "I captured him, so his bounty is mine."

No one answered.

Jones ordered his men to bind the four beastmen and then roughly shoved them out the door and into the open. The party was joined by the soldiers who had been guarding the rear of the house. They formed themselves into a line with four prisoners in the middle and started toward the woods.

Suddenly the private who was leading the column stopped and started looking along the edge of the woods. He was joined by the rest of the soldiers.

"What's going on?" Santiago asked Parker.

It was Longtooth who answered, "They're looking for the strips of cloth. They're not there anymore."

Jones heard this and turned to Longtooth, glaring once again.

"Did you really think it would be that easy?" Longtooth asked.

Without a word, Jones drew his pistol.

"I wouldn't do that if I were you," Longtooth advised. And with that he let out a shrill bark.

The beasts seemed to appear out of thin air. They rose from the tall grass, less than thirty feet away and stepped from behind trees right in front of the party. There were about fifty of them and they were all armed.

"Drop your guns, slowly," Longtooth said, while one of the beastmen moved forward and cut the rope that bound his hands.

Everyone complied but Jones. He stood with his pistol in his right hand and his left hand resting on his saber. Hate burned in his eyes.

Dillon pointed a thick stubby finger at Jones as soon as he was free, "We oughta kill that one."

"No," Longtooth said, "We're not going to stoop to that level ever again. We'll bring them with us. All of them."

Despite the fact he knew he wasn't going to die, Jones didn't drop his gun until Santiago ordered him to do so.

Chapter 15

Night had fallen for some time and Cole still stood on the upper deck of the *Gabby*. Two hours before, he had finally called for a chair. Now he sat with Dog's head in his lap, alternating between watching the woods and watching the sky. The weather had finally cleared and the stars were out.

Thompson approached the colonel quietly and solemnly. He had been angry, now he just felt let down. In fact, he felt somewhat guilty. The way he saw it, if the colonel had respected him enough to send him instead of Jones none of this would have happened. Cole had been wrong to send Jones, but he knew the colonel had been right not to send him. He was a cartographer, not a leader. Some people were natural-born leaders. He was not one of those people.

"We need to get underway," Thompson said.

Cole sighed. "I guess they're not coming back," he said without turning.

"No, sir, I don't think they are."

"We've wasted a lot of time, but we'll still be able to reach their main camp before they can gather all of their forces. I just wish I knew a little more about what we're getting ourselves into."

Thompson didn't reply.

Cole sighed again. "Signal Morison. Tell him to get underway."

"Yes, sir."

As soon as the humans were relieved of their weapons they were forced into a column and the whole group started north under close guard. For the most part the soldiers were treated fairly well. Occasionally one would fall out of line and find himself roughly shoved back into place, but this was to be expected.

They were only on the trail for about an hour before the column stopped and Parker was separated from the other humans. He was led to the head of the column where Longtooth, Dillon, Gregory, and the tough-looking grey-coated dogbreed he would later learn was called 'Sid' were waiting. Longtooth bowed his head slightly in the way of a greeting, but nothing was said when Parker joined their company. As soon as he was with them, the column started moving north again.

As they moved along there was very little conversation between the beastmen, but combined with what he saw there was enough for Parker to pick up on some information on his captors. As far as he could tell, Dillon was a man, or rather a beast, of strong faith. Dillon also served as a sort of bodyguard for Longtooth. Gregory was what could best be described as a butler—in fact, unlike the other beastmen, Gregory was unarmed. They were joined by another dogbreed who seemed important; his name was Mouser. He was a brown and white dogbreed with a sharp nose, wearing a captured kepi. Like Sid, Mouser seemed to be something like a high-ranking officer in Longtooth's beastman army. In fact, his jaunty strut reminded Parker of a cavalry officer, even though the beastmen had no cavalry. Apparently Mouser had been in charge of the troops hidden in the forest when they had been captured.

After another hour, Parker decided to test the waters and speak, "It doesn't matter how fast we march, those steamers are going to beat you upriver."

"Getting tired?" Mouser asked, baring his teeth in what Parker assumed was a grin but could have been a snarl.

"A little," Parker admitted.

Dillon snorted what might have been a short burst of laughter.

They walked on in silence for a few seconds before Longtooth spoke, "They won't beat us. I've seen to that."

Morison stood at the bow of the *Baton Rouge*, staring at the superstructure of a partially sunken steamer blocking the river. The hulk was almost within arms reach of the captain. With her shallow draft, the *Marmora* had managed to find a path around the sunken wreck, but the three chartered steamers would be cutting it close and there was no way the *Baton Rouge* or the Army transports would make it.

The expedition's most experienced pilot was normally on the *Marmora* since it was the lead steamer. His young nephew, who was supposedly quiet experienced despite being only thirteen, was serving as the *Baton Rouge*'s pilot. Morison had taken to the younger pilot, but he decided that more experience was needed at the moment, so he had ordered the older pilot to come over to the *Baton Rouge* on the *Marmora*'s skiff. Currently the grey-bearded man was next to Morison, but instead of standing, he was sitting with his feet dangling in the water. He lowered a weighted rope into the water to gage the depth.

The old pilot spit a thick stream of tobacco into the water and turned to the captain. "Seems that there ship's the only one but they put her right war they needed to. The river's narrow and shallow here. As high as the White's runnin' they couldn't have blocked the river anywhere else with only one ship."

"There's no way around her?" Morison asked.

"Nope."

"Then we'll have to take her apart. That's going to take some time."

An ensign approached the two. "Excuse me, sir, but Colonel

Cole wants to know how long it'll take to clear the obstruction," he said.

"I'll tell him, but he's not going to like the answer," Morison replied.

"Two days?" Cole said. "Can't we just force our way past it?"

"Not without risking serious damage to the ships." The ensign replied.

Cole turned and walked toward the *Gabby*'s railing. "It's all falling apart. Everything." He said. "First the weather, then the attack on the *Roe*, then the parley, and now this. We're almost a week behind schedule already."

Thompson stepped forward and joined his colonel at the ship's railing. "We'll still be able to reach the enemy's camp before they are reinforced," he said, "They don't have telegraph. Word has to travel to the camp, from the camp to the outposts, then the outposts have to get back to the camp as best they can. There's no doubt that Longtooth knows we're coming and that he's sent messengers to all of the outposts, but I still don't think they've had time to alert all of them and I imagine very few, if any, have arrived at the camp."

"Two more days, though."

"We've come this far," Thompson replied. Although he was having doubts about the expedition, he kept them to himself. Right now he felt it was his job as chief of staff to see that his commander didn't sink into a self-defeating slump.

"I just wish I knew if their camp really was on the river. If it is, we should have no problem pounding it to pieces with the *Baton Rouge*, then cleaning up with the infantry."

"Exactly," Thompson said. "The only thing that can go wrong is if they move inland, and even then it won't be a total loss. We can keep steaming north and liberate Elizabeth."

Cole thought it over for a minute then nodded his head. "We'll tie off on the west bank. Tell the boys to dismount and set up camp. They need to form a double picket line and everyone is to sleep with their rifle handy. If the enemy attacks us here, I want to be ready for them."

"Yes, sir."

It was so dark Parker couldn't see his hand before his face. When he tripped and fell for the third time in ten minutes he finally became frustrated. "Y'all may can see in the dark but I can't," he snapped as he was roughly hauled back to his feet.

Somewhere to his left Dillon snorted.

"We'll stop here," he heard Longtooth say from somewhere up ahead.

"We need to keep going," Sid replied from somewhere in the darkness.

"No, we'll stop here. How far back did the other group stop?"

"About two miles," an unidentifiable voice answered.

"Go back and tell them we've stopped. Tell 'em to keep coming, but not to hurry. We've got plenty of time."

This was the first time Parker realized that not only had he been separated from the rest of the humans, but that he was also in an entirely different group altogether.

For a while they seemed to just leave Parker alone in the woods. He could hear them moving around and he could occasionally hear them talking, but he couldn't see a thing. It took some time before he realized they were making camp. They were all settling down on tattered blankets that were laid out on the wet ground.

Groping in the darkness he found a tree and lowered himself so that he was resting with his back to the trunk. The ground was wet, instantly soaking through his pants, but it was a welcome rest.

"You have a time of it in the dark, don't ya?" a rough yet friendly voice asked.

"Yeah," Parker replied.

"Even when da stars out?"

"The stars help some," Parker said.

"Us dawgs see better than you at night, but day's better for us too. I thought you's funny when you tripped then I tripped jus' like you did."

"But did you go face down in the mud?"

The voice seemed to laugh as it spoke. "No, guess not."

Parker found that he was extremely grateful for the stranger's conversation. He also noticed that this creature seemed curious about humans.

Parker was about to say something else when a soft hand fell on his shoulder. At first he thought it might be the beastman he had been talking to, but the voice was different. It wasn't as heavily accented, and it was also somewhat smoother and calmer. He recognized it as Gregory's voice. "Longtooth wants to see you."

"Okay," Parker answered, rising to his feet.

"See that light?"

At first he didn't. How could he when he couldn't even see which direction Gregory was pointing? Then he saw the flickering glow of a small campfire to his left.

Stepping cautiously through the brush, Parker made his way to the small opening. He found Longtooth sitting alone by a small fire that was little more than a few burning twigs and some glowing pine straw embers. Longtooth sat on a log with his elbows resting on his legs, his hands clasped before him, and his head lowered. If he had raised his hands to his face he would have looked as though he was deep in prayer, but with his hands lowered he simply looked as though he was deep in thought. He didn't even look up when Parker entered the clearing.

Another log had been placed opposite the small fire. Parker took a seat.

"How's David?" Longtooth finally asked.

"David?" at first the name didn't register. "Oh, David Donovan. He's fine. They won't hurt him."

"You sure?"

"Yeah," Parker replied. "I'm sure."

"He's a good man, you know," Longtooth said, "After my friends was killed I felt like humans was all devils. I ended up with this group of runaways headin' north. I went with them to Missouri, but when they said they was going to St Louis to meet a human, I turned back to Arkansas. They met this human and told him about me. He used them to find me, but instead of turning me in for the bounty he taught me to read and write."

"That was David Donovan?" Parker asked, though he knew the answer.

"Yeah. I didn't like him at first. I thought he was just another devil like the rest of them, but he stayed with me and proved me wrong. I tried to hate him but I couldn't. He left his good life with the humans to stay with me for months on end. Sure, he was one of them, but he really cared about me. I thought maybe I was wrong. Maybe not all human are demons."

"You can't fight the world alone." Parker said solemnly.

"Huh?"

"It's something my brother once told me—you can't fight the world alone."

"Your brother was right," Longtooth said, his voice raising in pitch just a touch. "After our master did what he did to Jewel, we killed him. I wanted to hurt him like he made her hurt, but I had a brother like yours; one with a heart in his

147

chest instead of dry lump of coal like I had in mine. He said we shouldn't become what he was. When the people came to capture us I wanted to fight, but my brother talked the others into giving up. I ran. I found out what happened later. The humans didn't even hang them; they beat my brother and my friends to death." Longtooth paused. "I hated humans then; still do a little."

"I understand," Parker replied. "Believe me, I do."

"David stayed with me for months, but he finally went back to his city. I didn't have as much hate, but I had enough. I started stealin' food, but I realized the real reason I stole wasn't because I was hungry. So I started stealin' money and anything else that would make humans mad. I even started killin'. Word got around and suddenly my folk saw me as a savior and yours saw me as the devil. I liked that. I started getting it into my head that I could lead some great revolt. Now, I was never so stupid to think I could win. I just thought I could cause so much pain and misery that the humans would really believe I was a devil. I wanted them to scare their children with stories about Longtooth coming to get them. I wanted a legacy of hate." Longtooth paused and glanced up at the stars. "That's how it started, anyway."

Throughout the afternoon Parker noticed a difference between the beastmen's method of communication and that of humans. Humans use tone to express themselves—a shouted word means something much different than a reverent whisper—but it seemed the beastmen took this to a new level. All of the expressions that are available through our faces and posture were present in the tone of their speech, perhaps even more. He actually began to feel the sorrow in this poor creature's heart.

Longtooth continued with his story, "Then something happened. I went to kill a human and one of my own stopped me—not just stopped me, but actually fought me. He was ready to die before he would let me kill his master. That made me think of David. I knew it would break his heart to see what I'd become. I decided to quit it all. I actually aimed to move west and leave it all behind me. Then the rebellion happened."

"Wait a minute, I thought you caused the rebellion."

"I did in a way. I gave them hope. But I didn't plan it. It surprised me when it happened. The plantation owners don't know it, but it's easy for us to talk even when we're far away. We can hear speech good enough—better than you—but we can hear barks and yelps for miles. There had been talk of all of the beastmen leaving their masters. They wanted me to lead them. I tried to say no, but when they revolted they had no one else. David found out and he tracked us down. With him by my side I decided we would fight, but we would fight honorably—only to defend ourselves and never to kill the innocent. Then came Clover Bend. I'm sure you heard what happened there."

"I heard," Parker said, "but what I've seen today has convinced me that what I heard was all lies. I can't see your people doing the terrible things I that the papers said they did."

Longtooth glanced up from the fire, tears were standing in his eyes. "You don't understand. It was true. All of it. After the battle I saw 'breeds killing, torturing, and even eating humans. It was terrible."

Parker didn't know what to say so he remained quiet.

"We were about six-thousand strong then, never even close to thirty-thousand like the papers said, but a lot more than we have now. I ordered anyone who had taken part in the horrors after the fight to leave my group. Some of my people thought this meant I was weak so they sided with the others. It was hard but I told about two thousand to leave and many more went with them. Then we fought another battle. We were better organized then and had begun to think we might be able to win, but this battle was much different. The humans stood and fought. Both sides bled that day. The papers said we won, that we beat the humans, but when I saw how many died it felt like we lost. We went to the White River and set up a permanent camp on the river there."

"And then you ambushed that steamer that was carrying weapons upriver." Parker said. "I've been wondering about how that happened, and don't tell me it was dumb luck. You knew that steamer was coming."

Longtooth's teeth showed and he panted a couple times, probably a smile. "Ella," he said.

"Who?"

More panting, and now Parker was sure it was a smile. "She's the governor's servant. You see David told me that when the Democrats freed the blacks, they only freed the workers. The servants were free in name only. Ella has access to all of the governor's business and he thinks she's loyal to him, but she hates not having her freedom. She sends messages to us. We even knew that Cole had orders to bring me in, but didn't know nothing about the order to kill me. We didn't see that one comin'."

"If you knew we were going to betray you, why did you ask for the parley?"

"So we could meet."

"What?" Parker said, completely startled and confused.

"Not you in particular, but I hoped they would send someone like you."

"I don't understand. Why?"

"Because it's all coming to an end. After the next fight I figure my people will either be dead or we'll be so weak that we'll have to disappear into the woods. Someone needs to tell what really happened. I mean David will give us a fair shake, but what human's going to believe a man who disappears into the Ozarks for months to teach renegade beastmen to read?"

"Probably the same people who'll believe a colored boy from the Mississippi Freeland," Parker said with a wry half-smile. "I'm tickled you picked me to pass along your story, but I don't think I'm a good choice."

"You'll do just fine."

Parker didn't say a word. He wished someone else had been burdened with this tale. Not only did he imagine no one would believe him, but he simply didn't know how he would go about telling it.

Longtooth continued, "Attacking the boats gave us supplies, so we kept to it. We even started using the cannons."

"How did you learn to use the cannons?" Parker asked. "Did someone help you?"

"You humans don't think we're smart." Longtooth said accusingly, his head rising from its solemn lowered position, "We are smart. We know how to work muskets and rifles; it didn't take much to figure out how the bigger guns worked."

"I didn't mean to insult you."

Longtooth lowered his head and gazed into his hands. He didn't actually say he accepted the apology, but Parker assumed by his posture that he had.

"So this Ella told you about the expedition?"

"Yeah."

"So you've had time to reinforce your camp," Parked said, suddenly concerned that his boys were steaming into a trap.

"Yeah, but we still only about fifteen hundred strong there. Many were tired of fighting. I sent them into the swamps. We can live better in the swamps than you. We don't get sick as easy and we can eat uncooked meat when we have to."

"You're tired of fighting too; I can tell it." Parker said, leaning

151

forward from his log. "Why don't you go with them?"

Longtooth looked up. "Would you leave your soldiers? Turn your back and just walk away? Even if you did know it was the right thing to do?"

"No I guess not."

"Duty," Longtooth said, as if that word summed it all up. And, in a way, it did.

Chapter 16

PARKER WAS REUNITED with the rest of the humans at dawn. From there Longtooth ordered Mouser and a handful of his troops to return the humans to their ships. Parker noticed that the beastman leader seemed rather confident that he knew exactly where the ships would be. The humans were gagged and their hands were tied behind their backs for the trip back to the river. All except Parker, that is. Since he had gained Longtooth's respect he was considered trustworthy.

They moved quickly at first, but as they approached the river they became more careful. Mouser's soldiers, they called themselves scouts, were generally smaller and more agile than the normal beastman. They moved through the woods without making so much as a sound.

Up ahead of the column Mouser motioned for them to halt. He then let out a series of whines and motioned to either side of him. The dogbreed grinned as two scouts spread out. He seemed to thrive on his role as Longtooth's chief scout. When the other two scouts entered the woods, Mouser went with them.

"Where they goin'?" Parker asked a nearby scout.

The scout first put a finger to his lips, but then answered the question. However, he apparently expected Parker's hearing to be as good as his—his whispers were so quiet Parker didn't catch a single word.

Another dogbreed caught on. He got the attention of the first dogbreed and pointed to his ears. They laughed quietly, shared a joke that was obviously at the humans' expense, but which was once again too quiet for Parker to hear.

The first beastman walked over to Parker and said quietly, but in a haltingly slow tone. "They going to see your pickets."

Now Parker realized why the others were bound and gagged. If they knew how close they were to the human lines they might make a break for it or at least call out—there was no doubt Jones would do so.

"If we're that close, why not let us go now?" Parker asked in a whisper.

The beastman smiled and panted. "Mouser likes to mess with them."

They waited a few more minutes and Mouser appeared followed by the two scouts that went with him. His smile was unmistakable. A canteen was hanging around his neck that hadn't been there before. He unslung the canteen took a drink, then held the canteen out. "Want a drink?"

"What's in it?"

"Water."

"Sure," Parker said.

He took the canteen chugged down a drink. The water was warm, but it was wet and that's what counted. When he finished he noticed Mouser was still grinning while he watched him drink. He suddenly felt he was the target of some joke.

Mouser pointed the direction he had come and whispered. "They just ahead. You'll see 'em as soon as you're past these bushes." Then he grinned and said, "Give them back their water and tell them Mouser says thanks."

"You didn't," a scout who had stayed behind whispered.

"Sure did," Mouser said, playfully pushing the doubter.

"I saw him," one of the scouts who went with him said, "It was hanging from a tree. He snuck right up and took it. They weren't even asleep."

"Might as well have been," Mouser added.

"Longtooth would kill you if he knew you got that close."

154

"That's why we won't tell him."

As Parker watched the playful conversation he felt a strange familiarity. It was just like watching his own men horsing about.

Some semblance of seriousness overcame Mouser and he whispered, "Okay, we've got to do this and head back." He pointed at Jones. "Leave him tied and gagged. He's apt to try to fight us as soon as he's free. They can untie him as soon as we're out of here."

Mouser turned to Parker and said, "Be sure and call out before you approach them. They might shoot you if you don't."

The scouts cut the ropes that bound their captives, then disappeared before the gags were off. It was probably an unneeded precaution, as the human soldiers were too excited about being free to want a scuffle at that point—all except Jones, that is, and he was still bound and gagged.

"Hullo!" Parker called.

There was a brief pause before the pickets answered, "Who's there?"

"Lieutenant-Colonel Santiago and Sergeant Parker of the 13th Colored," Parker called out. "The party that went to talk to Longtooth."

"Ain't no way, they downstream." A voice answered.

"And dead, too," another added.

One of Jones' soldiers grumbled something and started toward the pickets. Parker put his hand out to stop him, but the soldier pushed him away and kept walking.

"Soldier, unless you want to get shot, I'd sit tight." Santiago said, halting the soldier in his tracks.

"This is Captain Reginald Jones, Goddamn it," Jones shouted as soon as his gag was off. "Let us pass or I swear before the Almighty I'll drown your sorry asses in the river."

"Sounds like Jones all right," they heard one of the voices say to the other.

Finally they were joined by a third voice, probably their sergeant, "Y'all come on real slow like. And keep your hands up where we can see 'em."

They did as they were told. Parker stepped out of the brush first. He saw two militia soldiers with their rifles trained on him, a sergeant behind them and four more soldiers coming at a run. He felt relieved that they weren't his boys. At least he didn't have to chew anyone out for having their canteen stolen by the enemy while on picket duty.

Once the whole party was out of the brush the sergeant apologized for holding them, but said they had been on pins and needles over the last few days. He turned to lead the way back to the steamers, but not before Parker nonchalantly handed the soldiers their canteen.

The party was taken straight to the *Gabby*, but Parker refused to tell Colonel Cole what had happened until Haiber arrived. Cole accepted this trivial insubordination without complaint.

When the *Anne Marie's* skiff pulled alongside, Haiber was at the bow. A wide grin stretched across his face as Parker reached out to take the line and pull them in. "I thought I'd seen the last of you," he said.

Parker said nothing as he hauled the boat in. He returned the grin with a much more conservative smile, the corners of his lips barely turned up.

Haiber climbed onto the deck and immediately embraced Parker in a strong, unmilitary-like hug.

"Okay, that's enough," Parker said, embarrassed.

Haiber pulled away, still grinning. "How in the world did you get away? Cole said Pickering gave Jones orders to kill Longtooth. I figured once that happened they would tear you guys apart."

Parker shook his head. "They let us go."

Confusion caused Haiber's smile to falter. "What?"

"I kept Jones from killing Longtooth. I guess he felt he owed me."

"Was anyone else killed?"

"Naw, they let us all go. Even Jones."

"Damn."

Parker nodded. He too couldn't help but wish Longtooth had killed Jones, but he respected him for the decision.

"Well, we'd better go see Cole."

"He's waiting for us on the upper deck."

They started along the walk toward the stairs. As they made their way, several of the militia soldiers that lined the rails turned to watch Parker as he passed. Their eyes were wide and their faces pale as if they'd just seen a ghost.

Cole felt mildly feverish, however, he knew his body well enough to know that he wasn't about to come down with the crud. This was different. His body was frail and he felt groggy, but there was no chill to go with it. He was ill all right, but it wasn't any bug or pneumonia. The cancer was beginning to rear its head in force, sapping him of energy. He wondered briefly if it was clouding his judgment. Certainly there had been some questionable decisions along the way, but all in all he still felt he had acted properly on the information that had been on hand.

The old colonel leaned back against the railing. His legs were killing him, but he dared not request a chair. They were already questioning his leadership, there was no need to throw his failing health out there for them to see.

Cole, Santiago, Thompson, Jones, and a pair of soldiers from the militia stood in silence on the upper deck, waiting for Parker and Haiber to arrive. They weren't going to go over to the *Baton Rouge* for this meeting; Cole felt Morison's loud, brash demeanor was too much of a distraction. The problem was, the *Gabby* didn't have an officer's mess like the *Baton Rouge*, and the staterooms and the hold were occupied by soldiers. As a result the best meeting place on the ship was the open deck. This made Cole a little uneasy since the first order of this business was liable to turn hostile, and he hated for this to happen in full sight of the men but there was no way around it.

Cole could hear Parker and Haiber talking as they started up the stairs, but after their footfalls fell on the fourth step they too became quiet. In fact, only the lazy churning splash of the ship's wheel and the distant chatter of a mockingbird broke the tense silence.

The two men came onto the deck and joined Santiago. Haiber gave a respectful yet cold nod in Cole's direction. Parker didn't even go that far; of course all things considered simply holding his tongue could be considered respectful.

Cole got right down to business. "Captain Jones, I understand you received orders from a civilian observer that were not in keeping with the orders given you by your commanding officer." His tone was ridged and formal, almost as if Jones were already standing before a court marshal, "Furthermore, I understand that these orders could have jeopardized the lives of those under your command as well as the observers sent from Colonel Haiber's Regiment."

Jones cut his cold grey eyes in Cole's direction. He jaw clenched and unclenched, but he said nothing.

Cole turned to Parker and Santiago, continuing in his formal tone. "Did Captain Jones attempt to act upon orders that were not the intention of his commanding officer, including the execution of a prisoner without due process?"

"He did," Santiago replied, but Parker didn't say a word.

Still clinching his jaw in silence, Jones continued to cut his eyes at each person as they spoke. Perhaps he hoped to intimidate someone into taking his side, but Cole felt this wasn't really the case. He imagined this was nothing more than a hate-filled man's perpetual anger showing through its thin veil.

"Was he successful?"

"No, sir," Santiago said, "Sergeant Parker stopped him."

That was more than Jones could take. He thrust an angry finger at Parker shouted, "That damn field hand turned sergeant drew a gun on an officer while in the presence of the enemy. He sided with the enemy!"

Jones' face was red, his eyes were bugged and the veins bulged in his neck. Cole had to fight the urge to yell back at the insolent captain, but he knew this was a battle that he had already won. There was no need to stoop to Jones' level of incivility. He turned to Jones and rather politely said, "It appears to me that Sergeant Parker may have prevented you from committing murder. Perhaps you should thank him."

"Murder?" Jones shouted. "That dog has a prize on his head *dead or alive!*"

"And if you were a bounty hunter all would have been well," Cole said, smoothly at first, but his volume began to rise as he spoke, "but you were serving in the capacity of an officer in the United States Army and an officer does not take it upon himself to execute prisoners, and they certainly do not take orders from civilians who tell them to do so. You may not see it as murder, but you can bet your ass I would have seen you court marshaled under those charges."

While Cole spoke, Jones' arm remained hovering in the air still pointing at Parker, almost as if he had forgotten the appendage. Now it came down and joined the other arm at his sides trembling with fists clenched.

Cole continued, "As it is I will see you before a court marshal for dereliction of duty." He nodded to the two soldiers standing guard, "Gentlemen, if you would be so kind as to escort Captain Jones to his quarters and see that he does not set foot outside for the remainder of the expedition."

Fists still trembling, Jones took a step toward Cole. Thompson stepped forward, positioning himself between the two of them. Jones was almost a head taller and it was obvious by the look in his face that Thompson was terrified, but he didn't step aside. The captain's eyes bore into the one-armed lieutenant-colonel's. "I'll beat you down, militia-boy, don't think I won't," Jones said, teeth clenched in fury.

"Take him away," Cole said with a flourish of his hand. "The sight of him sickens me."

The soldiers hesitated. Jones took a few seconds to stare down Thompson, then, apparently satisfied that he'd struck enough terror, the captain turned on his heels and led the way down the stairs without a single glance behind him.

As soon as the captain was gone, Thompson let out a quavering sigh of relief then glanced around sheepishly as if hoping no one heard him.

Cole didn't even wait until Jones' footfalls reached the lower deck before he moved on to the second order of business. He turned to Parker. "I understand you spoke with the enemy leader."

"Yes, sir," Parkers replied.

"Could you tell us what was discussed?"

Parker started from when he was walking with the beastmen in the dark shortly after he was separated from the main group. Although Cole knew Parker was bitter, he also knew Parker would hold nothing back because this information was important to the expedition and therefore important to the welfare of his troops. The information was even more detailed that what he had expected from Hunter. In fact, it was so detailed, it made him wonder if they weren't being lead astray.

"Do you believe he was being truthful?" Cole asked.

"Yes, sir," Parker answered without pause.

Cole considered this. The stakes were high. If Longtooth had been lying and the enemy was well prepared with three to four thousand armed soldiers waiting for them when they dismounted form the steamers this expedition could quickly turn to a disaster.

"Sir," Parked offered. "There's little doubt that he didn't tell me everything—no leader worth their salt would do that—but he was bein' straight with me on what we did discuss. He wants this fight as much as we do. He's tired of running and he wants it to be over, one way or the other."

Cole stood in silence for a little longer before he took a breath and said, "Well, one way or another we'll find out when we reach their camp. We've gone too far to turn back now."

Almost as if on cue, Baxter appeared at the top of the stairs. He grinned and said, "The *Baton Rouge* got through, sir. Looks like we've cleared the obstruction."

"Good," Cole said with a smile. "Let's get moving then."

Chapter 17

THE *MARMORA*'S PILOTHOUSE was cramped and stuffy. The pilot, a grey-bearded man in civilian clothes, manned the wheel, while three of the ship's officers, including the commanding officer, looked on. The *Marmora* was Lieutenant J. R. McCammon's first command. Some might consider the gunboat squatty and ugly compared to the tall, colorful civilian paddle-wheelers that ran the Mississippi, but McCammon loved the little steamer like he'd never loved a woman, excepting perhaps his mother and even then it was close. The way he saw it, she was the perfect river gunboat. Her speed made up for her lack of armor, and her light draft meant she would have little trouble patrolling areas where the bigger ships would have to be left behind. And while she wasn't exactly a heavy hitter like the *Baton Rouge*, *Marmora* did have teeth. She mounted five twenty-four pounder naval guns, one forward and two on either side. Her only weakness was the fact that she was a sternwheeler, which meant she was fairly unmaneuverable and couldn't mount guns pointing aft. Of course, McCammon didn't see this as a disadvantage. Her big stern wheel was pushed by a powerful engine, making her one of the fastest river gunboats in the Navy. And as far as her inability to mount a stern gun, McCammon never expected to have to run from a fight so why would he need a gun in the rear?

Marmora was itching for a fight. Not just her captain and her crew, but the ship herself seemed to have an aura of eagerness about her. While the other ships struggled to push ahead against the current, *Marmora* swiftly sped forward, often ranging so far ahead of the column that Captain Morison would have to signal for her to slow down. Everyone on board the *Marmora* knew that the *Marmora's* officers, especially Lieutenant McCammon, were pushing ahead on purpose. They wanted to be the first to engage the enemy. McCammon was no fool, though. He knew the enemy had field pieces, and he was well aware that these guns could penetrate his ship's thin armor if they hit at just the right angle. However, he figured he could silence the smaller guns before the *Baton Rouge* came within range. As for the two 24-pounders the beasts supposedly had at their disposal, there was simply no way they had transported these heavy naval guns all the way up the river and even then, these animals certainly wouldn't have been able to figure out how to properly mount them.

"Comin' up on another bend," the pilot said, "River's gonna turn left then snake back, makin' another S 'fore headin' on to Acousta."

"Should we wait for Morison?" Ensign Rodgers asked with a knowing grin.

The answer wasn't as quick and confidant as Rodgers expected. McCammon stepped forward and peered through the armored slit at the sharp turn ahead. Although Morison seemed to expect the attack to come when they reached the Acousta Bluffs McCammon wasn't so sure. The Acousta Bluffs certainly would allow the guns to fire plunging shots down on the approaching ships, but the approach to the bluffs was a long straight stretch. The way the beastmen used their light 6-pounders seemed to indicate that they preferred masking batteries around bends in the river.

Bends such as the one ahead.

"Keep as far to the right as possible." McCammon told the pilot.

"What about our speed?" the pilot asked. Even though the

ship's speed was normally none of his concern, he too was apparently nervous about the approaching bend.

"We'll stay at three-quarters. Once we get in the turn we'll cut to a quarter and let the others catch up." McCammon answered. Then his eagerness seemed to return. "I want to see what's around the bend first."

No sooner had McCammon finished speaking than Ensign Rodgers pointed to the trees ahead of them and said, "Did you see that?"

"What?" McCammon asked. He hadn't seen anything, but he knew Rodger's eyes were much better than his.

"I saw someone. Couldn't tell if it was human or not, but I know I saw someone."

"Probably another bushwhacker." McCammon said.

Ever since they had passed the obstruction the transports had been harassed by sharpshooters and a solitary 6-pounder that would be fired once then disappear into the trees. McCammon figured Rodgers saw another ambush in the making. If this was the case, maybe it was that pesky little cannon. It would certainly make his day to finally silence that gun.

However, the lieutenant was also aware of how close they were to Elizabeth. What if Rodgers had seen an advance lookout for a battery of 12-pounders positioned right around the corner?

And what if those beasts had managed to mount one of the 24-pounders?

He turned to the brass tube that ran down to the engine room and spoke loudly, "Slow to one-half."

The slight reduction of speed made little difference since they were already only a few feet from rounding the bend.

The tree line stopped as more of the right bank came into view. The bank also became steeper as it rounded the bend. Although they were not quite what one would call bluffs they were still a good six feet out of the water. As they entered the turn, the lower part of a bald hill came into view; this hill was located on the second peninsula formed by the S in the river. At first McCammon thought there was no trees on the hill, then he realized that there were several stumps on the slope.

It didn't dawn on him that these stumps marked the places where trees had been cut to clear firing lanes until the battery itself came into view. Six notches in the earthen mound marked where six guns had been emplaced. McCammon barely had time to register what he was seeing and was unable to bark the first order before all six guns opened fire.

Four balls splashed into the water; two ahead and another pair fell just short of the *Marmora*, slashing in the water to her left. Another shot hit the pilothouse at just such an angle so that it peeled the iron roof back, exposing them to the sunlight above. Shards of wood and iron flew from the impact. Lieutenant McCammon and Ensign Rodgers were untouched and Ensign Williams only received a deep cut on his shoulder from the flying metal, but the pilot crumpled to the floor, clutching his neck; his long beard already soaked with blood.

The sixth shot crashed into the forward casemate. While the pilothouse was protected by a layer of wood covered with a sheet of half inch iron, the casemate was protected by wooden walls that were a foot thick. Even though there was no iron, the thick casemate walls could actually take more punishment than the pilothouse. However, this shot tore through the wood, showering the deck with splinters that were as big as a man's forearm. McCammon saw this shot when it hit; he felt the impact as it jarred the entire ship.

"Christ!" he exclaimed, "That was no field gun!"

"Hit!" Sid called out. He turned to one of the members of the gun crew and slapped him on the back, "Damn good shot!

Do it again!"

The gun crews had been drilling for this type of action for a month, before the guns had even been mounted. However, since powder was in short supply, they had very little experience actually firing the guns. Sid never doubted the crews could handle the guns, but their accuracy came as somewhat of a surprise. And it was a surprise that excited Sid to no end. He normally wasn't one for outward displays of emotion, excepting maybe anger, but he couldn't help himself. It was all too good to be true. The humans had stuck their neck out and the noose was tightening.

Sid stood between the two heavy guns, on either side of him the beastmen were at work swabbing the barrel, then reloading. Behind the gunners, eager beastmen were bringing cannon balls up the hill; in fact, the desire to help was so strong that the balls were being delivered much faster than the gunners could use them, causing a small pile of cannonballs to rise behind both big guns as well as the four smaller pieces.

Sid noticed one beastman hurrying up the hill with a sack of powder over each shoulder. "Hey! Don't bring powder up until we call for it," Sid snapped, "You want to blow us all up?"

The soldier quickly turned and started back down the hill, where he replaced the sacks of powder with a pair of cannon balls. Sid knew they probably wouldn't need so many, but he didn't say a word. There was a look of eager determination on all of their faces, as well as a look of pride. They wanted to be part of the action and Sid couldn't blame them.

As soon as the guns were loaded, the crews used heavy ropes and makeshift pulleys to heave the two heavy cannons back into place. Several of the soldiers who had been carrying cannon balls stopped what they were doing grabbed a rope.

Sid stepped up onto the parapet itself and took in the scene before him. The trees were still bright green from soaking up the recent rain, the water in the river was running high, but from this vantage point it seemed nothing more than a lazy brook. Amid all of nature's splendor was a scene of death and carnage, yet it was a scene of triumphant vindication—it was beautiful.

When the next cannon fired Sid titled his head back and hollered; it was a sound that was somewhere between a howl and a cheer. Several others on the battlement took up the call with him.

McCammon grabbed the wheel, and turned to the starboard, trying to bring his port broadside to bear on the enemy fortification. "Full astern!" he shouted into the brass tube.

The big wheel came to a stop and reversed direction, but the forward momentum continued to carry them forward. The *Marmora's* stern-most gun returned fire, but too many men in the forward port gun had been injured by the initial hit they received from the enemy battery. It would be back in action as soon as the gunnery officer replaced the downed gunners with members of the forward and starboard guns.

Four more shots rang out from the smaller, easier to load guns in the battery. McCammon was surprised at how fast they had reloaded and was even more surprised at their accuracy as three of the four 12-pounders scored hits. One sheered off Marmora's stack and the other two slammed into the casemate, doing little damage. McCammon held his breath when the two big guns fired, but, luckily, they missed. He did notice, however, that they hadn't missed by much.

Below the pilothouse, the stern port gun fired again and was finally joined by the forward gun.

"They're shooting high! Both of them!" Rodgers yelled.

McCammon then shouted into the brass tube, "Both guns

are overshooting!"

"Aye-aye," a voice called from below.

With the wheel churning full to the rear, the *Marmora*'s moment was all but halted. She was coming to a stop and would soon begin reversing direction. So far the *Marmora* had been embarrassed and bruised, but not beaten. There were several men down and bleeding, but she had yet to lose a single member of her crew. This all changed when a twelve-pounder fired a shot that passed through the hole that the bigger gun made in the casemate. The ball traveled low across the gun deck, removing the right leg of the port gunnery officer before slamming into one of the cannons on the starboard side, killing three gunners and disabling the gun. This shot was followed by yet another hit by one of the twenty-four pounders; this time the gun scored a hit toward the rear of the *Marmora*, penetrating her side and knocking her wheel off its axle. The ship was now dead in the water, relying on the current to bring her to safety.

The guns below replied again. The first shot scoring a hit on the battery, but failing to take out an enemy gun. The second shot was high again.

"Stern gun's on target! Forward gun is still high!" Rodgers yelled.

McCammon turned to the brass tube and opened his mouth to pass on the information. The words never made it out of his throat. Twenty-four pounds of deadly iron slammed into the side of the pilothouse, killing all inside.

In the river ahead of the *Baton Rouge*, a cannon ball plowed into the pilothouse of the *Marmora*, caving in its side and then over turning the square structure like an upended outhouse. The *Marmora* had been staying close to the east bank as she entered the turn then she had turned right in order to bring her guns to bear. This brought her too close to the shore. Despite her shallow draft, her bottom caught on an overturned tree. She was aground and the battery was tearing her apart. Soon both guns on her port side were silenced and she was completely helpless.

"Goddamn them!" Morison swore. It was the first time he could remember having used the Lord's name in vain, but he was unconcerned about his lapse into blasphemy. Surely the Lord agreed with his damnation of these hellish abominations that were part beast and part human.

Despite the horrible sight in the river ahead, or perhaps because of it, Morison was excited. Like McCammon, he was itching for a fight. Unlike McCammon, he had the right machine for the job.

"We'll position ourselves between the battery and the *Marmora*," Morison bellowed.

Morison's own pilot, a sandy-haired boy with bad teeth, glanced at Morison like the captain had lost his mind.

"Never fear, son," The Morison boomed. He slapped his big palm on the iron wall of the pilothouse. "They can't get us in here."

Mouser's grin spread to his back teeth and his tongue lolled out of his mouth as he eagerly watched the *Marmora* drifted closer to the bank. Longtooth had instructed him to keep his men in the woods and only to attack if they tried to come ashore, but surely their leader had never expected one of their gunboats to come upriver ahead of the others and then to run aground right in front of them. There was no doubt that this was the moment he had been waiting for—that golden chance to recapture the glory of Clover Bend. How could he pass up such an opportunity?

His scouts were all around him, staring at him with eager

faces. They understood the situation and were every bit as excited as he was.

"Let's do it," one of the nearby scouts said anxiously.

"It'll be just like Clover Bend," another added.

A round of anxious yips and barks followed the mention of the scouts', and therefore Mouser's, crowning moment.

Mouser turned to them, he could see, even smell, their excitement. "We're going to move to the bank and harass them as planned."

Several groans, sad faces, and even a few low growls answered this declaration. They wanted more. They wanted glory. And Mouser knew it.

"But you know," Mouser said, his tone thoughtful but loud enough that they all could hear him, "It is a shame that those guys back there in the camp are having all the fun. I mean, is it fair that all we get to do is shoot a few humans who are stupid enough to try to swim to shore?"

"No!" several voices answered. More barks and yips followed.

Mouser thrust a finger upward like a brilliant thought had just crossed him mind, "But, wait a minute. If we could get on board that boat there's no telling how many weapons we could capture. Come to think of it, it would be just like Clover Bend."

The yips and barks changed to all out cheering.

"Okay, everyone get into position," he turned toward the river. "Wait until I give the signal, then we'll take it to them."

The beastmen cheered and howled.

Teams of marksmen moved into position behind trees at the water's edge while the gun crew moved Mouser's remaining light cannon into position. By now, the *Marmora* was hardly even fighting back. In fact, the scouts had more to fear from the occasional overshot from their own battery than they did from the crippled gunboat's cannons. It was only a matter of waiting until Mouser gave the signal, then the steamer would be theirs.

On board the *Baton Rouge* it seemed to take hours to get upstream to aid the *Marmora*, but it was an eternity for the poor souls trapped in that wooden hell. Several members of the gunboat's crew clamored out of the gunports in order to jump into the river. As soon as they were on the outer deck, they came under fire from bushwhackers hiding in the woods. And just when it seemed the situation couldn't get any worse, the enemy's battery switched from shot to shell and were then joined by another smaller gun on the near shore. Now the *Marmora*'s walls were weakened to the point that they could no longer prevent most of the shells from tearing their way into the casemate and exploding among the crew.

By the time the *Baton Rouge* started pulling alongside the *Marmora* smoke was beginning to boil out of the disabled steamer's gunports. There would be no saving her now. It was only a matter of rescuing as many members of the crew as possible. However, with the bank only a few feet away, the beastman bushwhackers were having a turkey shoot, picking off anyone who tried to move between the two ships.

"Bring us along side her," Morison said to the pilot.

"Ain't a good idea," the young pilot replied. "She got stuck and we a lot heavier than she is."

"Get as close as you can." Morison said, then he started down the ladder into the main part of the ship.

The casemate was hot and loud. The *Baton Rouge*'s four broadside guns roared while officers shouted orders and corrected fire. Heat rose out of the boiler room below in waves as the firemen poured on as much coal as possible. Morison found the commander of his marine detachment,

Sergeant Shumaker, standing near one of the guns watching the show. Known to his men as Sergeant Shoe, or sometimes just Shoe, the big Dutchman was as loud and overbearing as his commanding officer. However, the similarity ended there. Shoe was a drunkard who prided himself on being able to out-swear, out-fight, and out-drink any man on either side of the Atlantic.

Shoe and Morison had an odd relationship. The captain was a strict disciplinarian. He allowed no drinking or swearing on his ship. However, it was widely known that Shoe was the exception to this rule so long as he kept his indulgences to a minimum or at least kept them out of the captain's sight.

"Sergeant Shumaker," Morison yelled, and when he wasn't heard over the roar of the cannons he started toward the sergeant. "Sergeant Shumaker!" he tried again.

Shoe finally heard the captain and met him halfway across room. His eyes were bloodshot and his big nose was so red it looked like an overgrown radish. He seemed sober enough, but he probably had a hangover.

"We can't get alongside; it's too shallow," Morison explained. "I need you and your men to take the boats over to the *Marmora* and pick up survivors."

Shoe grunted. He started across the deck to the opposite side of the ship where he could see the battered *Marmora*. His eyes moved on to the shoreline where he occasionally caught a brief glimpse of one of what was surely dozens of bushwhackers keeping the *Marmora* under steady fire.

"You can take both boats over. We can cover you with canister fire." Morison explained over the sergeant's shoulder.

Shoe shook his head, "We got one boat left," he said in a deep rumbling voice. "That battery's done shot the portside boat all to hell and back. And you can't use canister without hitting the *Marmora*."

"We can cover you with the carbines."

"If I go I'm taking all my marines over with me with their carbines. Your sailors are just as likely to hit us as they are the enemy. Hell, your brown water babies couldn't hit an outhouse if they were sitting on the crapper." Shoe nodded toward the *Marmora*. "I think it's a bad idea; there's a whole lot of hell between here and there."

Shumaker was right, but, still something had to be done. They couldn't just leave those men on that ship.

"You've got to go," Morison said, his voice loud but serious, without its usual aplomb.

Shoe grumbled, but nodded in agreement.

"It will probably take more than one trip," Morison added.

Still gazing out the gunport, Shoe took a flask from his coat pocket.

"Is that really necessary?" Morison asked.

"You're goddamn right it is." Shoe took a long drink before returning the flask to his pocket.

"Yeah!" Sid yelled when a shot slammed into the side of the bigger gunboat. His enthusiasm faltered a somewhat when the solid iron shot shattered without making much more than a dent.

Longtooth had arrived at the battery just after the engagement started. He could feel the excitement in the air; hell, even Sid's normal dour disposition had changed to loud outward expressions of enthusiasm. For some reason, Longtooth found he was unable to fully enjoy the scene on the river below. He briefly thought that maybe had been around Gregory too much, that he could no longer revel in the bloodshed. Perhaps that was part of the reason he felt such a dark cloud hanging over this shining moment, but the real reason was he had a nagging feeling that everything was going too well. Not only that, but it was quickly becoming obvious that this new gunboat was going to be a much tougher nut to crack.

On either side of him the gun crews of the big guns were panting from exertion and excitement. The steady breeze blew most of the smoke away from the battery, but after several minutes of hard fighting a light black fog had developed around the guns themselves. Not enough to obscure their target, but enough to make mid-afternoon seem much later. The crewmen with lighter colored fur now looked dark; those with dark fur looked black. Longtooth remembered how after the battle of Berkley the beastmen found that the close proximity to powder flashes from their muskets had darkened, and sometimes even singed the hair on the right side of the faces of the riflemen. After the battle this had become a badge of honor among the beastmen to the point that after it wore off some of them took to darkening their right cheek with charcoal. He imagined dark fur would become quite popular by tomorrow.

Sure enough, as Longtooth watched, one the exhausted gunners stepped aside to take a break. However, instead of finding a drink of water, or even taking a seat, he took his grimy hands and ran them through his fur, causing dark streaks to appear in his tan coat. As he watched this, Longtooth felt a strong pang of familiarity. At once it reminded him of what he loved and what he feared about his people. Quite often they seemed simple, almost childlike, yet there was no denying what had happened after the fight at Clover Bend. All visions of innocence had been swept away when he witnessed beastmen killing, torturing, and even eating humans. He remembered one particularly grotesque sight; three beastmen fighting among themselves to see who got to eat a wounded soldier. When he tried to intervene, one of them attacked him. Of course, he knew war often brought out the worst in humans as well, but what scared him was how many had behaved so wildly. It wasn't the act of a few ruining the name of the majority. What scared him was almost half of them had turned savage and the few who hadn't had been too afraid to take a stand.

In fact, as he watched this beastman rub powder into his fur he couldn't help but recall seeing another beastman playfully rubbing the blood of a fallen human into his fur just after Clover Bend.

The beastman looked up and noticed Longtooth watching him. At first he seemed overjoyed at having caught the attention of their revered leader, but must have noticed the dour expression on Longtooth's face because no sooner had his face lit up than his long tail sagged to the ground. He turned and practically tripped over himself getting back to his position at the gun.

Longtooth turned from the gunners to the scene below. The first human ship was little more than a shattered hulk now, but the second one seemed to be able to take everything they could dish out. Even the heavy guns had little effect on the iron sides of this vessel.

As his sharp eyes scanned the tree line, he noticed something that was out of place.

A shell from one of the enemy's big guns burst in front of their position, sending dirt flying into the air. Some of the nearby gunners dove behind the earthworks, but Longtooth didn't flinch. Something had caught his eye. He turned to Sid, "You got those field glasses with you?"

"Sure," Sid said. He reached into a pouch on his belt and produced an ornate pair of field glasses that had stolen from a plantation house near Elizabeth. "Here you go."

Longtooth took the glasses and scanned the tree line behind the enemy vessel for some time. He grunted.

"What is it?" Sid asked.

"Mouser."

"Damn," Sid said, instantly returning to his normal grumpiness. "What the hell is he doing?"

"I don't know," Longtooth replied without taking his eyes from the field glasses. Then after a pause he finally added, "But he's gathering his scouts near the river. All of them."

Sid shrugged, "As much as I hate to admit it, he's doing a pretty fine job of keeping their heads down."

"But it shouldn't take that many of them to harass the enemy," Longtooth said, solemnly shaking his head. "He's up to something."

It was only about fifty yards from the *Baton Rouge* to the *Marmora*, but it was fifty yards of pure hell. There were only a dozen marines on the ironclad to begin with; by the time they got the boat in the water and started toward the *Marmora* only eight were left. The remaining marines tried to stay as low as possible, while rowing as fast as they could. The result was sloppy rowing. This didn't please Shoe in the least. He alternated between swearing at his marines and swearing at the beastmen who were firing at them from the banks. The big Dutchman had already taken a bullet in the thigh and one in the arm, but he seemed to suffer no ill effects from these wounds.

Sitting at the back of the boat, Shoe was the only man who could see where they were going. He saw another dogbreed take aim from behind a tree. Quickly throwing his carbine to his shoulder, he fired three shots in rapid succession. He could see the bark flying from the tree the beastman was using as cover. The dogbreed didn't so much as flinch.

A puff of black smoke, a sharp report, and the bullet stuck the side of the boat, piecing through the wood and hitting a marine in the leg. The marine yelped and dropped his paddle.

"Get that damn paddle you worthless bastard!" Shoe roared at the marine then he turned his attention back to the tree line and fired his remaining two shots.

Despite his pain, the wounded marine reached into the water and retrieved the paddle before it drifted too far away. Gritting his teeth against the pain, he immediately resumed paddling.

Shoe handed the carbine to the man sitting in the boat in front of him. The marine handed a loaded gun to his sergeant and then went to work reloading the empty one.

Two more shots rang out from the bank. A bullet splashed in the water nearby, but the other bullet struck a marine in the back of the head—his lifeless body slumped to the side, leaving his bottom half in the boat and his top half lying over the side. A marine stopped rowing and reached across to pull the body back into the boat.

"Never mind him! Keep paddling, you whore-loving bastards! Keep paddling!" Shoe roared.

A sailor swam by the boat on his way to the *Baton Rouge*. He was one of about a dozen who had made it into the water uninjured and were now swimming to safety.

"Damn cowards," Shoe said, and he meant it. He couldn't understand someone who would leave wounded comrades behind. However, he could tell by the look on their faces that his marines wished they could join the swimmers in the water. "Almost there, you bastards. If you quit on me now, I'll stomp a mudhole in every one of your worthless asses," he said, encouraging them the only way he knew how.

Another bullet hit a marine in the hand, but after a few more pulls they were close enough to the *Marmora* that her hull shielded them from the bank. Several men were already crowded on the near side of the gunboat. They were relatively safe there, as the superstructure shielded them from the marksmen on the banks and the *Baton Rouge* was positioned between them and the fort. A sailor threw a line to the marines. With several sailors hauling them in, the boat sped up considerably and gave the rowers a chance to drop their oars and pick up their carbines.

Panicked sailors crowded the deck near the boat as soon as they were alongside.

"The wounded come off first," Shoe barked, using his carbine to motion for them to step back. "How many wounded?" he asked.

A wild-eyed sailor in a blood-soaked shirt answered in a high-pitched voice, "We all wounded. You got to take us all."

"We ain't got the room, jackass," Shoe growled.

"The hell you don't," Another panicked sailor said as he tried to board the boat.

Shoe grabbed him by the throat and hurled him into the water.

"Come on, boys," the big sergeant said as he pulled himself onto the gunboat. "We want the serious wounded first, but not those who won't make it anyway. We can take about twelve to fifteen a trip."

The six remaining marines climbed onto the gunboat and started into the shattered casemate. Shoe stayed topside to make sure none of the sailors tried to leave with the skiff.

The marines in the casemate went to work immediately, passing the first wounded sailor out the gunport almost as soon as they had entered the ship. Two more wounded sailors had been hauled up through the gunports, and Shoe was reaching for another when he heard someone on the other side of the gunboat yell, "They coming! Oh dear Lord Jesus, they comin'!"

Shoe couldn't see what was going on, but he could hear the fire on the other side of the ship increase. Down the river, the *Gabby* was still far enough back so that the bend would hide her from the fort. However, despite the range, she fired a shot with the little 6-pounder on her bow. Shoe cursed the men on the *Gabby* at first, knowing full well they stood a better chance of accidentally hitting that *Marmora* than of hitting one of the beastmen hiding in the woods.

Then the he realized what was happening. The beastmen were no longer hiding in the woods. They were wading into the river in an attempt to board the *Marmora*.

Shoe leaned down and yelled through a gunport, "Spike the guns!"

"We already done it," an old wounded sailor who had been hauled up from the casemate answered, his voice amazingly calm tone.

Shoe leapt into the gunport and joined his men. The marines, along with a handful of armed sailors were firing their carbines out of the gunports on the opposite side. Even if the cannons hadn't been spiked the range would have been too close for them to have any effect since the beastmen were apparently too sharp to approach right into the mouths of the guns.

A sailor dropped his carbine, turned and fled, shouting, "There's too many of them!"

Shoe caught this man in the jaw with butt of his own carbine, sending him to the ground. "Damn cowards," Shoe growled as he stepped over limp sailor.

One of his marines turned to Shoe and frantically shouted, "We're holdin' 'em here, sir, but they comin' up on the bow."

Shoe nodded, his face stern and serious. "You and you," he said, his big hand slapping two marines on their backs in turn as he spoke, "With me."

No sooner had the three men started toward front of

the casemate than a beastman jumped in through the bow gunport, followed quickly by four more. Shoe smiled as he took aim; there was no tree for them to hide behind this time. He fired twice, both shots hitting the first one in the chest. His two marines opened fire and three more fell dead.

The remaining beastman leaped behind the *Marmora*'s dismounted bow gun, firing a pistol as he dove for cover. Shoe managed to hit this adversary in the leg, but one of the pistol shots hit a marine in the gut.

"I'm hit!" the wounded marine groaned.

"Keep fighting," Shoe growled.

Shoe started over toward the fallen cannon to finish off the beastman hiding there. He was almost there when a smoking iron ball was rolled into the casemate from the bow gunport; fire sputtered from the smoking cannonball as it wobbled along the blood-soaked wooden floor. It was a six-pounder shell that had apparently been lit and hurled inside like a grenade.

"Bomb!" Shoe shouted.

The explosion knocked the big man off his feet, but he was lucky. Two nearby sailors were killed by the blast.

Three more makeshift bombs flew in through the gunport. These were hurled with more force in an apparent attempt to sling them across the deck toward the starboard side, where the marines and sailors had pinned down the first boarding attempt. The resulting explosions cleared out both starboard gunports. Shoe could hear victorious shouts from the bank as more beastmen surged into the water and started toward the wrecked gunboat.

As the sergeant got to his feet the all but forgotten beastman came from behind the bow cannon with his pistol raised. He fired before Shoe had time to react. The bullet found its mark in the sergeant's chest, but if there was pain, it failed to register. The beastman squeezed the trigger again but the pistol misfired. Shoe took aim with his carbine, but was only rewarded with a dry click—he was empty.

The dogbreed let out a shrill growl as he charged forward, drawing a bowie knife as he ran. Shoe drew his pistol, but he wasn't able to get off a shot before his enemy was on him. They came together with such force that Shoe was slammed into the wall. The big knife sank deep into his shoulder, but when the beastman attempted to pull it free he found that it had become stuck in the big man's collar bone. Chest to chest, they grappled, the beastman desperately trying to free his knife with his right hand while he hung on to Shoe's pistol with his left. Shoe's attacker was a full head shorter than he was, which ruled out a headbutt. But the wily old marine wasn't out of tricks. He lunged forward and bit down on the dogbreed's ear and was rewarded with a shrill yelp. Twisting his head and biting as hard as he could, Shoe felt a grim satisfaction when half of the furry ear came off in his mouth. The dogbreed was startled and injured just enough to loosen his grip on the pistol; Shoe pointed the barrel into the beast's side and fired twice.

He tossed the dying dogbreed aside and spit the ear to the ground beside him. The big knife still protruding from his left shoulder, he quickly took in his surroundings. The beastmen were swarming the ship. There were only a handful of sailors and marines left and every one of them was wounded in some way.

Still, the few remaining marines were fighting back.

And so was Shoe.

The big Dutchman took aim with his pistol and dropped a nearby swinebreed before taking another bullet in his side. He spotted his latest attacker as the dogbreed attempted to reload his rifle.

"Son of a bitch!" he shouted, and fired twice dropping the beastman on the second shot. A smile lined with blood made its way across Shoe's face as he morbidly realized that most of his enemies were, in fact, sons of bitches.

There was no lull in the fighting. Shoe took aim at another target. Across the room a marine was frantically trying to reload, but he was too late; one of the sons of bitches clubbed him in the head with the stock of a rifle. Shoe put a bullet into the back of this murdering dog. Then he saw another beastman running toward him with a pistol in each hand. He took another bullet in the hip, but dropped this beastman before he could fire again.

While his thoughts were cloudy, the warrior part of his mind was still sharp and seemed to be running on its own. He knew he had to get out of there, but then he realized that he was no long standing on his own. At some point he had leaned back onto the wall behind him and he found that when he tried to move he almost fell.

Barely visible across the smoke filled room, Shoe saw a beastman taking aim at him with a rifle. Shoe took aim and pulled the trigger but his pistol was empty. Fire and black smoke erupted from the rifle; he figured the bullet must have hit him, but he wasn't sure where. He rolled to his left and collapsed on the floor. The smoke was thick now, providing cover as he pulled himself out of one of the holes in the side of the gunboat. Only a handful of wounded remained on the deck. A group of cowards had taken the boat and everyone else was either dead or they were swimming for it. There were no beastmen in this side of the shop, though. They were staying out of sight of the *Baton Rouge*.

The old sailor who had so calmly told Shoe that they had already spiked the guns had pulled himself up and taken a pipe out of his pocket for a last smoke.

"Swim for it," Shoe said as he pulled himself out of the hole.

"Can't," the old salt calmly replied. He nodded toward his legs, which were both ruined from the knees down.

Shoe smiled. "Then we'll die together."

"Suits me," the old sailor said. He took a couple more puffs on his pipe.

With great effort, Shoe managed to haul himself to his feet.

From the *Baton Rouge's* forwardmost starboard gunport, Morison watched the scene unfold. He had a good idea what was going on, but he wasn't certain. Or perhaps he couldn't bring himself to believe what he was seeing. He occasionally caught a glimpse of a beastman on the top of the *Marmora* or on her bow and he could hear the increase in gunfire. There was little doubt the *Marmora* had been boarded, but he couldn't tell who was winning. When wounded sailors began leaping into the water, taking their chances with the river rather than staying in the ship there was no more denying it. The enemy had boarded the ship and apparently they were winning.

All of the starboard guns were loaded and the crews stood by.

"Is that Shoe?" one of the gunners asked.

"Jesus Christ, I think it is," another gunner answered.

Morison started to reprimand the second gunner for his blaspheme, but then he saw the old sergeant and his breath was taken away. Shoe was covered in blood. Even at this distance he could tell that it was taking everything he had to rise to his feet.

Shoe started yelling something, but Morison's hearing wasn't as good as it had been. He turned to the gunnery officer, who was standing nearby with his mouth agape. "What's he saying?"

At first the officer didn't answer, as if he was unwilling for the words to come out of his mouth. Surely others among the gun crew heard what was being said, but they too held their tongues.

"What is it, lieutenant?" Morison asked, now forceful.

The gunnery officer swallowed hard and said, "He's telling us to open fire on the *Marmora*."

Everyone on the ship became quiet. Now Morison could hear him as well. Almost every other word was a swear word, but there was no doubt that the big man was calling for them to open fire.

"What do we do?" a nearby gunner officer asked.

Morison gazed out the gunport again. A beastman casually walked along the top of the *Marmora*. He could see another climbing on the ship near the bow. There was no doubt about it now; the *Marmora* and everyone on board her was lost.

"Prepare to fire!" Morison bellowed.

There was a murmur among the gunners, but the gunnery officer managed to get everyone to their stations.

Morison whispered a brief prayer then yelled, "Fire!"

Chapter 18

A LONE SQUIRREL made its way along the edge of the woods, moving with frantic speed for several feet, then stopping and remaining still for a few breaths before taking off again. Overhead a red-tailed hawk watched in stern silence. When time was right the predator left its perch. Wings splayed, talons forward, the hawk plummeted down toward its prey. At first the startled rodent froze, then it made a break for the trees. The bird struck, grasping the squirrel in his unforgiving claws. For a moment the hawk had the squirrel, but as he lifted it a sudden burst from the terrified rodent propelled his quarry out of its grasp and into the air. For an instant both predator and prey were airborne, the panicked squirrel clawing for the ground, the hungry hawk clawing for the squirrel. The rodent's feet found the ground first, and with it, traction. The hawk spread its wings and rose into the air as its would-be dinner scurried away into the woods.

Standing alone near the edge of the woods, Longtooth wasn't sure if he identified more with the hawk or the squirrel today. Behind him he could hear the cheering and howling from the camp, but he didn't feel like celebrating. His people were excited about the victory over the first steamer, but the way the second steamer, the one that seemed to be made of iron, had taken everything they could throw at it gave him the feeling that it wouldn't be as easy to deal with. In fact, judging from the damage to the battery after just a small exchange with this warship, Longtooth had a feeling that if it decided to poke its head around the bend it could casually knock out each of their guns one by one.

And that wasn't the only reason he didn't like joining in the festive spirit. Watching through the field glasses, he had witnessed what had happened to the scouts. The battery had devastated the ship with shot and shell from a hundreds of yards away, but when that human steamer opened fire with canister from only fifty yards or so it had obliterated the vessel. He didn't see how anyone could have lived through that maelstrom.

From a distance behind him, he could hear Gregory's voice calling out to him, "I'm sorry, sir. I tried to tell him you wished to be alone." He turned and saw Sid and Gregory approaching from the direction of camp.

Sid motioned behind him as he approached. "You need to get back to camp, oh Great One," he said, his voice an odd combination of his usual sarcasm mixed with a healthy dose of excitement over today's engagement, "Pig-boy is up there telling everyone about the will of God. You need to remind them about the will of Longtooth or the whole camp is going to turn into a revival. I normally don't mind Dillon so much, but we've got one hell of a fight coming up and this ain't the time to be rambling on about how we're the new Israelites."

"I plan on speaking to them tonight," Longtooth said dryly, "Right now I have something else I need to take care of."

"You need to talk right now," Sid insisted. "By nightfall Dillon'll have them all convinced you're going to part the river or walk on water or something."

"Longtooth really wants to be alone right now," Gregory meekly ventured.

Sid spun toward Gregory. "I've heard about enough out of you!" he snapped. "Get out of my sight, right now!"

Despite being almost a foot and a half taller than Sid, Gregory lowered his head and sulked away.

"Was that necessary?" Longtooth asked.

"He gets on my nerves. Hell, he's almost as bad as Dillon."

Longtooth sighed. "Sid, you need to go back to camp."

Sid paused, looking honestly confused.

Longtooth wasn't sure how to explain, then he found he didn't have to. Sid's eyes turned away from him and toward the woods. His expression darkened and his tail lowered. "Mouser," he growled.

Longtooth turned and saw that it wasn't actually Mouser himself, but three of his scouts. All three of them were wounded. One had his arm in a makeshift sling and was using his arm to support the weight of a friend who was limping along with a bloody bandage wrapped around his lower leg. The third, smaller beastman was walking with a limp and the fur on his head was matted with blood; Longtooth recognized him.

"Cedar, you okay?" Longtooth asked as he approached.

The young scout lowered his head and whined, but as Longtooth walked up to him he slowly nodded his head. "Yes," he said.

"What happened?" Longtooth asked.

"We were trying to get stuff off that boat," Cedar replied solemnly. "You know, guns and the like. The humans fought harder than we figured they would, then once we finally got on the boat they started shooting at us with those big guns on that other boat."

"What?" Sid cried with a yelp, "The scouts were on that ship?"

Longtooth turned to Sid and nodded grimly.

"There ain't many of us left," Cedar added.

"Where's Mouser?" Longtooth asked.

Cedar didn't answer at first. Then he nodded back the way he came.

"Is he okay?"

"He's fine, I guess. He ain't hurt or nothin'." Cedar said still looking at the ground. He paused again, then looked up before continuing. "After we killed all the men that were still fighting he got some of us together to carry stuff back to the camp. He went back to the land to make sure we was organized. He wasn't on the boat when they started shooting the big guns."

Sid's growl increased at Cedar spoke. As soon as the small beastman was finished he said, "Damn shame he wasn't still on that boat, if you ask me."

Cedar turned to Sid. "He wanted to go back onboard," he said, his voice becoming shrill and defiant as he spoke. "Even after the shooting started. He wanted to go back and help get the wounded off."

"They wouldn't have been on that boat if he'd done like he was told," Sid snapped.

Cedar drew himself up. He was tiny specimen, a full head shorter than Sid, who wasn't exactly a tall dogbreed himself, but he held himself proudly, "Mouser saw a chance we had to take. And it wasn't just him; we all wanted go. Mouser's scouts ain't scared of no humans."

Longtooth held his hand up for them to stop, but Sid was determined to have the last word.

"Maybe if you had more than a few loose rocks in your head you would be a little scared of them," Sid popped back.

It was all he could take. "That is *enough!*" Longtooth shouted.

A stunned silence followed, neither Cedar nor even Sid had ever heard Longtooth raise his voice in such a manner.

Longtooth took a deep breath and turned to Sid. "I need you to return to the camp," he said in a calm voice. Sid started to protest but Longtooth raised his hand and continued. "I'm not asking you."

Sid scowled for a moment, shot Cedar an angry glare, then

stalked away in silence.

As soon as Sid was out of earshot, Longtooth turned to Cedar. "How far is he?"

"Not far." Cedar replied.

"Take me to him."

Cedar nodded then wordlessly led the way. As they entered the woods, about a dozen more wounded scouts passed them on their way to the camp. They all hung their heads and couldn't bring themselves to look Longtooth in the eyes, as if it was their fault.

Barely fifty yards into the woods, Longtooth noticed a gathering of about a dozen beastmen, all standing with their heads hung low. These must have been some of the scouts that Mouser had sent ashore to handle the captured supplies; most of them were unwounded, at least physically. Mouser sat on a stump in the center of the small knot of warriors, his elbows on his knees and his head in his hands.

"Mouser?" Longtooth asked as he approached.

Mouser looked up, saw his leader approaching and burst into tears, literally howling in anguish.

"There's no time for that, Mouser," Longtooth said sternly.

"I just ... I'm so sorry," he sobbed.

"It's behind us. We've got to move on."

Mouser seemed to pull himself together. That is, he at least stopped blubbering, but he remained seated with his shoulders slumped.

"What happened?"

Mouser drew in a breath and explained. "I thought we could take the ship and come off with their weapons before they could react."

"I told you to try to take one of their ships on downriver, but if that failed you were to only harass them from there on out. And I told you not to get into a serious scrape."

"But it could have been like Clover Bend."

And therein lay the source of the problem. Mouser's laurels had never hung higher than they did at Clover Bend. He had reveled in the attention, and there was little doubt he wanted to relive the glory of that day.

Longtooth sighed. "Mouser, you outdid yourself at Clover Bend, but there's a world of difference between coming up with a good plan like you did that day and not doing what you're told." Mouser looked as if he was about to break into another emotional apology, but Longtooth held up his hand, stopping him short. "What's done is done. I need you, Mouser, but you ain't worth spit if you can't get a grip on yourself. Understand?"

Mouser nodded, then he rose to his feet.

"How many do you have left? Not counting the wounded."

"I don't know. Less than a hundred; probably less than fifty."

Longtooth's heart fell to his stomach—he had just lost over two-hundred of his best soldiers on the eve of battle. However, he only nodded at the news, trying hard not to show any emotion. "I need an exact count of how many scouts are left. Meet me at my cabin before nightfall."

Longtooth turned on his heels and started back toward camp.

Behind him, Mouser called out, "I won't let you down again."

Chapter 19

SOLDIERS WITH RIFLES to their shoulders lined the side of the transport steamers, cautiously watching the bank as the planks were lowered onto the muddy east bank of the river. From the middle of the river, the *Baton Rouge* looked on with her deadly battery, ready to saturate the tree line with a deadly barrage of canister-fire should the beastmen attempt any sort of attack during the initial stages of unloading transports. As soon as the planks on every streamer were secured, soldiers began hurrying to shore. Once the first company from each ship was ashore, they began spreading out as they pushed inward. Other companies were rushed ashore and added to either side of the swelling formation. The entire movement was precise and if everything kept moving smoothly the perimeter would be secured in less than an hour, but this was a very delicate operation. An enemy attack at the proper time with the sufficient force could spell disaster.

"No resistance as yet," Thompson said nervously as he watched trees for any sign of movement.

Cole walked over to Thompson and leaned on the railing beside him. He said nothing, but his overall demeanor wasn't one of a man overly concerned with the operation.

Thompson knew Cole wasn't one to take such a serious undertaking lightly. He eyeballed the colonel curiously and said, "You know, it's strange that they haven't tried anything, what with us all strung out and vulnerable while disembarking."

"Oh, it's not really all that strange. In fact, I'd be surprised if we received more than a musket shot or two here and there along the line." Cole replied with a knowing smile.

Thompson paused. The colonel had one of the sharpest military minds he'd ever known—and this said a lot since he had served on John Reynold's staff in the war—but it just didn't make sense that the beastmen wouldn't try something during this, the most vulnerable part of their operation. "What makes you so sure they won't try anything? They've played it pretty smart up to now."

"I don't think those soldiers were supposed to board the *Marmora*, and when they did they really took a beating. I'd wager that those beastmen were the troops Longtooth wanted to use to attack us when we tried to unload. From the looks of things, there's not enough of them left for a full scale attack, and they're probably too rattled to give us any sort of organized harassment. They're going to have to lick their wounds and regroup."

It made sense, but Thompson was still uneasy. "Are you certain?" he asked.

Cole shrugged, "Nothing's certain in war, but I'm about as sure as I can be."

"I hope you're right."

"So do I."

As if to accent their worries a shot rang out on the right flank. This shot was followed by what could have been a brisk light exchange of gunfire. Then a stern shout seemed to cut through the noise. The distance was great, but it sounded as though the voice was calling for them to hold their fire. Sure enough, there were only one or two more shots, then all was silent.

"Hold your fire!" Parker yelled again as he strode out in front of the line, holstering his unfired pistol.

A thin waft of black smoke drifted across a sunbeam in the damp forest, a dark stain in an otherwise perfect natural surrounding.

The men of Company H were jittery; their eyes were wide as they scanned the woods, but all eyes turned to Parker when the sergeant stepped before them, between them and the trees which could hide any number of beastmen with guns.

Parker was furious. Not only was he upset about the unneeded shooting that might have given away their position and intentions, but it also bothered him that if he hadn't been with Company H at the time and seen that there was nothing to shoot at this little incident could have spread all along the line with smoke adding to the confusion until the entire regiment was blazing away at nothing. As it was he had been there, but they had still failed to cease fire when he told them to. These boys were better than this and he knew it.

"Next time I say hold your fire you best listen!" Parker was furious, "You're firing at shadows! Nothin' but shadows!"

The company was silent and still. Only the nervous rustle of fidgety boots on twigs and grass broke the silence. Parker wanted to say more but the companies on either side of them were advancing and Company H was still in place.

"Get moving!" he shouted, and Company H hurried past him.

As he turned to watch them disappear into the woods he felt as though his stomach wanted to do flips. His boys would see real action soon, perhaps as soon as tomorrow. He kept telling himself they would do just fine, but he couldn't help but worry. This was his family. They were all his boys.

The bridge and decks of the *Baton Rouge* had been remarkably quiet ever since the ironclad had devastated what was left of the *Marmora*. Neither man nor beast could have survived that hail of iron, and a dark cloud seemed to hang over the entire ship as every man wondered how many of their own had still been alive when they opened fire. Of course it wouldn't have mattered; whoever was still on that ship would have been killed by the beastmen anyway.

Even their normally boisterous captain was uncharacteristically quiet as he paced back and forth on the bridge. It wasn't until he received the signal that all of the soldiers had landed that his old loud aggressiveness began to show signs of returning.

Now it was time for a little payback.

Steam was up, guns were loaded with gunners standing by.

"Full speed ahead and may the good Lord in Heaven bless us in this, our noble endeavor," he called out. It was something he had come up with a couple of days ago, something he felt was worthy of the papers and maybe even the historians. Saying it aloud seemed to stir a little life into him. He smiled for the first time in hours, walked up to the front of the bridge and clapped a heavy hand on the shoulder of his young pilot. "Steady at the wheel, my boy."

"You wanna keep right?" the boys asked.

"Keep to the center. We'll let our port guns have the first few rounds then we'll take the turn and pound them to pieces with the big boys up front."

"All right," the boy said, then he attempted to spit a manly stream of tobacco out the slit before him and missed, leaving a dark splatter just above the hole. The brown spittle started slowly dripping down, thin tendrils extending across the slit itself. This almost ruined the mood for the captain, but it had the opposite effect on everyone else on the bridge. It was just the tension-breaker they needed. They hid their snickers and smiles as they watched the captain slowly remove his hand from the boy's back.

River pilots are normally given a little more leeway than regular Navy sailors, but there was a limit. "Spit the wad out, boy." Morison said disgustedly, more like a deep throated school marm who's never been around tobacco than an old captain who had seen action on four different warships.

"Sir, I been chewin' since I's off the tit."

"Just spit it out," the captain said. His nose still wrinkled in disgust, he reached inside his coat, removed his white handkerchief and attempted to clean the massive splotch on the inside of his pilothouse.

It was all they could stand. The two ensigns and the mate on the bridge with him almost collapsed to the floor laughing. His face red, Morison continued staring at the river before him, trying to keep up a dignified air.

Soon the *Baton Rouge* poked her head around the corner and the battery came into view. Just as when the *Marmora* made the turn earlier in the day, the battery opened fire as soon as the ship was around the corner. This time, however, the balls had no effect. Even the heavy 24-pounders failed to penetrate the *Baton Rouge*'s thick armor. The only chance the beastmen had was scoring a direct hit on one of the gunports, and these were covered with thick iron shutters except when the guns were run out and fired. Before the *Baton Rouge* was even able to bring her big bow guns into play two of the enemy's guns were knocked out, one of them a 24-pounder.

The *Baton Rouge* entered the curve in the river then slowed considerably until its forward momentum was just enough to offset the current, effectively keeping it in one place. The second shot from the big 10-inch gun scored a direct his on the remaining 24-pounder. Morison smiled as he watched the heavy gun leap from its makeshift carriage in the explosion. After that all of the battery's guns were silent as whoever was in charge up there wisely ordered his soldiers to withdraw away from the now impotent battery.

A voice called up the brass tube from below, "The enemy's guns are silent, sir! Shall we start shelling the trenches?" The

197

cheering gun crews could be heard in the background.

"No," Morison said into the tube, his voice stern his stern and businesslike, "You are to continue firing at the guns until each one has been dismounted. Fire slow for accuracy; I don't want to waste powder, but I want every gun on that hill dismounted and destroyed, not just abandoned."

An ensign leaned forward and asked the captain, "Do we call up the *Gabby* yet?"

"Not until I'm sure all of those guns are knocked out," he said, as he extended his telescope for another look, "No more haste. Drop both anchors and as soon as we're sure they're holding bring the engines to stop. We've got all the time in the world to exact our revenge."

When the *Gabby* was finally given the order to move forward only Thompson and Cole were in the pilot room with the pilot. This was the way Thompson wanted it. Many of the maps he had drawn for the IV Corps during the French and Mexican War had been created in fields, tents, and ruined houses, wherever the headquarters happened to be at the time, with literally hundreds of people coming and going, bumping and jostling about. He had managed to work that way and even turned out some maps he was quite proud of. However, that wasn't how he preferred to work. Some might have said that this map was considerably less important than, say, his map of the western approach to Ciudad Madera, which had been drawn on scrap piece of paper while sitting in the saddle with Mexican skirmishers' bullets whizzing by his head, but the way he saw it any map in which battle plans were to be laid was worth doing right.

Cole sat in a chair near the rear of the pilothouse. He didn't say a word. He wanted to be present, but this was Thompson's show.

Thompson stood beside the pilot with field glasses in hand, then he placed the binoculars to his eyes for several minutes before setting them down and making a few new notes and drawing a few lines, and then he started the whole process over again—first he used his eyes; then he amplified what he saw; then he put it in his notes; then he added to the map. He always felt his meticulous routine was why his maps were so accurate. In the war he would have had the binoculars in his right hand while he drew with his left. Now his right hand had to pull double service. Still, considering his surroundings he couldn't have asked for more.

The White River turned in a shallow S here with the fort—or rather the battery, since the works seemed to be open in the rear—situated on the hill that made up the peninsula formed by the second turn. The position was good. The hill rose high on the southern portion of the peninsula, protecting the solders and possibly the encampment on the other side from heavy guns. Also the battery was positioned near the beginning of the peninsula rather than at its head, enabling it to guard the landward approaches along the river. Unlike the mostly wooded area around them, the hill and the approaches to the hill were clear, open firing lanes. A shallow creek ran across the base of the peninsula; logs had been piled here to provide cover troops defending from a possible attack from inland. This was probably the best approach, but even then the soldiers would have to wade through the woods before crossing open ground to attack across a creek in the face of a fortified opponent.

After almost an hour of drawing and writing Thompson decided to take a break. "They're in an excellent position."

"I was afraid of that," Cole said without rising.

"There's only one fault; there's no way out of it. The river's too deep to ford and the current's too swift to swim. They got themselves hemmed in," Thompson continued, "If we can break them here, we ought to bag the lot of them."

"It's going to be one hell of a fight, but with the *Baton Rouge*'s firepower, I have no doubt we can beat them so long as they don't use nightfall to slip away."

Thompson took another long look at the fortifications then replied, "These aren't temporary works. I think they aim to stay and fight."

"Good."

Chapter 20

HIS NAME HAD BEEN WALTER a lifetime ago, but he could remember when he didn't even have that name. He couldn't remember anything before the procedure, before they used surgery and slime and transformed him from beast into something that resembled man—something both beast *and* man. His first memory was of pain—blood, bandages and excruciating pain like fire in his veins. There was a burning under his skin, and his joints—all of them—ached.

He wasn't alone; screams of agony filled his ears. He had glanced around and saw many other twisted forms lying on tables in that foul hell that appeared to be part factory and part hospital. Men in white coats moved among them like ghosts, or perhaps demons. This memory was but a flash in his mind. He had slipped back unconscious not long after raising his head from the table.

When he next awoke he was in a crowded, windowless room that smelled of stale blood, urine and feces. But at least he wasn't alone. Several other frightened, twisted forms milled about in the room. None of them spoke; they didn't know how. They only whimpered and cried in pain.

It was here that the beast who would soon be named Walter met his brother. At least everyone always assumed they were brothers, since they looked so much alike. He could remember that his brother never cried and whined like the others. He bore his pain in silent dignity.

After some time the demons in white coats came for them. They were all told to rise and walk on two legs. It was difficult at first. Fresh incisions on his legs wept blood and his hips ached, but he found that once he got used to the pain he could stand and walk with little difficulty. This was, he later learned, in the early days of the creation process, before men learned about Mendel, and he was among the first beastmen to be created, rather than born, in America. He was, he also found out, reasonably lucky to have even survived.

Others weren't so lucky. He remembered hearing a sharp crack as one pitiful soul next to him tried to rise. The creature fell to the floor, clutching his leg where an unhealed bone had fractured, causing a sharp point to pierce out of a poorly sutured incision. The newly created beastman, now crippled, was considered a loss. A white coated demon walked over, casually lifted the poor creature's chin and slit its throat.

The remaining creatures were led out of the foul room and brought into a larger, marginally cleaner, room. They were then given random names; he had received Walter and his brother received Jack. It was there that a man in a suit gave them their first instructions in speech. On pained legs they stood for hours while they were made to use their new vocal cords to sound out the letters of the alphabet. They would return to this room every day for a year, learning more and more about speech and the ways of their human masters. Walter came to like the trips to The Big Room, as they called it. He had a natural curiosity about him and often found himself receiving beatings for asking questions out of turn.

But there were other lessons in The Big Room, such as discipline. Of the many rules they were taught, one of the most important was to never bare their fangs at a human. The white coated demons would walk down the files, cursing, slapping and spitting into the faces of their creations, trying their best to incite the beasts to react. And anyone who so much as snarled was beaten down with canes.

He could plainly recall a whiskered man with thick glasses

screaming and spitting in his face. He could still remember the first time, fighting the strong impulse not just to growl or bark, but to bite—to lunge forward and take this man's face in his mouth and rip it from his skull. After the months passed, most of them grew accustomed to the routine, but a part of him still wanted to lash out. By now it had become less of a desire for violent resolution and more of a need to show that he was not so inferior. One day this led to a minor rebellion on his part. The scraggly whiskered man had just finished slapping him around and had turned away to start on the next in line when Walter briefly flashed his teeth and just as quickly closed his mouth. The whiskered man caught the movement out of the corner of his eye, and spun to face him. Walter stood rigid, as if he was a soldier at attention. However, one solitary tooth had caught on his upper lip when he closed his mouth, leaving a lower pointed canine protruding like a telltale sign of guilt. The whiskered man already held a special hatred for Walter, so the beating was severe, lasting until well after the others had left The Big Room.

He was hauled back into their dark dungeon and tossed into the corner, beaten but proud of what he had done. He remembered Jack coming over to him and chiding him, saying, "You got to do something about that long tooth."

And that was how he came about the nickname Longtooth. Truth was, Walter's teeth were no longer than any other beastman's; he had just dared to show them.

"It's almost dark."

Longtooth jumped at the sound of the voice.

"I'm sorry. You told me to let you know when it was dark," Gregory said from the doorway, "I sincerely apologize if I startled you."

Longtooth shook his head. "I was just thinking of old

times."

Gregory smiled. "Better times?"

"No, just old times."

Gregory ducked his head and stepped into the small cabin that served as Longtooth's home and quite often as the as the impromptu headquarters for the camp. It was an unadorned log structure with a sheet hung near the middle that hid the hammock where Longtooth slept—when he did sleep, that is.

"I thought you were going to get some rest."

Longtooth shrugged. "I couldn't."

Gregory gave Longtooth a look of concern that was tempered with a heavy dose of sadness. A slight whine unintentionally escaped, but the proper butler-like dogbreed quickly covered the slip by clearing his throat. He did not, however, attempt to cover his concern.

"I tried to rest, honest," Longtooth said with a weary smile.

"Sid, Mouser and Cooney are waiting outside. Would you like me to send them away? I can tell them to come back after you've rested."

"No, I'm fine."

The concerned whimper escaped again and this time Gregory didn't bother to make an attempt at hiding it.

"Thank you for your concern, but I feel better than I look."

"You haven't slept well in days."

More like months, Longtooth thought, but he didn't say as much. "I'm fine, really. I just don't need as much sleep as I used to," Longtooth explained calmly.

Gregory paused then finally said, "Shall I send the guests in?"

It all seemed so ironic. Here they were in a one-room shack in the middle of rebel refugee camp and this habitual servant was acting as if there were gentlemen outside calling on a fellow gentleman at his estate. Tomorrow hundreds, perhaps thousands, would die, and this gentle giant was concerned about his master's sleep. And if he were to stick around much longer he would no doubt bring up Longtooth's diet as well. None of this was for show; it was all honest, good-natured concern.

"No, don't send them in just yet. I need to talk to you first," Longtooth motioned to a makeshift bench made of a log resting on two short stumps.

Gregory seemed to hesitate at first. He was no fool; he probably knew what was coming.

As soon as the big dogbreed was seated Longtooth got right to the point. "Tonight I'm sending the women, children and those who don't want to fight into the swamp. I want you to go with them."

Without hesitation, Gregory shook his head.

"They need you to lead them."

"No, they don't. You know as well as I do that I'm not a leader."

Longtooth sighed. "It don't matter. You're going with them."

"No, I'm staying here," Gregory said, flatly refusing Longtooth for the first time since they'd first met.

"Tomorrow is going to be bad, Gregory. You've got the purest heart I've ever known, but you're no warrior."

"I'm staying and it has nothing to do with whether I can shoot a gun or not. I could never live with myself if I left you now. I'll never raise a hand in anger but I need this as much as you do."

Longtooth looked at Gregory curiously. The statement caught him off guard, but he knew what Gregory meant. "Okay, then," Longtooth said. He reached into his coat and produced a pistol. Taking it by the barrel, he held it out for

Gregory. "If you're going to stay, you need to be armed."

Gregory stared at the gun for a second, then said, "Thank you, but no. I don't believe in taking the lives of others."

"They're going to try to take yours."

"I know, but that don't mean I have to be like them."

Longtooth raised his eyebrows at this comment, but his ears lowered, as did his tail. He wasn't consciously angry, though; he doubted very seriously Gregory realized that what he was saying was quite insulting.

Gregory caught the look, but instead of his normal servile backtracking, he reached out and placed a hand on Longtooth's shoulder in a gesture borne more of friendship than servitude. He smiled and said, "I respect you more than you'll ever know, and I truly believe in what you're doing here. But our ways are different."

"I reckon I can respect that." Longtooth put the pistol back into his coat then motioned toward the door. "I do wish you'd leave before it gets bad, though. You deserve better than this."

"I'm staying."

Longtooth nodded, "Okay, then. I guess you'd better tell them to come in before Sid throws a fit at having to wait."

Gregory dutifully rose to his feet, dusted his slacks and tweaked the seams straight before he turned toward the door. He was an odd sight to behold, a tall canine butler in a muddy cabin in the middle of an armed refuge camp. Longtooth wished there were more like him, not for his habitual servitude, but for his nobility.

The dirt floor was thick with mud in the main area, so Longtooth pulled back the sheet that separated the cabin into two rooms and led them into his sleeping area where the floor was drier. He then took his hammock down, rolled it up and placed it in the corner. The only ornamentation in the entire cabin hung on the wall in the back where he slept—a United States Army officer's infantry saber. Mouser had presented the saber to Longtooth after Clover Bend, and usually couldn't help but ramble on about the saber—any opportunity to bring up Clover Bend would suffice. However, now when Longtooth took the saber from the wall, Mouser remained silent.

Longtooth used the point of the saber to draw a large horseshoe in the dirt. "This is where we are," he said, pointing to the center of the horseshoe.

He then drew a circle inside horseshoe, near one of the outer legs of the horseshoe. "This is the battery," he said. He then drew a then line from the outer part of the hill to the other leg of the horseshoe, "and this line is the trench covering our backdoor.

"There's three ways to get to us, they can come up the shoreline and straight up the hill, they can come around through the woods and fall on our rear, or they can use their steamers, come upriver, and land behind the battery," he said, pointing at each approach as he mentioned it. "I don't think that last one's going to be an option, though."

"What about that big iron steamer?" Sid said, "You saw what it did to the guns we had on the hill."

"That steamer's not going to be a problem after tonight," Longtooth said. He turned to Cooney, "Ain't that right?"

Clooney nodded, and the good side of his face stretched to match the warped side, forming a wicked smile. "Leave the steamer to me."

"Still, they may use the river along with another approach," Longtooth said. "We'll set Mouser's little cannon up near the point, just in case. That should buy us enough time to react to whatever they send upriver."

Longtooth turned to Mouser, "How many scouts are there?"

"Thirty-eight unwounded, plus another twenty-three who ain't hurt bad."

"I imagine their main attack will fall on our rear, but they'll have to move through the woods to get there. I want you to harass them every step of the way. Don't get drawn into a standup fight—shoot, fall back, shoot again."

"You can count on me," Mouser said without any sign of his usual joking spirit, nor without the slightest hint of his earlier breakdown. This was a good sign.

Longtooth turned to Sid, "We're going to have weak forces up front at first, only about three-hundred in our rear and two-hundred in the fort on the hill. This should be enough to hang on until we can bring up more. Everybody else will be organized in groups of about fifty. We can add as many groups as we need to the rear, the hill, or the river when we need to. When they make the first attack, I'll go to that position and you'll stay with the groups, sending them to me as I call for them. If they come at us from two places, you'll take over at the second place they attack. Understand?"

Staring down at the crude map drawn into the floor, Sid was silent at first. Then he looked up and said, "You know, I think we can win this thing."

Chapter 21

CRICKETS CHIRPED IN THE DISTANCE as a whippoorwill sang its lonely song. Nightfall had come and all was silent along the White. At dusk the *Baton Rouge* had ceased her relentless pounding and withdrawn behind the curtain of trees that obscured the fort, and so far there had been no incidents in the woods.

Colonel Haiber sat on the upper deck of the *Anne Marie*, perched on a camp stool, composing letters and reports with only the moon and a solitary candle as his light. He finished his final report for the night, then rummaged through the other papers until he found three other papers he needed, folded them together and placed them in an envelope. He had been delighted at the prospect of finally getting off the stuffy steamer but there hadn't been enough room on the tiny strip of land that they had managed to secure before nightfall, so Haiber had compromised; he set up his headquarters on the open upper deck.

"Parker?" he said, turning to his sergeant, who was standing near the railing looking at the stars.

"Yes, sir?" Parker said, turning from the railing and making his way over to the desk.

"These are the reports Cole requested. I need you to take them to him and see if he needs anything else."

Parker paused. Haiber could tell the sergeant was still bitter about the whole parley fiasco. He hadn't forgiven Cole and the rest of the Southerners; Haiber couldn't blame him. In truth Haiber found it hard to forgive as well. However, in a day or two they would have to fight side by side and there was no time for personal squabbles.

"Why don't you send Smith? He's—" Parker began.

"Lieutenant Smith is not my chief of staff." Haiber said uncharacteristic bluntness. Without another word he handed the envelope to Parker.

"Yes, sir," Parker replied. He took the envelope and started down the stairs.

When Parker left Haiber was alone. The colonel turned his head up and gazed at the starry sky above. As long as he could remember he had wanted to be an army officer. Growing up among aristocratic society in Massachusetts it was hard to find friends who were willing to play the parts of soldiers while he played the officer, so he had often entertained himself commanding imaginary armies. He and his imaginary soldiers had pushed the villainous redcoats out of the family garden hundreds of times. Not once had they failed, and not once had an imaginary soldier questioned his brilliant commands. He grew up and eventually went to West Point, but his dreams remained the same. Loyal soldiers would follow his every command unquestionably, and together they would drive the enemy before them.

Reality was nothing like he had imagined it. He felt so terribly alone.

Parker wordlessly handed the envelope to Thompson.

"Thank you, sergeant," the brevet Lieutenant-Colonel said with a friendly smile, but Parker's reply was a crisp salute, after which he turned on his heels and left without saying a word. He had nothing personal against Thompson. It was just that he had rather not talk to anyone from the Arkansas Militia.

Parker was making his way toward the plank when he noticed something above the trees to the north. He turned and watched as twin pillars of smoke, barely visible in the against the night sky, rose above the trees in the bend of the river. Probably just smoke from large campfires, but something about these pillars didn't set well with Parker, so he stopped and watched them. They seemed to be moving, but that wasn't possible. Another solitary pillar, smaller than the other two, appeared just to the left of the first two. After watching for a few more seconds there was no doubt about it; these black pillars were moving.

Suddenly flaming sparks flew upward into the first two pillars of smoke, causing them to glow red. Parker suddenly realized what he was seeing, but for a split second he was too stunned to react. His jaw fell open as he stared in disbelief.

On the *Baton Rouge*, a few hundred yards ahead an alert lookout noticed the smoke and apparently reached the same conclusion. "Steamers ho!" a voice called out.

Just then a massive steamer around the bend, picking up speed as it made the turn. All lights were out on this vessel, but there was enough starlight for Parker to tell this was no small river barge—a full sized steamer was bearing down on them.

The commotion had already stirred Morison from his slumber, but he was still getting dressed when someone banged on the door to his stateroom.

"Captain, sir?" the panicked voice called from the other side of the door. "Unknown vessel approaching from upriver."

"What's the status?" Morison replied gruffly.

"We're building steam, trying to get underway. The steamer is running without lights. Lieutenant Walther wants to know if we should open fire?"

"Certainly not!" Morison snapped. "It's probably a boat trying to escape from above Elizabeth."

"Walther wants you to have a look."

"I'm on my way!" Morison shot back as he pulled his trousers up. He didn't even bother buttoning his jacket before he burst out of his room, almost knocking the startled mate to the floor.

On his way down the hall he called out to a nearby ensign, "Tell Walther to slip the cables, but stay near the bank. They probably have their lanterns out so they can sneak by the beasts. They may not even know we're here. We can't afford a collision." Morison didn't join his lieutenant in the pilothouse—the forward gunports were closer. As he ran forward he saw his chief gunner, Lieutenant Harold Cooper, standing by the starboard-most forward gun. He too had been roused from bed and was currently dressed in his long johns. Although he had just arrived, he was taking immediate action.

He held his hand up and called out, "Ready!"

"Hold right there, lieutenant! What on earth are you doing?" Morison bellowed. "That's not the enemy!"

"Just a warning shot, sir," Cooper replied. "We've blown the whistle, but they won't respond. I don't think they see us."

Morison's face was red, his cheeks puffed as he breathed heavily. He peered out the gunport and could see two steamers in the river ahead. The first one was big, and at first glance it appeared to be an Army transport, but Morison knew there weren't supposed to be any up the White River. The second one was a rather small steamer with only one stack. The lead steamer was still two hundred yards away. It was certainly running dangerously close, but it didn't seem to be bearing down on them.

"Go ahead and send them a warning shot."

"Ready!" Cooper continued. "Fire!"

The big 32-pounder roared into the night.

A tongue of flame leapt out of the squatty ironclad's leftmost gunport. The roar of the cannon echoed across the water. Cooney winced, waiting for shot or shell to tear into their steamer, but it didn't. Perhaps it had been a warning shot. If that was the case then Longtooth had been right in that the enemy wouldn't even realize they were under attack until the last second.

Beside him an anxious dogbreed leveled a rifle at the ironclad.

"Not yet!" Cooney snapped. "Longtooth said not to fire until they started shooting at us with rifles."

There were only about two dozen marksmen on *Big Dog* and even fewer on *Little Dog*. Longtooth had told them to sink the ironclad and a random transport, then swim to safety, but it was a suicide mission and Cooney knew it.

As per Longtooth's specific instructions, Cooney stayed to the left, but he wasn't to steam directly toward the ironclad until the last possible minute.

The wind blew Cooney's ears flat on the side of his head. To lighten the topside, the roof of the pilothouse had been cut away. The wind in his hair was so much better than sticky heat of the engine room where Cooney had spent years shoveling coal. Cooney cast a glance upwards at the starry sky. The wind blew under his twisted chin and he smiled with the good side of his face. He felt free.

He turned to check on the little steamer following in his wake. The beastmen who had escaped from Memphis were all part of *Big Dog*'s crew. As a result, *Little Dog*'s crew didn't have the experience his did, but they had been given specific instruction and so far they were performing quite well—they made it around both bends without incident.

The ironclad loomed ahead. He could see men scattering about her deck. They were close now.

"Here goes!" Cooney called out. He smiled as he cut the wheel to the port, sending the big transport on a collision course with the enemy warship.

Morison had taken the time to button his coat, but his hair was still in wild disarray as he and his chief gunner officer watched the big vessel in the river ahead. The mysterious steamer seemed to be keeping to the left, but it was beginning to look as if it would miss them. The *Baton Rouge* had been drifting into the river when Morison had ordered her to continue building steam as rapidly as possible but to drop anchor in order to give the big steamer plenty of room to pass.

"Something's not right, sir." Walther's voice came down the brass pipe to the gun deck where Morison and Cooper watched the ship making its way down the river.

Morison was about to reply when the big transport suddenly wheeled to port and headed straight for them.

"Oh Hell!" Cooper swore. Then without waiting for orders he called out, "Fire!"

The two guns that hadn't fired, the other 32 pounder and the big ten inch gun, roared to life, sending shells pointblank into the approaching vessel. The effect on her superstructure was devastating, but did nothing to stop the momentum of the massive steamer. A few crewmen who were topside opened fire with their carbines a handful of enemy sharpshooters returned fire.

"Brace for impact!" Morison bellowed as he grabbed a solid timber than ran from the ceiling to the floor through the gun deck.

Sailors pressed themselves against the walls of the ship, while the older salts tried to get as far away from the big guns as they could—many of these veterans of the French and Mexican War had witnessed what several tons of iron could do if it came loose from its mount and rolled across the deck.

Suddenly a powerful impact seemed to shove the entire world back fifty feet. Men fell to the floor, stacks of cannonballs

214

rolled forward, gun mounts cracked and at least one deposited its cannon on the deck, but it was wedged between its mount and wall so it didn't roll freely across the deck. From all around iron groaned and strained while heavy timbers popped. The bow was pushed downward, as the taller, lighter steamer rode on top of the ironclad as far back as the pilot house. Planks on the gun deck snapped under the strain, leaving jagged teeth along the floor. A sailor rolled forward along the deck until his body came into contact with one such row of unforgiving wooden teeth—pierced in the torso several times, the poor sailor was dead before he could scream. Water poured in through the forward and starboard gunports.

Cooper had been killed when he was thrown headlong into one his cannons upon impact. Judging from the way his head lay flopping down on his chest the impact had broke his neck. The timber Morison held on to snapped near the ceiling but was sturdy enough to remain upright; when the deck itself began fracturing a piece forced itself up and into the captain's calf, pinning him in place. However, Morison was able to hang on and survive the initial impact.

He glanced about the deck could tell by the tilt that the ship's nose had been forced down hard. Considering how close they had been to the bank, there was no doubt that the nose was wedged between what remained of the enemy's steamer and the river's floor. Only a few feet away the ceiling had collapsed over the starboard-most forward gun; the water was mostly red there.

Water was rising fast, but Morison didn't panic. They were in a river, not at sea. The water would rise only so far. "Secure the upper deck then start getting the wounded topside," Morison bellowed. Chaos still reigned and order was a long way off, but at least the men in the immediate vicinity seemed to be calming down.

Then Morison heard a sound that made his heart plummet.

A metallic explosion echoed from the open door that led down to the fire room below. The explosion was followed by a demonic hissing punctuated by pained screams.

Morison's eyes grew wide. "No," he muttered. He glanced down at his injured leg. The jagged plank penetrated into his leg; there was no way he could move on his own. He was doomed.

A wave of heat washed over the gun deck as a deadly mist rose from the engine room. Horribly burned men staggered out of the mist, their reddened flesh peeling from their bodies as they tried to flee.

"Abandon ship!" Morison yelled at the top of his lungs. "Ruptured boiler! Every man for himself!"

By the time the mysterious steamer slammed into the *Baton Rouge* all of the transports had raised their planks and were getting underway. But the transports took longer to build steam than the ironclad, and the civilian steamers longer than that.

Parker found himself stuck on board the *Gabby*. With the ironclad barely a hundred yards away, he heard the screams all too well when the boiler exploded. The deadly steam knew neither friend nor foe. The howls and yelps of the sharpshooters and crew of the enemy steamer soon joined the anguished cries of the sailors.

The second steamer stayed straight ahead and as soon as it was clear of the two dying giants, she started veering to the left, in the direction of the *Gabby*.

Most of the soldiers were with their companies on land, leaving behind only a handful to guard the transports. Of the few guards who were still onboard, many had witnessed horror of what had happened on the *Baton Rouge* and were now unceremoniously jumping overboard.

"Open fire at the steamer!" Parker called out to the few militiamen who remained on the deck.

Major Thompson came running from the staterooms, "What's happening?"

"They're using captured steamers," Parker said. He pointed toward the tangled mass in the river before them. "*Baton Rouge* is gone."

"My God," Thompson gasped.

The second steamer was still in the process of turning, but there was little doubt that the *Gabby* their intended target.

A scraggly looking man ran up to the rail beside them. Judging from his lack of a uniform, Parker assumed he was a member of the *Gabby*'s civilian crew. He turned to Parker and Thompson and said, "They goin' too fast. They gonna overshoot." With that, the crewman picked up a discarded rifle and fired at the approaching steamer.

Sure enough the steamer streaked by, passing so close to their stern that Parker felt someone could have reached out and touched her. The steamer tried to straighten out as whoever was at the wheel must have realized the mistake and attempted to steer into the next ship in line. The last minute change of course wasn't enough to keep the vessel from slamming into the bank. Her momentum forced her to skid along the shallows until her bow actually crashed into unforgiving trees lining the shore. A few beastmen sprang from the deck heading toward the woods, but they were cut down as soon as their feet touched the ground. Another handful of survivors jumped into the water and attempted to swim the river to the opposite bank.

"Fire into the water!" Parker called out, as he too found a discarded rifle and started firing at swimmers who were attempting to get away.

The few remaining crewmen—those who hadn't panicked and tried to swim—grabbed rifles and carbines and started making life miserable for the swimmers.

Cooney pulled himself out of the water on the far side of the river. His neck and shoulder ached from the collision and his thigh was burning from where he'd been shot while swimming the river, but he was alive. For several minutes he lay on the thin beach waiting for others to climb out of the water. None did. Perhaps they swam further downstream or maybe instead of crossing the river they tried to swim upstream, back to the camp.

Then again, maybe he was the only survivor.

He was about to drag himself further into the woods when he heard someone coughing near the water's edge. He squinted and could faintly see a shape clinging to a piece of floating debris near the bank.

"Over here," he said in a hoarse whisper.

The shape didn't move.

Cooney rose and loped back into the water, dragging his wounded leg behind him. He located the floating figure among a rough tangle of debris. At first he thought he'd found a wounded human, then he realized it was a dogbreed with all of its hair scalded off along with a considerable portion of its skin. How it had survived thus far he didn't know.

"Cooney? That you?"

"Yeah, it's me," he said, hesitantly reaching for the pitiful creature. He didn't know where he could touch it without having the skin come away in his hands. Finally he grabbed the debris his poor comrade was laying on and used it to pull him ashore.

"Never thought we'd get this far," the poor beast said.

Finally Cooney recognized the poor fellow as Scratch, one

of his mates from his days shoveling coal.

"We did it, though," Cooney replied.

Scratch coughed again. "They're beautiful."

"What is Scratch?"

"The stars...there's...so many…"

Scratch was gone.

Cooney gently pushed his old friend back into the river. He turned and limped inland.

Chapter 22

IT WAS ANOTHER two hours before the steamers finished fishing what was left of the *Baton Rouge*'s crew out of the river. Ninety-seven of her one-hundred-and-fifty-five man crew had died either in the collision or when the boiler ruptured shortly thereafter. Of the survivors, over half were so terribly scalded that they wouldn't survive to see sunrise. All in all, there would be less than two dozen survivors. Still, there was enough wounded and dying to require the transfer of all surgeons from both regiments to the Isabella as they converted her to a temporary hospital ship.

Everyone assumed the beastmen didn't have anymore steamers at their disposal, but there was no way to know for sure. With no gunboats, the small group of ships had to do what they could for defense for the rest of the night. The best they could manage was to position the *John F. Roe* in the river with steam up. With only one gun and no ram, the transport would be hard pressed against any attack, so Haiber assigned a company from his regiment to serve on the ship as sharpshooters.

When the *Gabby* was finally tied off at the bank it was all Parker could do to keep from running down the plank. He had seen enough for one night and didn't care if he ever set foot on a steamer again. However, he only made it halfway to shore when a voice called out from behind him.

"Sergeant, might I have a word with you?"

Parker recognized Colonel Cole's southern accented drawl and almost kept walking. Military discipline overcame personal feelings. He stopped in his tracks and turned to face the old Colonel.

Cole stood with his hand on the rail for support, his cheeks were frail and thin. It looked as though he had lost as much as ten pounds since the expedition began only a couple weeks ago—and he had been rail-thin then. Still, Parker found it hard to have any sympathy for the man who had been responsible for the parley fiasco which had almost cost him his life.

The old colonel motioned for Parker to come closer.

Parker nodded and walked back up the plank, then stood ridged before the colonel.

"At ease, sergeant. I'm worried about Haiber," Cole said as soon as Parker was close enough were they could talk without being overheard. "Tomorrow's going to be a rough affair now that we don't have the *Baton Rouge* for support."

Cole paused, apparently hoping Parker would inject something, but the sergeant held his tongue. He was at ease, yet he stood there rigid, as if he was still at attention.

"Can Haiber lead his regiment?" Cole asked finally.

"He was trained at West Point and has commanded the regiment for four months now."

"That's not what I'm asking."

Parker was silent for a moment before saying, "Permission to speak freely, sir."

"Granted."

"Colonel Haiber is no worse than the rest of the leadership of this expedition."

Cole's cheeks reddened but he didn't reply.

"Is that all, sir?"

"No, it most certainly is not," Cole said, his voice stern. "Sergeant, I could care less if you have a problem with me, but we both have a heavy task ahead of us tomorrow and right now we don't have time for personal feelings to get in the way. Back in Mexico I didn't take kindly to petty sniping from officers and I'll be damned if I'm going to take it from a sergeant. Understand?"

"Yes, sir," Parker said crisply.

"Tomorrow a lot of people are going to die and I don't want their blood on my hands because I let an incompetent officer lead half of my command. Now, I'm asking you a question, sergeant and I'm asking you one soldier to another—can Haiber lead his regiment?"

"Yes, sir," Parker replied without hesitation.

"Dismissed," Cole said and without another word he turned and walked away.

Parker felt his heart sink as he made his way back down the plank. He hoped he was right about Haiber.

"You wanted to see me, sir?" Thompson said, poking his head through the door to Cole's stateroom.

The lantern in the room was burning dim and the candle on the colonel's small, tidy desk had been snuffed out. Cole sat in a chair, looking out a porthole. He motioned for Thompson to come in, but didn't turn from the view outside.

Thompson stepped in the small room, closed the door behind him, but remained standing.

Cole turned from the window and motioned to a chair. "Have a seat."

Thompson took a seat across from the small desk while the colonel concentrated on lighting a match with his shaking hands. Finally bringing a flame to the match he carefully used it to light the candle on his desk. All of this took a surprising amount of time and concentration. It appeared as though the colonel's condition was getting worse. Thompson felt an attachment that was more than a subordinate staff officer; he felt Colonel Cole was a friend. Friends were supposed to enquire about the health of their companions. Thompson felt like he should saying something, but what would he say? The colonel was a proud man and he might take a question on his health the wrong way. Not that Cole would lose his temper, just that it might quietly injure the old man's spirits.

Thompson held his tongue, but it didn't matter. Cole read the look on his face and smiled wanly, "I'm not well, my dear Thompson."

"You do look a little pale around the gills, sir," Thompson said cautiously.

"I knew I was getting worse when we set out, but there was no way I could step down. When you've seen men ride into battle with more blood on their coats than they have in their veins it's hard to complain of illness on the eve of a battle."

Unsure of what to say, Thompson simply nodded.

"Let me cut to the chase," Cole said, "I'm still sharp enough to draw up a battle plan, but I don't think there's enough left in me to carry it out."

"I don't understand."

"You're going to have to lead the militia into battle tomorrow."

Thompson shifted uncomfortably in his chair. He smiled nervously and said, "I'm not so sure I'm cut out for command, sir."

"You are, or I wouldn't have recommended you for Lieutenant-Colonel," Cole said flatly.

"Lieutenant-Colonel's one thing, sir. Commanding the regiment's another. I just don't think I've got what it takes."

"You knew when you were promoted that you'd be second in command of the regiment and you knew I had my hands full running the expedition."

Thompson nodded, his face still stretched in a nervous smile. "Behind the scenes, sure. I can handle that. But actually leading the men into battle?" He shook his head, "I just don't think I can do it."

Cole was silent and for a second Thompson began to think he may have actually won the argument. Then the old colonel spoke again, "I'm not going to lie to you; it ain't easy." He turned and gazed out the porthole again, his eyes fixed on the trees only a few feet away, but his mind was thousands of miles into the past.

"There's this young lady back home, her name's Mildred Campbell. She's got three boys, eldest's probably gettin' close to ten by now. I see them up town quite often," still looking out the window, he smiled distantly, "Those boys're a handful. Only two years between the oldest and the youngest.

"Her husband served under me in the French and Mexican war. He came from a poor family, but a good one; I knew his father well. He enlisted in my old regiment, the 7th Arkansas, served under me throughout the war. He was a good soldier. Made corporal within a few months and I would have given him sergeant stripes, but I didn't want anyone to think I was showing favors to a hometown boy. Of course he was a volunteer and I was a general of volunteers, so we spoke when our paths crossed but I didn't see him quite as often as I had back home.

"I don't need to tell you how rough things got at Palo Gaucho," Cole said with a nod toward Thompson's missing arm. "It was the hardest fight we'd see in the entire war and my brigade was in thick of it. Hell, the papers called me the Rock of Palo Gaucho, but after my second horse was shot out from under me I couldn't find a third; all I did was stay behind the main line telling the shirkers to get back to the front.

"That's when I saw him ambling to the rear. He'd taken one in the leg, but it wasn't bad. I could tell he just wanted out of there. Hell, we all did." Cole sighed heavily. "I called him down in front of everyone. Told him how I knew his father and that his father would fall over dead if he could see his only boy walking away from a fight with his tail tucked between his legs. I asked him what his pretty little wife would think if he came knocking on her door with the brand of a coward burned into his cheek. I asked him how he would explain that to those three boys of his.

"You could see the hurt all over his face. He turned and went back to the line and a good number of men who had been hiding about went with him. They felt if I'd threaten to brand the son of an old friend I was apt to shoot them on the spot.

"I didn't see it happen, but they told me he never even got to fire another shot. As soon as he got in line a French bullet hit him in the neck. He died thrashing on the ground gasping for air.

Cole turned from the window and looked into Thompson's eyes. "I lied to that boy. His wife wouldn't have given a damn if he'd come home a coward, she just wanted him to come home. His daddy might have put on a show to save face in the community, but he would have felt the same way. And those boys..." Cole closed his eyes and slowly shook his head, "A dead daddy's pride doesn't teach a boy to fish on a cool summer day."

"Every time I see Mrs. Campbell she tells me how proud her husband was to serve under me. How highly he spoke of me in all of his letters, but, you know what? She never can bring herself to look me in the eyes. I know deep inside she's thinking how her husband went to war under my care and I failed to bring him home to her. Hell, truth be known you might say I killed the boy."

Cole lowered his head and paused again. Thompson was moved by the story, but he certainly didn't see how this was helping him decide to take command. In fact, the old man had just lined out exactly the reasons why he didn't want the responsibility.

Then Cole raised his head and looked Thompson square in the eyes once more and said, "There's not a day that goes by that I don't think of that boy or one of the other thousands that went to their grave following me into battle. But I don't regret it. Not one bit. I did the right thing. If I hadn't told those boys to hold the line we might not have carried the day and if we hadn't carried the day we would have just had to do it all over again and there would have been even more widows back home. A good leader doesn't fight for the flags and the glory. A good leader does his job because if he doesn't someone else will step into his place and that someone might not know what the hell they're doing. That's why you're the perfect man for the job. I know you; you could care less about what the papers say, you just want to do your job and do it right."

"Well, sure," Thompson said finally, "but I don't have the experience."

"You have plenty."

Thompson started to protest, but while he could think of hundreds of excuses, truth be known, he couldn't think of anyone else to suggest in his place.

"Besides," Cole added, his former softness gone like it had never been there. "It's not a request; it's an order. You will command the Arkansas militia regiment in tomorrow's engagement."

Thompson sighed. That settled it then.

"This brings us to one pressing issue."

This time, Thompson wasn't caught off guard. He knew exactly what the Colonel wanted to talk about. "Jones," he said.

"Exactly. What do we do about Captain Jones. He's an ass, but he's charmed the men of Company A into thinking he's some sort of idol; they worship him. I spoke to the lieutenant in Company A; they say the men won't go into action unless Jones leads them. Company A has more Mexican War veterans than all the other companies combined," he said. "Not only that, but they're the only militia company with modern arms."

Despite the fact that he had no idea he would be taking over the regiment, Thompson had fully expected Cole to ask him his opinion on this matter. He had spent some time thinking of the situation. Jones was the type of man who was fueled by a deep and burning hatred and his men seemed to feed off of that hatred; they loved him. Thompson's first impulse was to leave Jones locked up, but, as much as he hated the man, if living with Jones meant the difference between having the best one-hundred men in his regiment in the line or under arrest for dereliction of duty, then Jones was an asset.

"I say we let him out," Thompson said.

Cole raised his eyebrows.

"We need A Company in the line tomorrow. We're going to need every man we can get our hands on, but we *really* need A Company."

Cole nodded. "That settles it then. We'll let him out first thing in the morning. I think we should let him stay another night under guard though. It's killing him that he might miss the big show and it may do him some good to spend the night worrying about whether he'll be part of it or not."

"Agreed."

Cole straightened in his chair. "Now, if you would be so kind as to send a messenger for Colonel Haiber. I want to meet with the two of you to discuss tomorrow's battle plan."

Unlike the previous councils which had been held in the *Baton Rouge*'s spacious officer's mess or on the upper deck of the *Gabby*, this meeting was held in Colonel Cole's stateroom. The small table that had been serving as the colonel's desk sat in the middle of the room with Thompson's small, yet detailed map of the enemy's position spread on the surface. An extra chair had been brought in, bringing the grand total to three chairs around the small table. Still, the room felt cramped.

Cole cut to the chase. "The enemy wants us to attack here," he said, using his finger to indicate the most direct approach, coming along the shoreline and up the hill. "And that's exactly what I plan on doing."

Haiber squinted as he pored over the map, "Casualties will be high if we hit them dead on. It might have worked when he had the Navy's big guns backing us up, but now I just don't know if we can do it."

"You won't have to worry about this approach. That'll be Thompson's job. Roughly an hour after daybreak he's to take the Militia Regiment and move out in what our enemy will believe will be a frontal assault, but will, in fact, only be a diversion. He will stop at the foot of the hill and draw them into a firefight. Meanwhile, your regiment will have already begun on a wide flanking maneuver." Cole began tracing the second route on the map as he spoke. "You will move through the woods directly ahead of our current position coming in on the enemy's flank."

Haiber raised his eyebrows, it was bold but simple. However, he could see several problems with the plan, so he spoke up, "The enemy has proven themselves quite adept at harassing us at every corner. What makes you think our column won't come under heavy fire as we perform such a long flanking maneuver so near the enemy's main base of operations?"

"Oh, I have little doubt you will come under fire. That's why I suggest you cover the ground in line or in separate columns of companies arranged in line."

"Might work, but covering that much ground in such a short time won't be easy."

"I never said it would be. And timing is of the essence. Thompson will be engaged in an open firefight with an entrenched enemy. If you leave him exposed too long, his men will break."

Rather than addressing Cole, Haiber turned to Thompson. "We won't let you down."

Cole turned to Thompson. "And your job won't be as cut and dried as it sounds. You've got to make sure that you draw the enemy's attention away from their flank. If your diversion fails to pull sufficient forces away, Haiber here will be charging headlong into a wall of lead."

Thompson swallowed hard against the butterflies in his stomach. He turned to Haiber. Not trusting his voice to words, he extended his hand. Haiber took it.

"All right then," Cole said, "Get back to your units. Try to get a little sleep if you can, but be sure and have your regiments up and moving at first light."

Chapter 23

IT WAS MORNING, but the sun had yet to make its way around from the other side of the planet. It was still another hour before the eastern sky would begin to glow and yet another hour before the sun would begin ascending through the trees.

Joshua Jenkins sat near the dying campfire with his drum in his lap. While they were at Montgomery Point there had only been two drummer boys in the Arkansas militia, and when Brandon Ruggles started got a serious case of the crud before they even started up river Joshua knew he would be the only one. Brandon was twelve years old, only two years older than Joshua, so it was nice having someone around close to his age, but Joshua had found that he was actually glad when Brandon left. The idea of being the only drummer in the whole regiment thrilled Joshua to no end. Just wait until the boys back at school heard that he, and he alone, had drummed the men into battle.

Joshua placed his ear to the drumhead and softly tapped the head with one of his sticks. It just didn't sound right. He had tightened the drum yesterday, but it seemed like it already needed tightened again. Maybe it was the damp weather. With his ear still pressed to the drum, he tapped the drumhead again.

"Ain't gonna do no good," a hoarse voice croaked from under a nearby blanket.

Joshua raised his head so fast he almost spilled his drum out of his lap, which certainly would have made more noise that his light tapping. Just a few feet away, on the other side of the campfire, a thin, grey-bearded old man swung his calloused feet out from under the blanket and pointed them at the fire.

"I'm sorry Sergeant Thayer," Joshua said, "I sure didn't mean to wake you."

"I's already up," Thayer drawled.

Joshua spun his drum around and once again, ever so lightly, he tested it with a stick.

Thayer smiled. "I'm tellin' you. It ain't gonna do no good," He said, his voice hushed to a half whisper. "I fought in Mexico, seen dozens of battles, and I ain't never seen a drummer boy who thought his drum sounded right the day before a battle. It's called the jitters."

The little boy sat up bolt straight. "I ain't yeller, if that's what you're sayin'," he said, his voice bold and defensive, yet still hushed so as not to wake the rest of the soldiers sleeping near the fire.

Thayer smiled wanly. "I didn't say you's yeller. I said you had the jitters. They ain't the same thing. Gabriel would swear his horn wasn't carryin' the right tune if he tried it before a fight, and he stood up to Ol' Scratch."

Joshua's thin eyebrows wrinkled. He didn't understand.

Thayer leaned into the fire, cupped his hand to his ear, and motioned around them "Listen, and tell me what you hear."

Joshua listened a while and said, "Crickets, a couple frogs out by the river."

His hand still cupped to his ear, Thayer asked, "Now tell me what you *don't* hear?"

Joshua was really confused now. In fact, he was beginning to think old Thayer was making fun.

"I'll tell you," Thayer said as he removed his hand from his ear and leaned back away from the fire, "Snoring."

"Huh?"

"Snoring. Oh, there's a little, but not as much racket as there usually is in camp. Most of the boys out there ain't sleeping and those who are ain't sleeping very hard. They got the jitters too, but they ain't got no drum they can tune. So they lay there, some talkin' to God, some thinkin' about their families, some tryin' not to think at all. But every man out there that's got a lick of sense has got the jitters."

"What about you?" Joshua asked, "You been in more fights than George Washington."

"Son, I got the jitters somethin' terrible, or I wouldn't be up right now."

Joshua thought about this for a moment, then set the drum aside. Old Sergeant Thayer was right, there was no way to make it sound perfect. He started to ask the old sergeant something else, but Thayer nodded into the night and said, "Officer on the prowl. You best at least act like your getting some sleep."

Thayer spun his feet back under the blanket and lay his head down, while Joshua lay on his side, drew his knees to his chest and thought of his mother.

Thompson walked slowly and quietly through the camp. The men were mostly still and quiet, but he was surprised at how many eyes glanced back at him as he walked by. Near a campfire up ahead he saw the regimental drummer trying his best to tune his drum without waking anyone. Thompson didn't approach. He watched the boy from the darkness. He watched as an old soldier joined the boy at the fire. He couldn't hear what was said, but he imagined the old veteran was giving words of advice to the youngster. Only a few minutes into the conversation the sergeant noticed Thompson standing away from the fire. The conversation ended immediately.

Thompson stayed long enough to watch as the boy lay his drum aside and curled into a ball for warmth. A chill came over him as he realized that this boy's life would be in his hands tomorrow. He wished more than anything that he could go back to just being a cartographer, or better yet go all the way back to when he was a civilian surveyor in Southern Arkansas. Back when he had two arms and long before he had ever heard the roar of a cannon.

Thompson turned and started back to the river. He located his makeshift desk, a camp stool sitting next to an empty wooden keg. He took a map out of his pocket, a small, quickly sketched copy of the map he made yesterday, placed it on the makeshift desk and slowly he began moving his finger along the ink lines that made up the edge of the river until he reached the bottom of the hill. He then raised his head and looked up the river. The hill itself was obscured by the bend, and the shoreline ahead was barely visible in the darkness. He turned back to the map and retraced the approach again. For a second he was tempted to return to Cole's stateroom and ask the colonel if he could have a look at his original map, but he knew he was just worrying—fretting as Cole would have said.

He slowly folded the tiny map, no easy task for a man with only one arm, then placed it in his coat pocket. He rose from his chair and started walking through the camp again.

It was just a fleeting thought, but somewhere in the back of his mind he felt the urge to simply run away, to throw away his blue officer's coat and run back to Southern Arkansas and let someone else shoulder this burden.

But who? Jones? Thompson snorted at the thought. Jones might be a good company commander, but it takes more than hatred to command a regiment.

No, this was his burden and he would have to bear it.

Captain Jones's knuckles were white and his teeth were clenched as he watched out the small room's only porthole.

Today would be the day they had been waiting for and here he was, the only active Regular Army officer in the expedition. Well, the only active officer who wasn't a damned Negro wearing white skin. That damn Haiber didn't deserve his commission and nor did any of the other officers who stooped to serving in that godforsaken Colored Regiment.

And those worthless bastards would be fighting while Jones was cramped in this damn little room.

Jones swore and spun on his heels and began pacing the room once more. He kept telling himself that it was all for the better, that Cole and Haiber would make such a mess of this fight that he was better off not having his name attached to it. In fact, in the wake of the disaster he might come off smelling like roses since he would freely tell anyone who listened that he had been against the way the expedition had been run from the get-go.

He stopped at the porthole and clenched his fists again.

None of that mattered, and he knew it. There was going to be a fight and he wasn't going to be part of it.

Reginald Jones hadn't always been a fighter. When he was a child he had been quite the momma's boy, but all that had changed one fine summer afternoon. His older brother and his cousin tormented him when he was young, but one day he had turned the tables on them. Jones still recalled with pride how he found an equalizer in the form of an axe handle. He beat both boys until they were unconscious; then he just kept on beating them. It had taken weeks for his brother to recover and his and his cousin never fully did. His mother had been horrified, but Jones still recalled the thrill, the power, of that first fight.

Later Jones had been expelled from West Point for assaulting a fellow cadet. By then he didn't need an axe handle, his fists worked just fine. He probably could have kissed his military career goodbye if the French and Mexican War hadn't brought up the need for young, aggressive officers. Still, his penchant for fighting made his ascension in the ranks a slow one.

They just didn't understand. He was a fighter and that's what the Army needed.

A knock came at the door.

"What?" Jones snapped.

"Captain, it's Corporal Fontaine," the voice whispered.

Jones couldn't put a face on him, but the name rang a bell.

"From your company," the voice added in a whisper.

Jones's temper flared. He wanted to yell that his company was Company I of the 5th Regular Infantry, currently stationed on the Canadian border. The bunch of misfits that made up Company A of the only militia regiment in the entire state of Arkansas had been a temporary pain in the ass, but they were someone else's problem now. Instead, he gritted his teeth and growled, "What do you want, corporal?"

Apparently not noticing the venom in the Captain's voice, Fontaine still sounded eager and excited when he whispered, "I got good news. I heard they gonna let you out so you can lead us into battle."

A smile slowly crept across Jones's face. He wouldn't be missing the fight after all.

Haiber watched intently as the last of the horses made its way down the plank. He knew the men could unload the horses without his help, but he needed something to occupy his mind.

The *Anne Marie*'s hold was designed to carry horses and horse fodder as well as the supplies and stores for her human cargo. However, most of her below deck stables were currently occupied by ammunition, spare rifles, medical supplies and barrels of hard tack. That is, all except a handful of stalls near the back. There were five horses in all, one for the colonel of the 13th Colored and another for the lieutenant-colonel. Haiber also insisted on three extra mounts, one for his chief of staff and two for the messengers that would be attached during combat. Unlike the popular notion of a lazy officer who had rather ride than walk, who used his mount as a sort of status symbol that kept him above the common rabble, these horses served a very important role. Unlike a company commander, who was expected to stay with his company throughout the battle, the upper echelon officers might be needed at any given location throughout the regiment. Haiber intended to stay as mobile as possible during the battle.

Stuffed in tiny unfamiliar stalls for days on end, the horses were more than anxious to get out for a breath fresh air. Haiber watched as the last horse was lead down the *Anne Marie*'s ramp during the predawn hours. One horse had already reared on its way down, causing it and one of the handlers to take an unscheduled bath. Luckily neither man nor beast was hurt.

Haiber smiled as he approached his horse, a dark roan stallion named Ironwood.

"Woody, old boy, it's been a while," Haiber said softly as he ran his hand up the horse's neck.

Haiber didn't see Parker approach, but he heard him clear his throat. Horses made the sergeant nervous. There hadn't been any horses back in the Freeland, only a few scrawny mules and they were used for pulling plows and carts. Over the years in the Army he had become somewhat accustomed to the big beasts, but he only rode them when it was absolutely necessary.

"Yes, sergeant?" Haiber asked.

"Perhaps I should walk with the boys today," he said cautiously.

"No. Today I'm going to have to be everywhere at once, and

you're going to be with me."

Parker turned and walked away without replying.

Haiber didn't mind. He was enjoying the company of an old friend.

As a child his famous senator grandfather had presented him with a pony named Whig on his ninth birthday, but he didn't have a real horse until he was sixteen. Nevertheless, he proved to be a natural equestrian. It was a trait that came as something of a shock at West Point. Even though many of the Southern cadets had been riding almost since they could walk Haiber had managed to rise to the top of his class in the field. In fact, he would have signed on for cavalry if there had been a Colored cavalry regiment in the Army at the time.

Woody pawed the ground nervously.

"Easy, boy," Haiber said, he fished a carrot out of his pocket and gave presented it to the horse who eagerly bit it in half. "Save your energy. Today's going to be a hard day."

Parker followed the light of the campfire away from the river and into the woods. Barely fifty feet into the trees he found a cluster of blanket-covered bodies situated around the last glowing embers of last night's campfire. The sergeant quietly lowered himself down at the foot of a tree. He leaned forward and rested his head in his hands but he knew he wasn't going to get any sleep tonight.

A soldier peered from under the cover of a nearby blanket. "Um, sergeant," the voice whispered hesitantly.

"Yes, Micah?" Parker said without looking up. As with just about all of his boys he could not only recognize their face, but he could recognize them by their voice. Parker recalled Micah's family back home and what kind of boy he'd been on the Freeland. Although his father had been prone to drink too much, Micah Yates came from a good family. He had been quiet boy, perhaps a bit slow, but he was a good kid. He recalled that Micah had an uncanny knack for catching catfish, which was quite an asset in a near-starving community. Micah's family had taught him well; he never failed to share his catch with the less fortune members of the community.

"I can't sleep, sergeant," Micah said, his voice scarcely louder than a whisper.

"What do you want me to do about it? Sing to you?"

Hushed laughter sounded from under several nearby blankets. Obviously Micah wasn't the only soldier unable to sleep.

"Um, no, suh," Micah whispered, "I's just wonderin' if ... Well, seeings I can't sleep nohow maybe I could swap out with someone on the picket line and they could get a little shuteye."

The offer didn't come as a surprise, Micah had always been a thoughtful boy. Parker thought about it for a while, then said, "No, Micah, I don't think they would have any better luck sleeping than you are. Just lay still and rest as best you can."

Then Parker tried to follow his own advice. He closed his eyes and tried to even his breathing. Maybe, just maybe, he could coax himself into sleeping at least a few minutes.

He sat at the base of the tree for no more than five minutes before he was up, pacing the camp once again.

Cole's legs ached and he was short of breath; still, he couldn't sit in his stateroom and stare at the walls any longer. He braced himself and slowly rose to his feet. Once he was standing he waited until he was sure his feet weren't going to give way. His legs always seemed weaker when he tried to rise at night, but tonight they seemed worse than ever. The last thing he wanted to fall once he was outside of his room; soldiers were superstitious lot and those who saw him take a spill might take it as a bad omen.

As soon as his feet were steady, or at least as steady as they had been over the last few days, Cole put on his coat. Once out the door he started down the hall toward the deck.

The guard at the end of the hall turned and saluted. He then propped his rifle against the wall and instinctively reached out as any man with a proper upbringing might reach out to help the elderly. The soldier caught himself and flushed red. He suddenly seemed unsure what was appropriate—should he retrieve his rifle and return to attention, apologizing for treating his commanding officer like a doddering old man, or go with his first impulse and help the feeble gentleman through the door.

Cole saw the soldier's predicament and respected it for what it was. "My old legs ain't what they used to be," he said with a friendly smile.

The poor soldier still seemed confused. He wasn't sure how to reply.

Cole nodded at a tin cup on the rail in front of the soldier. "Coffee?"

"Yes, suh."

"You mind fetching me a cup?"

"No, suh, not at all. Someone brought me this here cup from camp, but I hear they got some in the pilothouse."

"Either is fine," Cole said.

As soon as the soldier left Cole stepped to the edge of the deck and leaned against the rail. He was lost in his thoughts when Dog nudged his leg and whined.

"Yeah, old friend," Cole said, "I feel it, too."

Longtooth stood alone near the river's edge, gazing at his own reflection in the water below. When he was alone he often wondered things like whether he was more dog or man at heart, what it was like to be human, what his mother had been like, and what would his life have been like if he had never undergone the alteration? Today he just gazed into the water and wondered how it had ever come to this.

He had never wanted to be a leader. Oh, sure there was a time when his blood was up and he wanted revenge, but that emotion had been borne of hatred and fear. Deep inside, all he ever wanted was a simple life with no more worries than what the crops would yield in the coming year. Now he was the leader of thousands, and quite possibly the idol of tens of thousands, maybe more. In fact, it was quite possible— probable, in fact—that he was known to more than just those of his kind inside their small community. It was conceivable that the future of his entire race, hundreds of thousands of souls, rested on his weary shoulders. Others might revel in the thought that they had risen from nowhere to take such a central role in the lives of their people, but not Longtooth; he detested it. However, he had no choice in the matter. The cards had been dealt and there was nothing he could do but play his hand to the end. It was far too late into the game to fold and walk away.

Longtooth turned east and could see the horizon already had a faint bluish glow to it. Sunrise wouldn't be long in coming.

He sighed as he turned and started back up the hill. This fight would be different than the two before—today everything hung in the balance.

Chapter 24

COLONEL HAIBER, Lieutenant-Colonel Santiago, Major Rogers and the regimental surgeon, and all ten company commanders stood around a recently rekindled campfire just before sunrise. Despite the fact that the 13th Colored Regiment was composed entirely of black enlisted men, Sergeant Parker found that, as usual, he was the only black man at the meeting. Normally when Haiber called the company commanders together the chatter was nonstop as the captains talked among themselves, in a subtle yet noticeable rebellion against their young colonel's command. Today was different. Parker thought that some of this might have to do with the fact that in less than an hour they would be going into battle, but he had to admit that Haiber was at least partially responsible for the change. While he hadn't quite turned into a ramrod leader with a fire and brimstone demeanor, he had suddenly become remarkably no-nonsense. And not like his old businesslike, by-the-books self. He wasn't sheepishly reading from the manuals—today, for the first time since he'd made colonel, he wasn't just commanding the regiment, he was *leading* the regiment.

"Listen and listen good," Haiber said, his voice high and strained, but still holding a commanding air. "We'll step off at sunrise. So you'll need to get your men into line as soon as you return to your commands. Once we move, we've got to move fast. As soon as we're in line we'll wheel left, pivoting on Company K. Once we're in position we'll dress the regiment. We'll have to work fast. This will be the last time we'll dress our lines until we prepare to charge the enemy's main line, so we'll have to be precise as well. Just move fast and rely on your sergeants to work the details, don't try to do everything yourself."

Haiber paused and glanced around the circle of officers, probably to make sure everyone caught that last point. Some of the company commanders, all of whom were white, had little faith in their sergeants, all of whom were black, but today they had no choice but to work together. As for Parker, he had more faith in the sergeants and corporals of this regiment than he did the officers if for no other reason because they knew they'd have to answer to him if they fouled things up.

Haiber continued, "Once we step off again we'll move straight ahead. The underbrush isn't heavy here, but it's still thick enough so that you'll only be able to see the company to your immediate left and right. Just keep straight ahead and stay in line as best you can, dressing with the company on your right." He nodded toward the Lieutenant-Colonel, "Santiago, you will be on our right flank with K Company today. You'll keep the tempo and watch the progress. If K Company gets a little ahead it won't be a problem since we've got to wheel right again before we emerge from the woods, but if you fall behind it could set us back as much as a half an hour and that could be disastrous."

"You can count on me, sir," Santiago.

Haiber nodded briefly and continued addressing the company commanders, "We're probably going to be under light skirmish fire the whole way, but this engagement is on a strict time-table. We must not stop to engage the enemy. No one, and I mean on one, is to return fire."

"Excuse me," Captain Griffith, commander of C Company said, "but what if we come up on a formed battle line?"

Haiber nodded, this was a good question, one that he planned on addressing but the fact that Griffith brought it to his attention meant the captain was thinking on his toes. "That would be perfect, but it's not going to happen. If the enemy decided to give us battle in the woods, then we won't have to force them out of their trenches. Colonel Cole says the enemy doesn't have the manpower to face us in the open and in the trenches."

"What if he's wrong?" Captain Clarke of G Company asked. "His main source is one spy who's now dead and whatever the enemy commander told Sergeant Parker while he was captured, neither are exactly the best sources."

Parker tensed but said nothing. In truth, he too was worried that Longtooth might be using him to spread misinformation. "Captain, your job is to follow orders, not question them," Haiber said coldly. He scanned the faces of the other officers to see if anyone else had something to say. They didn't. "Lieutenant-Colonel Thompson was very thorough in his mapping of the enemy position. I saw this map myself and judging by the size of their camp, they can't have more than two-thousand soldiers, and the number is probably closer to fifteen hundred. Sure, they might have a second camp hidden in the swamp, and maybe there's ten-thousand British Grenadiers hiding up in the trees, but that's not our concern. We step off in less than an hour and I will not spend another second discussing problems that are out of our hands. Is that clear?"

Some muttered their answer and some spoke it proudly, but every officer present replied, "Yes, sir."

Parker was impressed. Clarke still seemed to be stewing over the sharp rebuttal, but for once the majority, if not all, of the company commanders seemed to be behind their colonel.

Haiber continued, "Near the edge of the woods we'll have to perform another wheel to the left. We'll probably be taking serious skirmish fire at this point, so we'll have to move fast.

We'll pivot on A Company again. After that we'll move to the edge of the woods and dress the regiment before we step into the open. Thompson was unable to get a good look at the woods from his position in the river, but he said that judging from the old maps in his possession we should have plenty of room to form up, but we won't quite have enough room to face the enemy before exiting the woods."

Haiber took a deep breath, "And this is where it gets tricky."

Some of the captains exchanged glances with one another in disbelief. The instructions the colonel had already told them were complex enough.

"We'll move out of the woods at route step, but to turn to face the enemy we'll have to wheel left a third time, this time while under the fire of the enemy line. I know what some of you are thinking, 'why not use a shorter line and attack in two waves?' I considered this, but I think we'd be better off if we hit them all at once, in one solid line. Not only that, but I plan on halting the line to deliver a volley at one-hundred yards before we charge." Haiber paused, then said, "Any questions?"

The officers exchanged glances back and forth again, but no one spoke.

"It sounds confusing, but I'll be there the whole time. I'm going to stay mounted and my messengers and staff will be mounted, so I'll be able to address any situation that arises along the length of the line."

Most of the officers seemed to accept this, and Parker could tell that a few even seemed genuinely excited. Haiber was asking a lot from everybody, but now everybody knew their role.

Captain Clarke, however, couldn't keep his peace. He was a young, proud officer from a well-connected Georgian family. He was serving in a Colored regiment until a more prestigious position opened up elsewhere, and he was none too fond of his regimental colonel. "Colonel, sir," he said, "Let me see if I get this straight. We're going to have wheel twice in less-than-optimal terrain, while under skirmish fire. Advance against opposition from bushwhackers without returning fire. Charge out of the woods oblique to the enemy line, wheel again while under fire of the main enemy position, move to within one-hundred yards, stop, deliver a volley, then charge home against an entrenched enemy."

"Yes, that's exactly what we will be doing today. Glad to see you were paying attention, captain," Haiber replied.

Clarke snorted. "This is outrageous. Europe's finest couldn't pull off such a complex series of maneuvers, and this regiment isn't exactly the Coldstream Guards."

A couple of the captains hesitantly nodded in agreement.

Parker was a good sergeant, so he generally knew when to speak and when not to speak. But he took a tremendous amount of pride in his boys. Before discipline could catch his tongue, he turned to Haiber and said, "Excuse me, sir, but the men in this regiment are more than up to the task. That is, if the officers are."

"That's enough, sergeant," Haiber said bluntly before turning to Clarke. "You've heard the orders. If you don't think you can follow them I'll find someone who can."

Clarke drew himself up, but didn't reply.

Haiber then dismissed the captains so they could start getting their companies in line. Santiago also left so he could join the right flank. As soon as they were out of earshot, Haiber pulled Major Rogers aside. "I want you to follow Clarke back to his company. He's a grumbler and that's something the men don't need to hear this morning."

Rogers nodded in agreement.

"If he complains in front of the men, pull him aside and give him a warning. If he persists send him to the rear under guard and take his place in command of the company."

Rogers smiled but Parker could tell the major was nervous. He had more rank and experience than Clarke, but that didn't always mean anything when it came to the pecking order in the Army. Clarke had good blood and connections, Rogers came from a dirt poor family in Eastern Kentucky.

"He won't go quietly, sir," Rogers said, "He's a proud man."

"I'll give you a written order to dismiss him at your discretion. Strip him of rank and arrest him if you have to. Try to do it as discretely as possible, but if he's not going to follow orders, then he's not going to lead a company of my boys."

"Yes, sir," Rogers replied and he stood by while Haiber jotted down a quick order to take with him if he needed it.

Parker couldn't conceal his smile. Haiber had always referred to the soldiers as 'the men'. It seemed odd to hear the young colonel refer to the soldiers, most of which were no younger than he was, as his boys. This was what Parker always called them and it warmed his heart to hear Haiber refer to them the same way.

As soon as Rogers was gone, Parker turned to Haiber and said, "If it's all the same to you, I'm going to walk the line and make sure the boys are up and ready this morning."

Haiber agreed, but before Parker left he added, "Mount up, though."

"Sir?"

"You can cover more ground that way. And you might as well start getting used to the saddle if you're going to keep up with me today."

"Yes, sir."

Mouser watched from the bushes as the line of soldiers formed less than fifty yards away. He had let Longtooth down yesterday back on the river. Even before Clover Bend, Longtooth had faith in him even when no one else did, and Mouser always felt as though he was trying to live up to his expectations. And sometimes maybe he just tried too hard.

This time would be different. He only had barely fifty scouts left, but that was more than enough. He had carefully placed each scout and given them fallback positions all long the enemy's likely line of approach. Today they would make the enemy bleed. In fact, considering the ground the humans had to cover, he imagined he could cause enough casualties to break the whole lot of them before they even set their eyes on Longtooth's main line. That would more than make up for yesterday's mishap.

He had ordered the scouts to let the enemy form up before they started shooting; it would be easier to hit them once they were formed into a solid line. To make sure no one fired out of turn, he ordered them to wait until he fired the first shot.

Mouser slowly leveled his rifle at the line of soldiers ahead. He took careful aim at a man in the front row and squeezed the trigger.

The first shot rang out just before the regiment began its first wheel right and a soldier near the center of the line fell with a bullet between his eyes. This shot was followed by about a dozen more, then the first group of bushwhackers withdrew behind another group which waited under cover as the soldiers approached. Another rattle of about a dozen shots fired not long after the regiment completed the wheel and started forward. From then on the firing seemed almost constant. The soldiers pressed forward, trying their best to keep up momentum. If they could keep moving the enemy would have less time to reload and fire again, but, dealing with underbrush and mud as well as bullets, this was easier said than done.

Parker temporarily left Haiber's side so he could ride closer to the line. He watched as his boys bravely plunged forward into the woods, taking casualties at a startlingly high rate.

A company sergeant turned to Parker, "We ain't gonna be able to keep this up."

"Keep moving. Stay on their heels and they won't be able to reload."

The sergeant shook his head. "They smarter than that. They working in teams, one loads while another shoots. And we all lined up so they can't miss."

As if to accent the problem a nearby soldier fell dropped with a bullet to his chest. Those close to him had seen enough. They stopped and fired back, but their attacker had already disappeared. On down the line Parker heard another brief rattle of gunfire as more soldiers stopped to return fire. The exchanges were taking their toll, but not on the enemy; the line was slowing, giving the enemy more time to load, aim, and kill.

Parker wheeled his horse and returned to Haiber at a gallop. He found the colonel was already beset by messengers from the company commanders informing him why the line was stalling.

"We've got to keep pushing," Haiber was explaining.

In the distance, a sudden burst of rifle fire was heard in the distance as the Arkansas Militia pressed their attack back at the river.

"Sir," Parker said as he reined in. "They're right. We're taking too many casualties. The enemy is firing into a wall of soldiers. They can't miss. We got to deploy skirmishers."

"If we slow down and start fighting their skirmishers, we'll be playing their game," Haiber replied, "By the time we get out of the woods, the diversion will have failed and the regiment will have to attack on its own."

"With all due respect, sir. If we don't deploy skirmishers we might not have a regiment to attack with."

Haiber became quiet. All eyes were on him, and all ears were listening to the increasing gunfire coming from back at the river. "Okay, then," Haiber said, "Deploy skirmishers, but tell them that they are not to return the fire of the enemy, nor slow the progress in any way."

Parker shook his head, "What good does it do if we deploy skirmishers, but don't allow them to shoot?"

"Because then the enemy will have to shoot at individual soldiers and not a solid line; they'll have to take more time to aim and they won't hit with every shot!" Haiber snapped, the pressure finally getting the better of his thus far restrained temper. He then turned to the gathered messengers and told them to relay the message back to their captains and then told his own messengers and staff to make sure the order was enforced.

Parker felt the full weight of the world right square on his shoulders as he returned to the line to implement the dreadful order. He knew Haiber was right, in fact the order was downright brilliant, but it was still a hard thing to do. It would save lives in the long run, and keep the advance moving, but it was going to be a death sentence to the poor soldiers who were sent forward as skirmishers.

For a moment Thompson felt his stomach turn and he began to think he might get sick. However, when he composed himself and finally spoke, the steady voice that came from his mouth surprised even himself, "We don't have enough room to form a full line of battle," he explained to the gathered militia captains. "We're going to advance in two lines of six companies each. Company A will anchor the left flank of the first line and Company F will anchor the right. Companies

G through M will make up the second line. The first line will engage in a firefight with the enemy. After several volleys have been exchanged, I will call up the second line. They will pass the line, allowing the first line to regroup before repeating the process."

As expected, Captain Jones interrupted by clearing his throat then spoke his piece, "Passage of the lines while under fire is a lot easier said than done, and we're dealing with militia here. I'm not sure they could complete the maneuver on a parade ground, much less in the heat of battle."

Thompson bit his tongue. While tact was certainly lacking, this was actually better than he had expected from Jones. In fact, it was a valid point. "We are going to open the engagement at one-hundred and fifty yards. That should get us close enough to give them the illusion that we are the main attack, but not so close that we will be unable to sustain a prolonged firefight. I feel that we'll be able to perform the maneuver under these circumstances."

As expected, Jones pressed on, obviously trying to impress those present. "Major Thompson," Jones said, no doubt intentionally forgetting Thompson's brevet rank. You may not have noticed, but a creek runs before the enemy works. There is little doubt that this obstruction will play hell on our lines."

Jones couldn't have picked a worse topic to try to match wits with his commander. Terrain was any cartographer's cup of tea. "Actually, the creek runs between eighty and ninety-five yards before the enemy works, so it won't be a liability to our formation. In fact, should the fire prove heavier than expected the high walls of that creek may be quite a blessing as we will be able to push closer to their works and use the ravine for cover."

Jones didn't seem too put out by the brief exchange, but he

didn't seem to have anything else to add either.

Thompson knew Jones was a good company commander and he knew if he ruffled the prideful officer's too much that asset could turn to a liability in a heartbeat. However, there was one point he did want to get across before he proceeded. "And, Captain, it's not Major Thompson; it's Colonel Thompson."

"Militia," Jones muttered under his breath.

"Captain, I didn't lose my arm on the parade ground at Little Rock."

Jones' hate filled eyes bore into Thompson's, but Thompson glared right back at him. Thompson's heart thundered in his chest. For a moment he actually thought Jones was going to strike him. Then, much to his surprise, Jones averted his eyes.

Thompson cleared his throat and hoped the exchange hadn't left a tremor in his voice when he spoke. "I know some of you might not like the idea of a firefight with an entrenched foe, but if we keep our distance we should come out on top. Our boys may be militia, but that's still more training with musket and rifle than the enemy has. I wouldn't want it to come to bayonets with those beasts, but in a firefight we should be able to hold our own even if they are fighting from behind logs. The steamers are going to move up and give us what little support they can, but for the most part we'll be on our own until Haiber comes in on their flank."

Jones grumbled something under his breath.

Thompson hadn't heard exactly what was said, but there was little doubt that he knew the gist of it. "Haiber will not let us down," Thompson said bluntly. With that, he took his watch out of his pocket, checked the time, then said, "Okay, back to your companies. We'll be stepping off shortly."

As they left he found himself thinking, *God, I hope Haiber doesn't let us down.* This thought was followed by another, *I hope I don't let Haiber down.*

At dawn a solitary drum rumbled to life from somewhere down-river. Longtooth climbed on top of the battlements for a better look. He had nothing to fear on his lofty perch. Humans simply didn't have the vision necessary to part the pre-dawn darkness and see the solitary figure on the hill.

Longtooth turned to the group of marksmen waiting behind the log and dirt earthworks. "They're coming in two lines. As soon as you have a clean shot at the first line, take it. Make them bleed."

Two hundred canine riflemen raised their guns and aimed them down the river at the advancing line.

The first shots rang out as Longtooth jumped down from his perch. He picked up his own rifle and joined in.

Thompson couldn't believe it. They had hardly stepped off before the bodies started falling. It was incredible, the beastmen were finding their mark at ranges of around five-hundred yards.

Unlike Haiber's command, Thompson and his staff lacked mounts. He and his tiny staff had taken position in the center of the formation, between the two lines. Since they had only one drummer for the entire regiment, the drummer and the color guard had also been moved to this position.

"Keep moving!" he called out, as he saw the company on the far right start to fall behind the rest of the line. He turned to a messenger and said, "Tell E Company to keep moving. Tell their captain that the sooner we move up the sooner we can fight back, and be sure to say it loud enough for the soldiers to hear you. They might need a little encouragement if their captain is losing heart."

The messenger started toward the right flank at a slow jog.

"Run, damn you! Run!" Thompson shouted after him and the messenger's feet seemed to sprout wings.

Barely ten feet way a member of the color guard went down with a bullet in his chest. The little drummer boy turned white as he spun to see the man fall, but he never stopped pounding on his drum.

It seemed like forever before they were finally in range and able to return fire, but when they released that first volley Thompson finally began to feel a glimmer of hope.

Then he turned and saw the bodies they'd left in their wake on the approach. There was simply no way they could stand and fight against such heavy fire. He had to do something.

He gathered his messengers around him and said, "Tell the captains that on my signal we are going to rush forward and take shelter in the creek. Tell them not to bother with order. When I give the signal, they are to run as best they can."

The messengers hurried off and Thompson waited, making sure to give them enough time to get the message to every company commander lest some portion of the line mistaken the sudden movement for a charge, or, worse yet, a route. Another member of the color guard fell and the drummer, who no longer had to play since they were no longer advancing, seemed scared as ever.

Thompson turned to the boy and said, "I want you to go to the rear, okay."

The boy seemed confused, "No sir, I can't do that. Who will drum the regiment forward?"

"We'll be moving at route step."

"You still need a drummer."

Thompson sighed. A bullet struck the ground nearby. "Just report to the rear. That's an order."

The boy shook his head, "No, sir. I ain't gonna do it."

Thompson was angered, confused, and more than a little impressed. But above all he didn't have time to argue with a ten year old. "Okay, then. But leave that drum here, it'll only get in the way. And when we move out, stay close to me."

"Can I keep my sticks?"

"Yes."

The boy unhitched the drum and just before it hit the ground a bullet struck the drum's wooden shell. The boy's eyes grew wide again, but before Thompson could say a word he said, "I still ain't leavin'."

Once he was sure the message was out, Thompson gave the word. The men broke and ran for the creek. There was no order in the movement. Every man was in an all out run for his life. Still, Thompson was impressed that when the order was given no one bolted for the rear. Especially considering the cover in question was almost halfway to the enemy battle line.

The fire became heavier as they approached the creek. With bullets whipping around him, Thompson half dove, half fell into the creek. With only one arm to catch his fall, he had to drop his sword to keep from landing face first in the ankle deep mud. As soon as he was in the creek, he turned to see if the drummer was still with him. As he did the boy dove into the mud beside him. The colonel and the little boy had been lucky. Apparently the beastmen had targeted the color guard and the staff during the rush; almost all of them had fallen before they reached the creek. The regimental flag lay about twenty yards behind them next to the dead color sergeant, and the state colors lay on the ground close to where they started their mad dash.

Thompson gathered his sword and rose to his knees. The creek turned out to be the first blessing of the entire morning. The bank facing the fortified hill was steep and the opposite bank was shallow, forming a muddy but otherwise perfect battlefield trench.

Despite the cover, the soldiers in the front line were still pinned by fire from the hill. Something had to be done to increase the pressure on the enemy works. The problem was, Thompson was now with the front line and had no staff remaining unless you counted the persist little drummer boy.

"What company is this?" he asked a pair of soldiers who were huddled nearby.

"Company D," one of the soldiers answered.

"Where's your captain?"

"Dead."

"Who's in charge?"

"First Lieutenant Hatcher." The soldier pointed to a clump of soldiers to their right.

Thompson crouched low and made his way over to the lieutenant. On his way he kept telling the soldiers he met to keep firing.

Hatcher's eyes were lined with pronounced crow's feet and his beard was flecked with grey; he looked a little old for a lieutenant in the militia. At first Thompson harbored hope that he was a veteran from the Mexican war who had been too old to qualify for the draft, then he saw the wild look on the lieutenant's face and the flecks of froth in the corner of his mouth and realized that this was probably a well connected shirker who had weaseled his way into an officers commission in the militia in order to avoid serving on the Canadian front.

"We got to get out of here!" the lieutenant screamed, with tears building in his eyes.

"Where's the second lieutenant?" Thompson asked.

"He's gone! Shot dead!"

"Third lieutenant?"

"Dead! They're all dead!"

Thompson turned and gazed out over the field behind him and noticed that an amazingly high percentage of the men who had been killed as they ran toward the creek had been officers. Not only could the beastmen handle their rifles, apparently they were good enough to pick individual targets at that range.

"What about the First Sergeant?"

A grizzled old veteran a few feet away called out, "That would be me."

Thompson turned to the sergeant and said, "You're in command of the company now."

The first lieutenant didn't protest. He nodded grimly while remaining huddled closer to the relative safety of the creek's wall.

The sergeant looked startled when he saw the young boy with the colonel. "Joshua, what you doing here?"

"I told you I wasn't yeller, Sergeant Thayer," the boy said defiantly.

"We need to get a message back to the second line." Thompson said, "We've got to get them to come up."

Sergeant Thayer nodded. "Sure, but I don't think they'll be able to relieve us. These here boys are doing good to hang on to what they got, you go and give them an order to fallback and regroup and they won't stop running 'til they reach the Gulf."

"Don't worry, I gave up the whole passage of lines idea not long after we stepped off," Thompson said, "but we just need more men up here so we can keep the enemy occupied. Can we get a messenger back?"

"Not across that much open ground."

Thompson had an idea, but he would have to get back to the center of the line. First, while he was on the right flank he decided to poke his head up briefly and try to take a look at the enemy's entrenched left. He found a small rise in the bank where he could raise his head and see the enemy's left without exposing himself to the marksmen on the hill. What he saw brought a lump in his throat. There were still at least three hundred beastmen guarding the left flank, with at least five hundred more positioned right behind them, ready to take their place on the line. If he couldn't do something to draw more soldiers away from that flank Haiber's regiment wouldn't stand a chance.

Thompson turned to the sergeant, "It's not working. There's still too many of them guarding the flank. Tell your men to pick up the firing."

The colonel started back toward the center of the line, running low with his drummer boy right on his heels. Once he reached the place where he had first stumbled into the creek he called out to all of the soldiers in the area to wait for his signal then rise up and fire at once. As soon as everyone was ready he called out, "Fire!"

The men in the center of the line rose up and let loose a ragged volley. Thompson used the fire, as well as the resulting smoke, to provide cover as he surged out of the creek and retrieved the regimental colors. He felt a bullet tug at his arm as it passed through the sleeve of his jacket, but he was otherwise unscathed. Once he returned to the creek he cradled the flagstaff to his chest and waved it as frantically as he could with only one arm.

The two Army steamers had moved up to support Thompson's attack, but with only one gun apiece it was doubtful they were doing much good. Since the steamers didn't have to worry about the enemy's battery anymore, the three chartered steamers had steamed moved forward and tied off just out of range of the rifle fire. From this position they could take on the wounded, and, if battle plan fell through, they could do their best to support an emergency evacuation.

Colonel Cole watched the scene unfold from the deck of the

Gabby. He brought his field glasses to his eyes and could see Thompson frantically waving the flag.

Baxter was standing nearby, watching through his own pair of field glasses. "What's he doing?" the major asked.

"He's trying to call up the second line," Cole answered without taking his eyes off the scene below. "Major Baxter, who's in charge of the second line?"

"Major Sloan."

"Go tell Sloan to get off his ass and get into the fight."

"Yes, sir."

Baxter turned to leave, but Cole caught him by the arm. "Tell him to move forward at route step and join the first line in the creek. It's a brawl down there. Tell him to try to extend the flanks, but otherwise don't worry about intermixing with the companies of the first line."

"Yes, sir."

The second line of the militia regiment started forward at route step, but as soon as they reached the initial position of the first line they started taking casualties. From that point on their route step turned into a mad dash for the relative safety of the creek. However, sporadic from the first line gave them some cover during the movement, not only causing the beastmen to keep their heads down, but also resulted in a semi-protective pall of battlefield smoke. They covered the ground in roughly half the time it took the first line. They took losses, but it was nowhere near the battering the first line had suffered through.

With the addition of the second line, the militia was able to lay down more fire on the enemy. The sputter of scattered shots back and forth escalated to the steady rip of a real firefight. But Thompson still wasn't sure if it was going to be enough to pull the enemy's reserves away from their flank.

Joshua crouched nearby, behind the wall of the ravine. His sticks tucked into his belt, he now held the battle flag aloft so it could be seen by the men up and down the line. It was a little heavy for him, but with one end thrust into the ground he was doing a fine job, even managing to wave it back and forth. The little drummer boy was all Thompson had left in the way of a staff. All messages to the companies where now sent by privates taken out of the battle line at random. Of course with the lines mixed together, there was little for Thompson to do besides cheer his men on.

Thompson took his watch from his pocket and checked the time. Haiber would be emerging from the woods soon, but so far he had been unable to tell if the diversion was pulling enough beastmen away from the flank. Thompson moved up to the bank of the creek. A nearby soldier saw the colonel and must have read what was on his mind. "Now, don't you go and get yourself shot," the soldier said.

Another soldier agreed, "Colonel, you just keep your head down and let us worry about them dawgs up thar."

Thompson ignored them. He removed his hat so he wouldn't be noticed as an officer, pressed his body against the muddy bank, and then raised his head up just enough to allow him to see the hill. Thirty minutes ago it would have been suicide for anyone to raise up long enough to do anything more than take a potshot then duck back into the creek bed. Now the smoke from the ongoing firefight had at least given him some cover, not to mention that the additional troops gave the beastmen more targets so they were less likely to notice him and single him out.

The fire coming from the hill was sporadic, but amazingly accurate. Thompson had already been impressed by the number of men that were being picked off. There was no denying the fact that these beastmen could shoot.

Then Thompson noticed a beige colored beastman raise his head above the works with a rifle in his arms. Unlike the humans, who were popping up and taking nervous potshots before diving back into the creek, this creature patiently waited for his shot. He was as steady as a rock as he slowly panned across the line looking for a suitable target. A bullet kicked up dirt within only a few inches away from him, and then shell from one of the transports burst over his head so close his pointed ears to sway with the concussion. The dogbreed never flinched.

Thompson recalled a birddog from his youth. He remembered how his dog remained steady and unflinching throughout the hunt. Much to his horror, Thompson began to realize that dogs were pack hunters and natural predators. In the rush to build the perfect worker, mankind had accidentally created the perfect soldier.

These dogs weren't as good as humans. They were better.

A dull glint of polished gunmetal just to the left of the dog he'd been watching caught his eye—a dogbreed had him in his sights. Thompson ducked; at the same moment fire and black smoke sprouted from the rifle. He felt pain in the top of his head, but he knew he wouldn't have felt a thing if the bullet had been on target. He reached up and found blood in his hair, but not a lot. The bullet cut a groove in his scalp.

As a rivulet of blood made its way from Thompson's hairline to his brow a cold calmness washed over him. The plan to draw about one-thousand of the enemy to defend a feint to their front was not working. The grim reality was that they weren't facing ragged subhumans who could barely work their weapons, but they were pinned down by about two-hundred excellent marksmen.

He recalled something Colonel Cole told him when they first met—that good leaders followed orders, but the best knew when to improvise.

He also recalled another saying he had picked up somewhere—desperate times call for desperate measures.

"Soldiers!" he called out at the top of his lungs. "Fix bayonets!"

Longtooth couldn't believe the sight before him. He had just fired a shot and was about to reload when a one-armed officer sprang out of creek and started up the hill with a young lad behind him carrying a flag. It would have been suicide had it not been for what happened a split second after they appeared. Before any beastman could take aim at this prime target, the creek came alive as every human soldier who wasn't wounded, and a few who were, suddenly rose up and charged. The ragged militia, some with uniforms that were little better than civilian cloths, surged forward, all of them running and all of them yelling like they were the animals in this fight.

"Here they come!" Longtooth called out.

Damn! He had been sure this wasn't the main attack.

He turned to a fleet-footed young messenger beside him and said, "Tell Sid to shift half the reserves to the hill as fast as he can get 'em here then stand by to send more."

Longtooth turned and prepared to meet the onslaught.

Thompson had always been a reader and he was well versed in the military theories of Clauswitz and Mahan; and, unlike many militia officers, he knew the drill manual from front to back. However, the rush up the hill had little in common with these modern battlefield evolutions. It had more in common with the ancient battle of Marathon where Miltiades's Athenians closed with the Persians at an all-out run so they could come to grips with the Persians before the enemy's archers could come into play.

The line had been somewhat compacted in the creek, but now that they were converging on the fortification centered on the top of the hill they became a shoulder to shoulder mass. The men propelled themselves over the over the log and dirt mound, hurling themselves at the enemy. With the beastman reserves pushing up from the other side of the hill, the two deadly masses locked together in swirling melee. Bayonets, knives, pistols, and rifles swung like clubs became the primary weapons of the soldiers on the front of their mass, while the soldiers in the rear constantly pushed forward against the efforts of their counterparts in the rear of the enemy's formation, causing the melee to slowly move seemingly of its own will like some hellish beast blanketing the top of the hill.

At some point during the charge Thompson lost the brave drummer boy. He didn't know when it happened, just that someone else had the flag now. He hoped the boy had simply fallen or someone had convinced him to return to the creek, but he doubted it. There was no time to dwell on the loss of the boy.

Thompson climbed onto the top of the battlement, raising himself above the melee. From there he could see the brutal, confused struggle on the hill. He raised his saber over his head and pointed it in the direction of the enemy. The militiamen in the front were too busy fighting to notice him, but those in the rear gave up a wild cheer and redoubled their efforts to come to grips with the enemy.

Thompson caught a glimpse of a beastman taking aim at him. There was nothing he could do; it was too late for him to dive for cover. He couldn't distinguish the sound of the shot from the wild melee around him, but he saw the puff of powder and felt the sudden tightness in his lower chest—no pain, only a strange tightness. He then heard a grunt beside him and saw his new flag bearer topple to the ground. Thompson dropped his saber and grabbed the flagstaff, bringing it to the top of the battlements with him.

The sounds of the melee were now distant and hollow, as if he was hearing them from down the end of a long tunnel. He found he was growing sleepy and somewhere in the recesses of his mind he knew what this meant, but he tried to push the thought away. There was no time for dying. Not yet. He still had a battle to fight.

He jabbed the flagstaff into the ground and leaned his weight on it to keep from falling. A man toppled backwards right at his feet as a dogbreed shoved a bayonet into his chest. No sooner had the beastman withdrew his bayonet than a soldier clubbed him in the head with the butt of a musket. Here a man and a dogbreed both armed with knives rolled around on the ground repeatedly stabbing each other, there a man fired a shot pointblank into a beastman's face only to receive a shot in the chest from another adversary.

More beastmen were pouring up the hill. Thompson turned and saw the entrenched flank was depleted and they were sending even more reserves to the hill. The diversion had worked. There was still enough on the flank to make one hell of a fight, but enough soldiers had been withdrawn to give Haiber's attack a chance of success.

Still atop the battlements, Thompson slid to his knees. He looked down and saw the front of his coat was soaked with blood. His thoughts seemed to drift; he was finding it hard to keep his mind focused. But he remembered why he was on the hill. He turned to the woods on their flank. The way was open, but if Haiber didn't come soon the beastmen would simply overwhelm the militia and then turn on the Colored regiment.

A lone rider rode out of woods on the flank and stopped near the edge. The rider seemed to survey the open field then withdraw to the woods. The Colored regiment had arrived; the attack would begin shortly. Thompson smiled, then collapsed. He felt the flag falling from his grip, but someone else grasped the staff before it touched the ground.

And now Henry Thompson was drifting away. The world was dark, but peaceful; he could no longer see or hear the sounds of battle. The scent of burnt powder was gone, replaced by the smells of spring. Somewhere in the distance he could faintly hear his mother calling him in for supper.

As soon as the soldiers of the 13th Colored Regiment reached the edge of the woods they started dressing ranks. This would be the last time they could do so before they pushed on toward the enemy position. Sergeants and officers barked orders as the companies shifted into place and individual soldiers dressed right. The men were apprehensive, but anxious. They had already faced death on the way up the river and in the woods they had just passed through, but this would be different. This time death wouldn't come in the form of a random shot from a hidden adversary. This time their enemy would have no choice but to stand and fight.

Parker was frustrated. He rode up and down the line, doing his best to encourage them, but there was little else he could do. He returned to Haiber at a gallop. "Sir, the companies are in line, but we need a little more time to form up."

Haiber didn't seem to hear him. He was intently staring into the trees in the direction of the hill, listening to the sounds of battle. "Something's different," he said. "Something's going on back at the river."

Then Parker noticed it too. The sounds of battle hadn't let up, but they seemed to have changed. It had been several minutes since they last heard the guns from the transports fire and the wild firefight had died down to sporadic firing. However, the screams and angry shouts of hundreds of men and beasts had taken up the vacancy left by the lessening musketry.

Haiber spurred his horse into the clearing. He stared in the direction of the hill for a few moments then wheeled his horse around and returned to the woods.

"Damn!" he swore as he wheeled his horse next to Parker's, "Something's gone wrong. It looks like the militia tried to take the hill. There's one hell of a fight going on up there. I saw the flag on the battlements, but I don't know how long they can hold out."

"Should we send a messenger back to Cole and see if the plans have changed?" Parker asked.

Haiber shook his head. "No time. From what I could tell, they're hard pressed. Even on horseback it'll take about a half hour to get a messenger to Cole, and then he'll have to get word back to us. By then the fight on that hill will be over."

Parker rose in his stirrups and glanced up and down the line. Here on the edge of the woods, the undergrowth was a little thicker and the trees somewhat younger and therefore smaller and bushier than they had been. He could see could see the company they were currently with, but he couldn't see far enough down the line to see much more.

"Are the men ready, sergeant?" Haiber asked.

Without pause, Parker replied, "Yes, sir."

Haiber gave the word and the drummers started beating the advance. The long blue line surged out of the woods at double time. Despite being unable to see the length of their line when they formed up in the woods, the regiment was remarkably straight and organized as they jogged into the opening.

"Parker," Haiber called out as they trotted after the regiment. "I need you to report to the pivot company to make sure everything comes off smoothly on that end, but as soon as the wheel is complete I want you to report back here."

"Yes, sir," Parker said, and he spurred his horse and started down the line toward Company A.

As he made his way down the line, he noticed his boys didn't seem their usual selves. Even when they were in the midst of maneuvers there were always a handful of cutups who would call out to him as he made his way down the line. Not this time. In fact, only a few soldiers even looked back to see him galloping across their rear. He was concerned, wondering if this meant their morale was weak, but the way they were moving forward certainly didn't seem like a unit that was ready to tuck tail and run.

Parker reached Company A just as the evolution started, but he found there was little he could do besides encourage the men. He watched as left flank of the Company A, the pivot in a wheel to the right, came to a halt while the rest of the company slowed to a walk. Now that they were in the clearing Parker could see all the way down the line. He could see the entire regiment carefully altering their speed. On the opposite side of side he could see Lieutenant-Colonel Santiago, hurrying Company K as they swung wide.

The line swung to face the entrenched position that ran along the enemy's flank; smoke rolled up from the enemy's line as they continued to rain fire down on the regiment. No sooner had the wheel stopped than the drummers once again thundered the advance. The men surged forward at a trot.

Parker spurred his horse and returned to Haiber's position at a full run. There were bodies along the way and some of the wounded were doing their best to make their way to the rear, but he could see no shirkers.

As he approached Haiber was telling the drummers to get ready. The colonel drew his sword and only seconds after Parker joined him he called out, "Halt!"

The drummers gave the signal.

Moving as one, the front rank dropped to a knee and took aim, while the second rank halted just behind them and the third rank behind the second with their rifles leveled over their shoulders of the second rank. Parker had never seen them this precise, not even on the parade ground. All three ranks, in perfect order aimed at the enemy which was only one-hundred yards away. Their familiar faces grim and serious, they scarcely flinched even when comrades fell around them.

"Fire!" Haiber called out.

The resulting volley sounded like the tearing of a massive piece of cloth as the fire ripped outwards from the center position to the flanks.

The volley tore through their position. Despite the logs and dirt earthworks, a surprising number of beastmen slumped over dead or wounded.

Sid felt a bullet clip his ear. Still, he never turned his hate-filled glare from the enemy before him.

"Tiger!" he called out.

"Yeah," a striped dogbreed replied from the wall before him.

"You see that officer on the horse?" Sid yelled.

"Sure do."

"Kill that bastard."

"No problem."

Even with the smoke from the volley rolling along the field, the mounted officer stuck out like a sore thumb. And Tiger seldom missed. Most beastmen were superior marksmen, and Tiger was even better than most, maybe the best. He would have been with the scouts if he had been able to get along with Mouser.

He drew careful aim, waiting for the right moment. His target moved out in from of the regiment and raised his sword.

Tiger squeezed the trigger.

As soon as the volley was fired, Haiber rode between E and F companies, positioning himself at the front and center of the entire regiment. His heart hammered in his chest. Perhaps somewhere in the back of his mind he was a little scared, but mostly he was proud and excited—proud of his boys and excited to have the opportunity to see them live up to the potential that he knew was there all along.

He was also excited to see he was living up to a potential that he honestly didn't even know he had.

Haiber raised his saber and turned to give the order to charge. When he did, a bullet struck him in the chest. He suddenly found he couldn't breathe, let along speak. The pain in his chest was excruciating. He gasped for air.

Parker saw what happened and charged into the gap positioning his horse along side Haiber's. He had no saber, so he drew his pistol, pointed it in the direction of the enemy and called out, "Charge!"

At that moment, Parker's horse took a bullet and collapsed. The sergeant was just able to jump free before the dying beast rolled over on him. As soon as he was clear of his dying mount, Parker ran to Haiber. The colonel was still mounted and his saber was still in his right hand, but his left clutched his chest, while he gasped for air. His startled horse spun and was about to bolt when Parker caught the reins. Without waiting for the horse to settle down, Parker reached up and grabbed Haiber by the coat. As he did a bullet hit the horse in the flank, causing it break and run. However, Parker's grip was strong and when Haiber tumbled from the saddle he was able to break his fall.

Haiber rolled onto his back. His coat was bloody, but not

near as bloody as it would have been had the bullet struck him in the heart.

"Go ... get ... back to ... the men," Haiber gasped.

"You okay?" Parker asked.

"Yes," Haiber said, his words coming a little better now that he was able to breathe. "The bullet struck at an angle ... winded me."

"But there's blood," Parker said, "I'll get the surgeon."

"I'm fine, damn it!" Haiber swore, then he gasped for air before continuing, "Get back to the men."

"But—"

"That's an order, sergeant," Haiber said, "They need you."

"Yes, sir," Parker said. He turned and ran after the regiment, but for the first time in ten years he had the feeling that the boys really didn't need him anymore, and that thought made him prouder than he had ever been in his life.

The massive hog snarled and screeched as yet another bullet slammed into his torso. Dillon's right arm hung limp at his side and bloody froth formed at his mouth, but he refused to go down. Swinging a two-handed woodsman's axe effortlessly with his off hand, he brought it down onto the skull of one of the militia soldiers.

Where was Longtooth? The leader, their savior, was his responsibility, but in the wild melee they had become separated. If something happened to Longtooth, it would be his fault. So Dillon waded through friend and foe like a mad juggernaut. He had already been hit several times, but it seemed nothing could stop him in his rage.

Two more soldiers charged down the hill with their bayonets fixed. Dillon sung his axe around his head, picking up momentum before his swung at the men in a power sweeping arc. The man on the right tried to use his musket to block the blow but the force was too great. The musket flew out of his hands and the axe bit deep into his chest, sending him flying into his partner beside him, bringing them both to the ground.

Dillon pressed on, but he made it no more than two steps before he felt a pain in his thigh. He looked down and saw that the soldier who had been knocked aside had thrust his bayonet into his hip. The massive pig whirled around and screeched again as he brought the big axe down onto his attacker, killing him with one massive blow.

He tried to continue, but found his leg no longer cooperated. He collapsed to his knees.

A man with a musket stood before him and fired. The bullet slammed into his chest, but didn't kill him.

"Longtooth!" Dillon roared, blood now flowing from his mouth.

A musket was swung like a club into the back his head. He fell forward and tried to rise, but not before three soldiers were on him thrusting their bayonets into his back.

Tiger reloaded as fast as he could. They were almost on top of him when he brought his rifle up. He didn't even have time to take aim, but at this range he could hardly miss. He fired.

The black humans were all around him. He tossed his empty rifle aside and grabbed a rifle from a beastman who had fallen nearby, taking hasty aim he was able to drop another soldier. Another black-faced human lunged at him. Tiger dropped his rifle and grabbed that of his onrushing opponent, pushing it aside and preventing the bayonet from sinking into his vitals. They hit the ground and rolled.

Tiger came out on top. He reached for the knife he kept strapped to his leg. He swung the knife downward, but his opponent grabbed his arm. Tiger then used his free hand to grasp the man's throat and squeeze. His opponent gasped for air, but before Tiger was able to chock the life out of him he felt a sharp pain between his shoulder blades. All of the strength went out of his arms; it was over and he knew it. He collapsed onto his side, wondering if he had been killed by a bullet or a bayonet. He hoped it had been a bullet—for some reason he thought it would be better to die the way he had so often killed.

Mouser was exhausted, but he had to see for himself. He staggered to the edge of the woods and watched as the human wave crashed into the camp's flank. He tried to tell himself that they still stood a chance, that maybe they could push the attackers out of the fort and win the day after all, but he knew better. It was over.

He stood near the edge of the woods, watching as the camp was overrun. He had tried to stop them, but he had failed. There were just too many of them. He took his kepi from his head and held it over his heart. He stood with his head down in silence for some time before he turned and disappeared into the woods.

There was too many of them. The black-faced humans swarmed over the log barrier and into their ranks. Sid did what he could, but there were no reserves left; they had all been sucked into the wild melee on the hill.

As he withdrew he attempted to gather a group for a counter attack.

"Over here!" Sid called out to a group of beastmen who seemed to be at a loss as to whether they wanted to run or join the fray.

The soldiers hesitated but then finally ran his way.

"If we push hard, maybe their center will collapse," he

explained to the small group gathered around him. The beastmen seemed scared but determined. Sid wondered if they realized just how hopeless the situation was.

"Let's go!" he called out.

The knot of perhaps twenty beastmen yelled and they charged into the onrushing line of humans.

The humans leveled their rifles and fired. Well over half of the beastmen went down. Despite the fact he was leading the charge, Sid wasn't hit. However, when he glanced around him, he found that he was all but alone. Perhaps five beastmen followed him by about ten steps, that was all.

It was over and he knew it, but maybe he could at least take one of them with him. He was still twenty feet from their line. A second group of soldiers took aim. He closed his eyes but never stopped charging.

The volley tore into his body. Sid was dead before he hit the ground.

When the wild melee gripped the hill, Gregory found that he had become separated from Longtooth. Though he was unarmed, he found himself making his way up the hill looking for his master. During a wild chaotic twist of melee he found himself swept along with a powerful beastman counter attack. They pushed deep into the enemy lines, actually penetrating to the other side of the hill before the charge stall. Then one by one the beastmen were overcome by their enemy who were simply too numerous on this side of the hill. Still, Gregory refused to fight. He lowered himself to his hands and knees and alternated between playing dead and crawling toward his own people. At one point he thought he was close enough to run for it, but as soon as he rose to his feet he was shot in the hip. He fell and rolled down the hill, finally coming to rest out of the fight, but on the wrong side of the engagement.

He spied a log and tried to crawl over to it. Perhaps he could hide underneath until the fighting was over.

As he dragged himself over he was surprised to find a young boy in a soldier's uniform. The boy had been shot in the leg. The wound was a terrible one. The boy's knee had been shattered and he had lost a lot of blood. Gregory crawled toward the boy.

"No!" the boy shouted. He was barely conscious, but he still had enough strength to rap Gregory several times on the head with what appeared to be a drumstick. "Stay away!" The boy shouted, his voice a shrill and terrified.

"Easy, there," Gregory said as he easily grabbed the stick and took it away from the weak boy, "I'm not going to hurt you."

"Please don't eat me," the boy cried.

Gregory pulled himself closer. "I promise, I'm not going to harm you in any way," he said in his softest and gentlest voice.

As he drew nearer Gregory looked into the scared boy's eyes and suddenly he felt as though he was looking into the eyes of little Timothy.

It was a terrible wound, there was little doubt the boy was going to lose his leg, but if Gregory could stop the bleeding perhaps he wouldn't lose his life as well. And Gregory knew just what to do; he had learned a lot about treating wounds by assisting his former owner who was a doctor and occasionally a surgeon. He tore a strip of cloth from his shirt and started bandaging the leg.

"I'm scared," the boy sobbed, now obviously more frightened by the wound than he was of Gregory.

"Everything's going to be okay, Timothy," Gregory said.

The boy didn't correct him. He lay still and let the dogbreed do what he could to stop the bleeding and save his life.

When he finished bandaging the wound, Gregory drew the

boy to him and held him tight in his arms.

"My name's Joshua," the boy said, with tears still in his eyes.

"Pleased to meet you. I'm Gregory McMillan," the dogbreed said, with tears of his own building.

With the flanking fortification crushed, the remaining rebel slaves on the north side of the hill were caught in a vise. The militia held the crest of the hill and the Colored regiment held the low ground to the north. Both forces were pushing hard to finish off the beastmen. However, despite the hopelessness of their situation, pockets of resistance all along the northern slope and inside the beastman camp itself continued holding out. One such pocket formed near the river, where a group of beastmen had attempted to carry Longtooth off the field on a makeshift litter. Less than two dozen beastmen stood to resist the onslaught of Captain Jones's Company A.

Longtooth had been hit early in the fight, but he remained on the hill trying to stem the irresistible blue tide. Finally his wound had overcome him and he began slipping in and out of consciousness. It was too late to get him out of the enclosed trap, but his loyal followers wouldn't leave without trying.

The two exhausted litter bearers set Longtooth down near the bank of the river, while their comrades formed a semi-circle around them, to protect them from the inevitable attack.

"Leave me here," Longtooth croaked weakly. "Swim for it."

"Never!" the shaggy dogbreed with a pointy snout who was holding the head of the litter answered.

The other litter bearer seemed less confident. His whole body trembled as he watched the bluecoats descend on the outnumbered beastmen guarding them. The firefight on the bank became heated and loud. Within a minutes only four beastmen remained and they were all wounded.

"Run for it!" The dogbreed at the foot called out.

They lifted the litter and tried to run for the river. White foam and spray surged around their legs as they ran through the knee-high water at the river's edge. Spouts of water marked where bullets slashed into the water around them. There was no way out. Even if they kept running, the black-faced soldiers held positions down river. Still, the two beastmen couldn't bear the thought of leaving their wounded leader.

The litter bearer at the foot took a bullet in the back. He went face first into the water and when he came back up he floated face down, drifting with the current. The stretcher collapsed into the river, but the remaining dogbreed pulled Longtooth out of the water by his armpits and started trying to pull him into deeper water. Apparently now that he had no one to help him with the stretcher he was going to try something else.

"Leave me," Longtooth said, his voice now a hoarse whisper.

"If we get to deep water, maybe I can swim and keep your head above the water."

No sooner had he spoke the words than a bullet hit him, then another. He fell into the water slowly then he too floated along with his face down in the river.

It took all of his strength, but Longtooth was able to roll onto his stomach and lift his head out of the water. He tried to drag himself to the shore, but when he reached the shallows where the river lapped up on the bank he found himself looking down the barrel of a pistol.

"Looks like I get to collect on that hide of yours after all," Captain Jones said.

Longtooth didn't reply.

"Tell me, dog. How does it feel to know you're about to die?"

"You can't kill a martyr," Longtooth said.

"Watch me."
Jones pulled the trigger.

Chapter 25

ELI PRODDED THE FIRE with a stick, causing the damp logs to hiss and crackle and sending a small shower of sparks into the air. The stick was in his left hand, since his right arm was in a sling. His group of friends had been fortunate. Of the four of them, he was the only one to take a bullet, and it proved to be little more than a flesh wound. Owen had been hit on the head by the butt of a rifle, and Seth had a long gash on his side which he claimed was where a bullet had nicked him, but Joel said he got it when he tripped and fell over the log entrenchments during the charge. As for Joel, he was completely untouched. Considering over a quarter of the regiment had been killed and half were wounded, the four boys were lucky indeed.

Rumor had it the militia was even worse off.

All around them the rest of the exhausted regiment slept. However, the four notorious night owls were too excited.

"It just ain't right," Eli said as he drew back from the fire.

"You been sayin' that all night, but there ain't a thing we can do about it." Joel said.

Eli turned his gaze to tree near the bank of the river where the body of a dead dogbreed swung lazily in the breeze. After killing him, Captain Jones had ordered Longtooth's body hung in clear sight of the prisoners, to show them what had happened to their leader and what would happen to them if they stepped out of line.

Seth turned to the tree as well. "I don't like it no more than you do, but it ain't none of our concern."

"Hell, let that dawg swing," Owen declared. "We'd be

swinging if we'd lost. Unless they ate us."

"Owen, I'm glad they hit you in the head; if they'd hit you anywhere else they might have hurt you," Eli snapped, "You heard what Sergeant Parker said about Longtooth. He said the beastmen had every right to kill him and Jones and everybody with them after what happened at that cabin, but Longtooth let them go. Parker said he had a lot of respect for Longtooth, and you know the sergeant don't go around respecting a whole hell of a lot of people."

Owen shrugged, "Okay, so Parker liked him and now he's hanging by the river. Big deal."

"That's not the worst of it. When they take him down they're going to skin him and parade his hide around for everyone to see." Eli leaned closer to the fire, "And guess who's going to get that reward money? That damn Captain Jones, that's who."

"I gotta agree with you on that," Seth said, "He done nothin' but cause trouble and he's gonna walk away rich while we get nothin' but our pay and rations."

Owen's face suddenly broke into a wide grin. "Hey, wait a minute." He turned to Eli, "Are you sayin' we ought to steal his body and get that reward ourselves?"

"No!" Eli replied furiously tossing the stick he'd been using to prod the fire into the fire itself. "Owen, why you always gotta be such a jackass?"

"Jesus, Eli, no sense in getting your feathers all ruffled. I just thought that's what you's gettin' at."

"Well, it ain't."

After the outburst, the group became quiet. Across the fire, Joel began to watch his old friend Eli. Finally he spoke. "Eli, you never carry on like this unless you up to something. Let's hear it. What you got on your mind?"

Eli paused for a second, as though he was making up his mind whether or not to tell them, then he finally said. "I think we ought to take him down and bury him."

"Whoa, now. Hold on right there," Owen said. "You know what kind of trouble we'd get into?"

"I don't care." Eli got to his feet. "It's the right thing to do."

"I'll help," Seth said. "I'll stay in the brig till my hair turns gray if it means I get to see the look on Jones's face when he realizes his prize is gone."

"What if we get caught?" Owens repeated.

"We won't get caught." Eli said. "All we gotta do is take him down and put him in the trench they buried their dead in. We toss a few bodies on top of him and they won't never notice. They supposed to finish covering the graves tomorrow morning. You saw how drunk Jones was. Ain't no way he'll be up before they finish covering the hole."

"But someone's bound to notice he ain't by the river no more."

"The prisoners are the ones digging the graves; you know they ain't gonna say a word. And our boys are supervising; you think they gonna talk?"

Owens thought about it, then shook his head. "No way. Parker'll know. He knows everything."

Eli rose to his feet. "I don't care. I'm doing it."

Joel and Seth stood as well. "I'm with you," Joel said.

"Me, too," Seth said.

The three friend turned and walked away, leaving Owen still sitting at the fire mumbling to himself.

"I know what it is, Eli," Owen turned and called out to the three shadows, "You a corporal with a hurt arm, so you just want to see if we'll do all the work for you. You want us to take him down while you point and act all important. That it?"

Eli didn't reply. The three continued into the darkness until Owen could barely make them out.

Owen muttered something under his breath, then rose to

his feet. "Wait for me."

Longtooth, the beastmen's greatest hope, dangled by a rope near the river, his tongue lolling out to the side of his mouth, his eyes wide and staring. Privates Lawton and Saunders were standing guard by the tree when four figures approached in the darkness. The four silhouettes stopped when they saw the guards and seemed to have a talk among themselves. Lawton overheard part of their conversation. One of them said, "You didn't say there'd be guards" and other replied "I didn't know there would be." One of them started back the way they came, then seemed to change his mind and return.

"They gonna try and rob us?" Saunders whispered nervously.

"Don't be such a ninny," Lawton replied, "They ain't got no guns. We do."

"What they doin' then?"

"I'll bet they want him," Lawton said, nodding toward the dangling dogbreed.

"Why?"

"We're fixin' to find out."

The four figures stopped their discussion and finally approached the two guards. As they drew near Lawton realized what he already assumed—they were soldiers from the Colored regiments, and, sure enough, they were unarmed.

Lawton cleared his throat, "What you boys up to?"

A soldier with corporal stripes on his shoulder and his right arm in a sling stepped forward. He nodded toward the dead dogbreed, "We gonna bury him."

Saunders smirked, "You gotta be kidding me," he said.

"I ain't pullin' your leg," the corporal said, "We gonna take him down and put him in the pit with the others. He don't deserve this."

Another of the Colored soldiers spoke up, "And that jackass of a captain don't deserve no reward, neither. I don't care if he is your captain."

"That bastard ain't our captain," Lawton said then he added, "We from H Company. We got screwed into guard duty since G Company had picket duty last time we was ashore." It was a point of contention with him. The way he saw it Longtooth's pelt was A Company's plunder, so they should be guarding him.

Saunders turned to Lawton, "What we gonna do?"

Lawton stretched his mouth in a wide yawn and said, "I don't know, but all this fightin's done wore me out. "I warned the sergeant that we was too tired to take guard duty tonight."

"What?" Saunders cried, his jaw dropping open and his rifle almost slipping from his hands.

Lawton propped his rifle, up against the tree and sat down with his back to a nearby stump. He smirked as he pulled his hat down over his eyes.

"You gonna end up in the brig," Saunders said.

"Been there before," Lawton said, "It ain't so bad."

"They gonna drum you out of the militia."

"I make better pay at home anyway." Lawton raised the brim of his kepi just enough so he could see Saunders' nervous face. The poor boy was as white as a sheet. "And to tell the truth, these boys got the right of it."

"You agree with them?" Saunders said incredulously.

"Yep." Lawton pulled his hat back over his eyes.

As the four Colored soldiers stepped forward one of them produced a knife. Saunders was too scared to make a peep, much less raise his rifle and shout for them to halt. But the soldiers didn't use the knife on him, they simply cut Longtooth down from the tree, wrapped him in a blanket, and carried him away into the darkness.

Eli led the way while his three friends carried Longtooth's wrapped body through the narrow, winding streets of the beastman's dilapidated old camp. Many of the weary militiamen had taken up temporary residence in these structures, but no one was out on the streets themselves. Everyone was too exhausted. Pickets had been established around the perimeter of the encampment, but no guards challenged the boys as they made their way to the burial pit on the other side of the camp. As they reached the other end of the old beastman camp the scattered tents of their own regiment came into view.

Although the recent battle had washed away most of the animosity between the two regiments, a few guards had been posted between the two camps, just to make sure. Eli spotted two men from their regiment on duty near a fire between the regiments. One soldier was already asleep and the other looked like he was ready to drop any second. When the second soldier's head slumped onto his chest, the men moved swiftly, passing just outside the flickering firelight as they moved into the tent village.

Eli stopped while the rest of their group continued through the tents. He took a cautious glance behind him and saw one of the guards raise his head and look in their direction as if he thought he heard something. He rose to his feet and even walked a few steps in their direction, but finally stopped and returned to the fire.

When Eli turned to catch up with the others he found his way was blocked by a stocky figure. It was too dark to see more than an outline. His heart leapt in his chest; there was no doubt about it—he was busted. The figure spoke, and, sure enough, he recognized the voice.

"Eli, remember what I said about those corporal stripes?" Parker said, his voice hoarse and quiet. "Didn't I say I expect you to set an example for the others?"

There were jokes that circulated camp that were a lot like tongue-in-cheek superstitions concerning Sergeant Parker. The men joked that he never slept, and that he always knew what they were up to because he knew how to talk to squirrels, rabbits, possums, and all manner of birds, and they did his spying for them. Now it seemed that either a swamp rat or maybe an owl betrayed them. Either that or Parker had been awake and saw them slipping around in the dark.

Eli hung his head, "I'm sorry, sir, but..."

Parker placed a hand on Eli's shoulder, "You're doing a fine job."

And with that Parker turned and walked away.

Eli stood dumbfounded for a few moments, then he hurried to catch up with the others.

The men passed through the pickets without incident. Like the guards stationed between the two camps, these sentries here at the outer edge of the encampment were bone tired and nodding off.

The newly dug burial trench lay just on the other side of the shallower trench the beastmen had used to cover their flank. It was a deep slit in the ground, ten feet wide and about two-hundred feet long, and probably close to six feet deep, though it was hard to tell since the bottom was concealed with the bodies and mud. Beastmen and humans alike lay intertwined in the bottom of the pit. There had been too many bodies to hope to carry them back downriver, so Cole ordered a mass burial. The original plan was for three trenches, one for the beastmen and one for each regiment. However, even with newly subdued slave labor there simply hadn't been enough manpower for that much digging. There were too few captured beastmen and the soldiers were just too exhausted from the fight. Worried that the damp conditions combined with the

285

masses of bodies in the open air would create an unhealthy environment for the already exhausted soldiers, Cole ordered that they all be buried together in the same pit. This outraged a few until they were offered a shovel and told they were free to start digging their own pits; it didn't take long for everyone to see the common sense in the colonel's order.

Seth, Joel and Owen carefully laid Longtooth's wrapped body at the edge of the trench.

"Take him out of the blanket before you push him in," Eli instructed, his voice just above a whisper—the pit was unguarded and outside of the picket line, so they had little to worry about so long as they kept their voices down. "Make sure he lands face down."

"Yes, sir, corporal, sir," Owen said with a mock salute, "Will there be anything else, sir?"

"Shut up, Owen," Eli replied.

"Whatever you say, corporal, sir."

Owen, Joel and Seth grabbed the blanket and pulled, rolling Longtooth into the spongy mixture of blood, mud, and corpses below. He landed hard, causing the bodies to shift. He was face up.

Seth turned and gagged as the smell hit him, he walked away from the trench with Owen right behind him, also gagging. Eli stared wordlessly down into the pit.

Joel looked over at Eli. "We go down there in that mess to roll him over, we gonna smell just like that when we get back to camp. We'll be caught for sure."

Eli didn't reply. He stood at the edge of the pit, trying to work out a solution. Having recovered from his nausea, Owen returned, popping his head between Eli and Joel. He smirked as he opened his mouth for one of his standard smart-ass comments, but then he saw something that caused his words to catch in his throat. At first Eli thought he was just getting sick again, then Owen pointed a trembling finger across the trench.

A pair of figures slowly walked into the dim moonlight. These first three figures were followed by three more, then another group behind them. As they drew closer, Eli realized they were beastmen. There were at least a dozen of them, probably more like two-dozen. A few, maybe three or four, were armed, but that was all. An old grey-faced, crooked back dogbreed stood near the front of the pack; he had glasses perched on his snout, but one of the lenses was cracked. A younger specimen stood just to the right of him, hiding partially behind him. A wolfish woman stood just out of the light with a bundle held to her breast. Another female stood next to her, wearing what had once been a lady's dress but was now torn and tattered. Next to her stood a tall narrow-faced wolf-like beastman with a bandage around his head and his arm; he was one of the few armed men among him, but despite his gun he carried himself with more fear than courage. These weren't viscous monsters; in fact, Eli was amazed how much they looked like his people back home at the Freelands.

"We gonna make a run for it," Owen gasped.

"No," Eli replied.

"You crazy?"

"They won't hurt us."

A short, wiry beastman wearing a kepi elbowed his way to the front. Unlike the others, this one appeared to be a fighter. Yet despite the jaunty black feather in his cap, the newcomer had an air of solemnity about him. He looked across the pit at Eli, their eyes met, but neither said a word.

The dogbreed then climbed into the pit and worked his way over to Longtooth. Four more followed his lead, dropping down into the pit with him.

"Here they come," Owen said, his voice a panicked whisper.

287

"We gotta do something."

"Shut up, Owen," Eli said then he added, "That's an order."

The four beastmen grabbed Longtooth and gently carried him back to their side of the pit. Once they were out the beastmen withdrew from the edge of the pit, all except the short one in the kepi. He stood there alone until the others were out of sight, then he looked directly at Eli and touched the brim of his cap.

Eli nodded in reply.

With that the lone beastman turned and rejoined his people.

Chapter 26

PARKER STOOD AT THE TOP of the hill, leaning on the earthworks as he watched the scene below him. The burial pit had been filled and the prisoners were being rounded up and formed into groups of twenty. These groups were the shackled together and led away. There couldn't be more than two hundred prisoners. That was all that was left out of somewhere around two thousand. It made Parker wonder just how many were killed and how many had escaped before the battle.

Jones had placed himself in charge of the prisoners. His face was red from a volatile combination of anger and a major hangover. He moved among the prisoners yelling, pushing, hitting and kicking all that came within his reach. He was truly a one-man army of hate this morning. Even his own company had turned on him after he ordered them into the burial pit to overturn every body in an attempt to find Longtooth.

Parker looked down the side of the hill and saw Baxter and Cole working their way up to his position. Cole looked haggard and weak as he leaned heavily on Baxter.

"Morning, Sergeant Parker," Baxter said with a beaming smile.

"Morning," Parker replied. While he had been enjoying having the hill to himself and hated to lose his solitude, he couldn't help but warm to Baxter's childlike enthusiasm. And truth be known he didn't have as much animosity toward Cole as before. Perhaps the battle had wore of some of the rough edges, or maybe seeing the colonel's plan come to fruition had given him new respect for the old gentleman.

Cole was out of breath by the time they reached the top of

the hill. He leaned against the earthworks and told Baxter, "Thank you, son. Now if you would be so kind as to return to the steamers and see to the loading of the prisoners. Jones is having a little too much fun for my tastes. See that his excesses cease once the slaves are loaded."

"Um, okay, sir," Baxter said hesitantly.

"There won't be any trouble. When you get the slaves below deck on the Isabella have the men unshackle them. I don't imagine Captain Jones will go down to the hold with that many of them loose, and if he does he deserves what he gets."

"Yes, sir," Baxter said. He gave quick salute that somehow seemed more boyish than military, and then returned down the hill.

"The boy wants me to pull some strings and get him into West Point," Cole said as soon as Baxter was out of earshot.

"He's a fine boy."

"You think he'll make a good officer, though?"

Parker was somewhat shocked that Cole had asked his opinion on the matter. "You want my opinion?" he asked.

"I asked, didn't I?"

Parker nodded. "Then yes, sir, I think he'll make a fine officer."

Cole nodded then asked another question, "How's Colonel Haiber?"

"He's in fine spirits. The regimental surgeon said he got a broke breastplate. It was hurting him something awful this morning, but it ain't going to kill him."

"Very good. The army's going to need officers like him if the fighting breaks out on the Canadian border."

They stood in silence that for some time, both men quietly overseeing the chaotic scene below them. While they looked on Jones made his way down one shackled line of beastmen, shouting and pushing. A slight smile crept to Cole face and he said, "I believe our dear captain is a bit upset about losing Longtooth's pelt."

"That he is."

"He wasn't even able to figure out who to throw in the brig. Company H seemed unable to decide who had been on duty when the body went missing. Officers and men alike, not a one could remember who was supposed to be on duty. Imagine that."

Despite the scene before him, Parker felt the corners of his own mouth twitch into a slight smile.

"Reckon who took Longtooth down?" Cole asked, this time turning to Parker as he spoke.

"Ain't no tellin', sir."

Cole turned his gaze back down the hill, "I wonder if someone else will try to claim the reward."

Parker paused then said, "No, sir. I don't believe that's going to happen."

"Good."

Parker motioned toward the prisoners below them. "What's going to happen to them?"

"They'll be taken back to their masters," Cole said, his voice registering no pleasure in the fact.

"What about the others?"

"What others?"

"The ones who slipped away before we closed the trap, and the few we didn't catch in the fight? Will there be another expedition?"

"We bagged all of them, at least that's what the report will say. There won't be any need for another expedition."

There was a long moment of silence again before Cole sighed wearily and said, "I'm just glad it's all over."

At that moment a beastman tripped over his chains and fell at Captain Jones' feet. The captain gave the beastman a kick with his boot, hauled him to his feet and worked him over with his fists before shoving him back in line with the rest. However, when Jones turned away there wasn't a look of passive obedience on the beastman's face—there was a look of raw hatred. The beastman flashed his teeth, for just an instant, almost as if to show himself that he was as good as the humans around him.

Parker shook his head, "It ain't over. It's just beginning."

About the Author

Byron Starr is the co-creator of Moreauvia, and author of several books from Creative Guy Publishing: *Insurrection*, *Flatheads*, and *Ace Hawkins and the Wrath of Santa Claus,* as well as *Finding Heroes*, from CGP's Liaison Press imprint. Byron resides in East Texas with his poor traumatized wife, Shelly, and their two kids, Abby and Jay, both of whom act just like him